THAT DANGEROUS
ENERGY

By Aya de León

That Dangerous Energy

Queen of Urban Prophecy

A Spy in the Struggle

Side Chick Nation

The Accidental Mistress

The Boss

Uptown Thief

THAT DANGEROUS ENERGY

ENERGY

AYA
de LEÓN

www.kensingtonbooks.com

DAFINA BOOKS are published by

Kensington Publishing Corp.
119 West 40th Street
New York, NY 10018

All Kensington titles, imprints, and distributed lines are available at special quantity discounts for bulk purchases for sales promotion, premiums, fund-raising, and educational or institutional use.

Special book excerpts or customized printings can also be created to fit specific needs. For details, write or phone the office of the Kensington Sales Manager: Kensington Publishing Corp., 119 West 40th Street, New York, NY 10018. Attn. Sales Department. Phone: 1-800-221-2647.

The Dafina logo is a trademark of Kensington Publishing Corp.

ISBN: 978-1-4967-4032-8
First Trade Paperback Printing: January 2023

ISBN: 978-1-4967-4034-2 (e-book)
First Electronic Edition: January 2023

10 9 8 7 6 5 4 3 2 1

Printed in the United States of America

"We need to continue holding leaders accountable for their actions. We cannot keep quiet about climate injustice. Three things should stay with us as we continue to organize and mobilize: Faith. Hope. And love. And the greatest of these is love."

—Vanessa Nakate, author of *A Bigger Picture: My Fight to Bring a New African Voice to the Climate Crisis*

"Humans created the climate emergency, and humans can solve it. We even know what to do to solve it, and the solutions are within our reach! We simply need to bring enough people along as we make demands that can't be ignored."

—Sustaining All Life, "Staying Hopeful and Engaged in the Climate Emergency"

Acknowledgments

With gratitude to all the usual folks . . . my literary team: Jenni, Norma, Rebecca, and Michelle. To my family and my Familia from Scratch. Plus special thanks to my Black Climate Support Group, my Black Hive folks at M4BL and the wonderful women at Climate Critical Earth. Finally, thanks to all the amazing creatives I worked with at Black Literature vs the Climate Emergency, who have all helped me to get bolder and bolder in my climate storytelling for the win. Here's to stories that not only predict our victory in the fight for climate justice, but also help speak it into existence.

Prologue

Lourdes Alarcón fled from her husband in the middle of the night. According to Spanish law in the 1930s, a woman could leave an abusive marriage, but she couldn't obtain a legal divorce, nor take anything with her—other than the clothes on her back—not even her children.

The Moors had been expelled from Spain hundreds of years before. The Moors had advanced Spain's economic prosperity, arts, science, and brought indoor plumbing from North Africa. Lourdes didn't know which African country her Moorish ancestors had came from. Algeria? Morocco? Tunisia? But the springing curls in her hair were definitive evidence that they had been there.

Before their exodus, the Moors had rebelled against the oppression of the Spanish crown, and so had Lourdes, against her husband, the brutal ruler of their household.

With a shaking hand, Lourdes had worked late into the night, sewing her jewelry into the waist of her skirts and petticoats. She had worked by candlelight, heart in her throat, terrified that her husband might *catch her, plotting to escape. He was on the other side of the house, smoking cigars and drinking with friends. Or what if the baby woke up? Her husband would hear the crying. She wouldn't be able to quiet the child and hide the evidence in time. But somehow she managed, and now she was ready, poised for flight. The next day she fled, gemstones pressing against the silvery stretch marks on her belly. She closed the heavy wooden door behind her and ran into the street with a plum-colored bruise on her cheek, her breasts already aching with the weight of the milk her youngest would never drink.*

Lourdes sold the diamond necklace to an old man for a fraction of its value. The rage smoldered silently in her belly. They both knew he was cheating her, but a woman alone would have to settle for whatever he offered. It was enough for a steamer ticket to America.

In New York, Lourdes worked in a garment factory until she learned a passable amount of English. She then committed bigamy by marrying an Irishman. They moved to Pennsylvania.

Mr. Tehan wasn't abusive. Mr. Tehan was quiet. She felt a tenderness and gratitude toward him for accepting her, despite her past. She had left three sons in Catalunya, and even after having two daughters in America, the ache of loss remained. She nursed her heartbreak quietly and raised her daughters with a nostalgic bitterness that would never quite leave the women of her family.

Chapter 1

Morgan Faraday had never heard the story of how her great-grandmother Lourdes left Spain, only heard whispers that things in the Old Country were somehow *bad*. But in the family tradition, Morgan fled The Excelsior, an Upper East Side apartment building, when things in her own life got *bad*.

This was nearly a century later, and no law forbade Morgan from taking some of her belongings—a backpack that held all her treasured possessions. Yet she carried contraband in the internal pocket of her sweatpants. It pressed against her hip bone, like a necklace of Spanish diamonds.

The December morning was bright. Morgan looked out onto Second Avenue for the compact silver hatchback, which was supposed to be across the street in the white loading zone. She couldn't see around a double-parked truck and walked briskly toward a silver hatchback on the corner. A mother exited the hatchback and lifted twin toddlers out of their child safety seats. Wrong car.

Morgan stepped into the street to look around the truck. At the far end on the other side of the block, a tall man opened the door of a silver hatchback. She turned toward him, but a pair of security guards came out of The Excelsior and cut her off.

Morgan felt a surge of panic. How did they know? She had been so careful! Casual clothes. Small backpack. Leisurely pace through the lobby.

Morgan pivoted and fled toward the opposite corner, maneuvering past the double stroller that took up nearly the whole sidewalk.

This end of the street was more sparsely populated, and she took it at a full sprint, dodging pedestrians and a man walking three dogs: a Chihuahua, a Shih Tzu, and a Pomeranian. When she hit the other corner, she glanced over her shoulder. The two guards were still chasing her, cutting out into the street to avoid the man and the dogs.

Around the next corner was the subway. She blended into the crowd moving toward the station.

Taking the stairs two at a time, she dug in her jacket pocket for a MetroCard. Four train lines stopped here. If she could make it through the turnstiles, she could disappear. No way for them to know where she had gone. She swiped the card once, her hand shaking, and had to do it again. But then she was through.

She waited on the platform for the downtown N or R train in a sea of late commuters. A man in front of her was half dancing to music blasting in his headphones, loud enough that she could hear the tinny techno. Beyond him, she saw frantic movement: the two guards. One of them was looking at an iPhone and the other was scanning in her direction. They pointed at her.

Her heart was in her throat. What the hell? What were the chances that they would know *exactly* how to find her when they couldn't have even seen her walk down into the subway? Had her cell phone been bugged with a GPS locator?

She threw the phone into the tracks, causing gasps among the bystanders, and backed away. She rushed toward the other end of the platform. Maybe she should run back out of the station. Maybe it was a coincidence. She could get lost on one of the other platforms. Or better yet, be just far enough ahead of them to jump onto a leaving train.

She ran down the stairs and ducked around a corner. She blended into the crowd heading to the 6 train. No way they could track her without the phone.

On the 6 platform, she looked into the tunnel to see if the train was coming on her side. Instead, she saw the two guards coming down the stairs. Panic twisted in her solar plexus. How the hell had they found her? Again?

She hustled past a trio of men in suits, past a large advertisement for diamond jewelry. And then she realized. The engagement ring. The setting was big enough for a GPS microchip. The diamond must be worth a million dollars, but it wasn't worth her life. She twisted off the ring and flung it into the tracks.

The security guards gaped, and the one with the phone put it in his pocket.

Now she didn't even try to be polite. She shoved past people to the edge of the platform. There were stairs to exit there. But a steady stream of people walked down, transferring from another train. If she tried to climb the stairs against the flow of traffic, the guards would certainly catch her. She was trapped. Except for the tunnel.

The next stop was maybe only six or eight blocks away. The guards were getting closer. She elbowed her way into the knot of people coming down the stairs and leaped off the end of the platform.

"Hey!" a woman yelled.

"Give me your hand and I'll pull you out," a man called after her. "Think about what you have to live for."

Fucking idiots. She was determined to live but calling attention to her was going to get her killed.

She kept to the outer edge of the tunnel and soon found a narrow path for subway workers. As she sprinted along the edge, her running footfalls were the loudest sound.

Her heart pounded with the exertion. But then, the voice of one of the guards: "She's down there." She felt a spike of fear.

The train came down the tunnel on the other side, the blast of sound and wind nearly knocking her back. Still, she continued to run, her breath burning in and out of her lungs. The train passed. She heard the guards behind her.

A rat skittered ahead, momentarily throwing off her gait. She stumbled but then righted herself and kept running. She saw the distant light of the next station. The tunnel was dim and dank with puddles of water. She ran on, splashing through them, hearing only one set of footfalls at her back. One of the guards had fallen behind. She said a silent prayer of thanks for her daily runs on the treadmill.

But the guard pursuing her was also in good shape. He was gaining.

A train came on her side. The noise was deafening as it passed her, but she kept running. She felt a stitch under her ribs. Her knees were getting weak. The train slowed up ahead for a moment. Could she jump onto it?

Morgan put on a burst of speed to catch up. Her chest was on fire. Her legs were fatiguing. She heard the running steps of the guard—closer now. The train ahead started to move. With her last ounce of strength, she accelerated, taking a final leap and reaching through space for the handle on the back of the train.

She caught it! The guard at her back reached for her, his hand stretching through air. His fingers slipped off the nylon of her jacket while the train lurched forward.

The train sped up. Morgan watched the guard stop and double over, elbows on his knees. Then the train slowed down. He was walk-jogging toward her as the train ground to a halt. Should she jump off, start running again? Could she still run? Her muscles were jangled from the adrenaline of the sprint, the leap, and the sudden cessation of movement in the cold air.

She was ready to jump when the train began to move again, picking up speed as the guard fell farther and farther behind. She pressed herself against the blessed metal of the car, panting, her body so weak with relief she nearly crumpled and lost her grip.

They pulled into the next station, and she slipped off the end of the car onto the platform. Her leg had cramped and she was limping, her head damp with sweat, the roots turning back to curls, destroying the expensive blowout. Revealing her African roots, the same way her great-grandmother's curls had exposed her Moorish blood.

Morgan hustled down the subway platform, looking back over her shoulder. This was how she bumped into the chest of a man in a suit.

"Excuse me," she said. And then her breath stopped as she looked up at the stony face of the very man who had given her the engagement ring.

Chapter 2

Ten months earlier . . .

The Midwestern landscape stretched out below her like the color blocks of a quilt. As the plane descended, Morgan saw patchwork patterns in the agricultural squares of brown and green. Her grandmother had taught her to sew, taught her to see quilting squares in everything around her. The darkening blue of the early evening sky added another color to the mix. The bright orange stripe on the plane's wing would look good, too. A contrast to the more earthen tones of the rest of the color scheme, but that was Morgan's strength—to add that one unexpected color that made the whole garment dazzle the eye.

The plane lurched down and took her stomach with it. She inhaled and focused on a man's biceps across the aisle. It was the opposite of the blocks of farmland. All sinewy and curving with muscle. Nothing noticeable about the color. Just a white guy with smooth, beige skin. A covering of fine, tawny hair on the forearm. She couldn't see his features under the cap he had pulled down over his face. The plane lurched again, but he didn't stir. How could anyone sleep through this landing? She couldn't imagine sleeping that soundly. She traced the lines up from his wrist to his shoulder as it disappeared into the sleeve of his T-shirt. A nice arm. Sexy. Focus on that. Breathe.

Her stomach settled.

By the time the plane landed, she felt calm. She avoided the eyes of the man whose arm she'd secretly used to soothe herself.

It was long past dinnertime when Morgan wheeled her Dilani Mara carry-on toward the gate in the St. Louis airport. The Dilani Mara stiletto pumps were killing her feet. Why hadn't she packed a pair of flats?

Her stomach growled. Her last meal had been a salad before she left Brooklyn. She had eaten the free pretzels on the flight from JFK. More of the same would keep her going all the way to Denver. When she got there, she could order room service at Sebastian's hotel.

"Are you hungry?" he would ask.

"Starving," she would say. "I never get airport food." Like it was beneath her, not unaffordable.

Everything about Morgan's exterior screamed money. The designer shoes, jacket, and luggage. The stylish clothes. Fashion forward. Not like anything people had seen. Were they right off the runway? Who was she wearing? There were no designer labels because she had sewn the clothes herself. The outside of her wardrobe said couture, but the inside said homespun. Just like the outside of her body said glam, but the inside of her stomach said airline snacks.

So, the twist in her gut that she felt when the monitor said her flight was delayed was 15 percent disappointment, 85 percent hunger.

Damn.

She had $7.43 in her designer wallet. Enough to take a bus or subway if Sebastian didn't send a car for her. He usually did. But she never asked. She acted as if she didn't care one way or another. Like if he didn't send one, she could just afford her own.

Morgan's best friend Dashawna had carefully schooled her: Don't act needy. Don't even act grateful. Act like it's just a fact of your life. Men always send cars for me. No big deal.

And Morgan had done as her friend suggested. Kept her eyes from popping at the prices of the restaurants where Sebastian took her. Kept herself from gushing when he gave her a designer scarf. Dashawna said scarves were an ambivalent gift. Something a man gave a woman to test her response. Morgan had smiled warmly, thanked him, and kissed him. But didn't gush. She acted like it really was the thought that counted.

Morgan had met Dashawna at fashion school. On her first day, Dashawna had squinted at Morgan like she was a swath of shimmering fabric that changed color.

"Girl," Dashawna said, "you're Black, right?"

Despite the blowout, despite her light skin and aquiline features, somebody had come to claim her in this big city. Back home, she had always said "mixed" or "biracial." Given the racism in Pennsylvania, she might have tried to pass for Italian or Portuguese. But it was a small town. Everyone knew her mother was Black. But in New York, in this teeming metropolis where all sorts of middle-range brown people wore wild hair and African prints, and Black Lives Matter T-shirts, she hadn't quite dared to dream that she could be claimed. And then this obviously "real" Black girl, with thick braids and shamelessly tight jeans on her big ass came to claim her.

"Yes," Morgan said, afraid she might cry and spoil her mascara. "I'm Black."

"Thank God there's another sister up in here," Dashawna said. "Because I was afraid it was gonna be a lonely four years."

And Dashawna had swept her up into a tight friendship. Occasionally Morgan was clueless, but Dashawna would just school her and keep it moving. Dashawna was from Houston. Not only was she bold and confident, she knew how to hustle to make things happen. They got Dilani Mara designer gear for pennies on the dollar from a school friend, Vivian, who worked there. They took home garments that were floor models, imperfect, or otherwise unable to be sold.

But in the St. Louis airport, there was nothing in Morgan's designer purse to eat. She wandered over to the bar. Maybe they'd have free snacks.

The bar was a long slab of fake dark wood, with black vinyl stools and an illuminated liquor shelf behind it.

She sat down on a stool and looked around. A bowl of peanuts at the end of the bar caught her eye. There were too many people gathered around them.

"What can I get for you?" the bartender asked.

"A glass of water?" she asked. "I may have had a few too many on my flight from New York," she lied. Liquor wasn't free in economy class.

"Bubbly or flat?" he asked.

"Bubbly, please."

He poured the water into a tall glass of ice from the soda machine and moved on to another customer. She put a lime wedge and a stirrer into her water. She would have eaten the lime if it hadn't looked bad. How was she going to get her hands on those peanuts?

She and Dashawna used to do this at bars in NYC. Sit around and wait for men to buy them drinks. It usually worked. But this was an airport, and men were in a hurry. She sipped her water.

Maybe if she got into Denver late enough, she could plead tired and skip the sex with Sebastian until tomorrow. Or at least until after she'd had a meal.

Sebastian Reid was not a very good lay. But that was what vibrators were for. What had *Forbes* said his time was worth? Ten thousand dollars a minute? That was how he made love, like he was losing money every minute. But no woman dated a billionaire for his sexual prowess. He could buy you a truckful of vibrators. If you married him? You could own a vibrator factory. Although his family empire wasn't built on sex toys. He had inherited an oil company and was in the process of making it more eco-friendly.

Marriage was not on their immediate horizon. He said he wanted to keep it casual. She hadn't slept with anyone else since they had gotten together, hoping he would take it to the next level, committing to sexual exclusivity as the first step toward marriage.

Sometimes she did long for something more intense with a man. Like the guy who had just walked into the airport bar. It was biceps guy. She blushed.

The rest of the body went nicely with his arm. Tall and slender, with a muscled build. But it was his face that drew her in. She hadn't seen it under the cap. Dark eyes, high cheekbones, and a full mouth. She revised her estimate of him. He wasn't white. Not with the tilt and shape of those eyes. He was mixed with something. Like she was.

The only empty stool was next to her. As he sat down, she dropped her eyes down to her soda and lime juice.

"You on the Denver flight?" he asked.

She nodded.

"I knew I should have flown direct," he said.

The bartender walked up. "I'll have an Earthbound," he said. "And can I get you another . . . ?" he asked. "What's the lady drinking?"

"Vodka and soda," she said. "But if I'm gonna drink anymore, I should probably put something in my stomach. Can we get some of those peanuts?"

The bartender reached out and brought over the bowl.

"That's a great idea," he said. "Let me buy you some real food."

"Nah," she said. "I'm not that hungry."

"I'm famished," he said. "You never know what's decent

at these airport bars. I'm gonna order a bunch of stuff. Feel free to help me finish it."

"Suit yourself," she said. She began to eat the peanuts.

"I'm Kevin," he said. They shook hands.

"Morgan."

"I wouldn't have pegged you as heading to Denver," he said. "The way you're dressed, you definitely look like you belong in New York. Or maybe Los Angeles or San Francisco."

She shrugged. "I sew my own clothes," she said. It was nice to be able to take credit for her work. She was always playing it down these days, trying to give the impression she was rich instead of talented.

"That's amazing," he said. "If you sew your own clothes, I guess I can tell you my secret. I'm a farm boy."

"In New York City?" she asked, laughing.

"I'm from Iowa," he said. "My family has a farm there."

"But you live in New York?" she asked.

"Brooklyn," he said with a beautiful smile.

"What brought you to the city?" she asked.

"A relationship," he said. "It didn't work out. But it's hard to imagine going back to Iowa after half a decade in New York. How about you?"

"Fashion school," she said. "But that didn't really work out, either."

"How is that possible? Your dress is amazing."

"It's New York," she said. "Amazing isn't enough. It's got to be amazing, plus you need all the right connections, the world's best timing, and a bunch of capital to invest."

"Ain't that the truth," he said.

"I'm from Pennsylvania," she said. "Small town. Nothing you'd know."

"Are you Amish? Did you escape? Come out on your Rumspringa?"

She snorted a laugh and nearly spit some of her drink on

him. "Not hardly." She thought of her mother, pregnant at seventeen by a local speed dealer. Her early years with their grandmother in public housing. Her mother doing okay with a factory job until the corporation started doing all their manufacturing offshore. The nightmare stepfather. Their family homeless briefly, then back at Grandma's house.

"I'm gonna tell you my secret," she said. "I never really cared that much about fashion. What I really love to make is quilts."

"Quilts?" he said. He looked closely at her outfit. "I can see it," he said. "In the geometry of the panels you put together."

"It's fine to put the clothes on someone's body, but I prefer the two-dimensional canvas, where you can really see the shapes."

The bartender set down a platter of jalapeño poppers and she dug in, forgetting to be modest.

"What takes you to Denver?" he asked.

"Just needed some time out of the city," she said. "A friend invited me, so I said yes."

"Same here," he said. "Some friends asked me to come and I couldn't resist."

A friend. Sebastian had made it clear that they were "just casual." But Sebastian also had her sleeping at his apartment every night. Initially, he had asked yes-or-no questions: "Would you like to come over tonight?" But now he would ask, "What time should I expect you?" She didn't have a key, but the presumption was that she would sleep there.

The first time he had texted her: **Will you be here for dinner? I'm ordering in Turkish food.**

Dashawna had high-fived her and they'd danced around the tiny studio apartment. "Bagging a billionaire! My girl is bagging a billionaire!"

"It's only dinner. We're just casual."

"Girl, get a clue," Dashawna said. "His actions speak louder than words. 'What u doing right now?' is what someone texts if it's casual. 'Will you be here for dinner?' That's what you text your wife."

"No," Morgan said. "'Will you be *home* for dinner' is what you text your wife."

"That's your mission, girl. Make that 'here' into a 'home.'"

The Buffalo wings were a little too spicy, but she was so hungry.

"What kind of farm does your family have?"

"Corn," he said. "We're trying to transition to organic, but it's hard. Like last year, when the US agricultural—" He stopped himself. "You know what? Let's not talk about national agriculture. Let me just tell you what's growing in my garden in Brooklyn. I have the most amazing kale crop this year."

"Kale?" she said. "What are you, a cliché?"

"Go ahead and laugh," he said. "Kale is delicious. Especially the way I cook it."

"An old Iowa recipe?"

"No, I stir-fry it in coconut amino acids and a little bit of red pepper."

"More of a gentrified Brooklyn cliché."

"My garden is part of a public school," he said. "I teach sixth and seventh graders part time."

"Oh wow," she said. "Okay, maybe less of a gentrifier and more of a do-gooder."

"I'll take that upgrade," Kevin said. "We built a greenhouse. The kale is doing great. So is the lettuce. If we're lucky, we'll have winter asparagus. And when it warms up, the Puerto Rican and Dominican kids bring out different plants I've never heard of. I'm getting organic seeds for a few different green vegetables. It'll be interesting to see if they'll grow in the summer."

The two of them talked about food, about New York, about being small-town people in the big city. They were so busy talking and laughing that they almost missed the announcement.

"Was that flight 783?" she asked.

"What?" he asked. "They weren't supposed to be leaving for another hour."

"Maybe they're leaving earlier," she said. "Let's go look."

"I'll settle the bill," he said. "You check."

They had become a unit, bonded over food and drink and kale and textiles and small-town stories.

At the gate, she learned the flight had been canceled. They would be rebooked in the morning.

"Can we get some kind of hotel voucher?" Morgan asked.

"The cancellation was due to weather," the woman said.

"What do you mean?" Morgan asked. "The weather's beautiful."

"Out of Chicago," the woman said. "Sorry."

Kevin caught up to her. "Canceled?" he said. "Damn. Well, I'm a rewards member at . . ." He rummaged through his wallet and pulled out a card for a hotel chain. "I always get a good deal. Wanna stay at the same spot? We can continue our conversation over some equally crappy hotel food."

"No," she said. "That's okay. I'm gonna just hang out here at the airport and see if anything changes."

He gestured to the women at the gate, shutting it down for the night.

"You know," he said, "I think I have an email for a free upgrade to a two-room stay. I think it's going to expire soon. I hate for things to go to waste. These damn corporations. Would you consider staying at their expense?"

Morgan thought about it. Was this a predatory move? Was he trying to set her up some kind of way? Her mom had taught her to be alert for men who would take advantage of this type of situation. But he wasn't from here, either. He couldn't have known the flight would be canceled. They would take the cab together. She would be able to decline at the hotel if the offer was shady. She looked around the airport at the seating with metal armrests in between each chair. She'd never get any sleep here.

She smiled. "Okay," she said. "Just to stick it to the man, right?"

"Let's go," he said. "It'll be a Midwestern corporate chain-hotel adventure."

When he took her hand, she felt a charge.

The hotel was a standard chain. Three star, maybe. Small lobby. Smiling Black woman with braids behind the counter. Kevin went to check in. She sat on one of the sofas. The colors were beige, tan, and salmon. They blended into one another. She couldn't find any color blocks, not even the framed paintings. She hated these quiet, pale combinations. But they were standard for places like this.

Would Kevin come back and say they only had one room? Would their rooms be adjoining? Would they have separate rooms, but he'd help himself to one of her keys? She took a deep breath and decided to take it one step at a time. Rooming together? She'd decline. Adjoining? She'd carefully bolt the door in between. If her room was totally separate, she'd put on the hotel-room security lock. However it went, she'd watch her drinks all night. Breathe. See what happens. She'd be okay.

"They got us on two different floors," Kevin said, handing her a pair of keycards. "But they gave us vouchers for their restaurant. Prepare for the worst."

But it wasn't the worst. The restaurant had a seafood theme, which was a little ridiculous for landlocked St. Louis. Behind Kevin was a net on the wall with plastic crabs and lobsters tangled in it. They decided to avoid seafood and picked foods that were hard to ruin. She had a steak and fries. He had a Caesar salad with grilled chicken.

"I usually don't eat steak," she said.

"Because of the environmental impact?"

She shook her head. "I can't afford it."

With Sebastian, she usually ate fish. Dashawna said it looked light and feminine.

"It really depends how the steak is raised," he said. "If it's factory farmed, then yeah. Totally destructive. But if it's a small local farm, it's not much worse than other foods. Really it's the corporate—" He broke off. "Sorry. No more farm talk tonight."

But they managed to talk easily about a lot of things.

He asked about her heritage. Instead of that awful "what are you?" question, he finessed it.

"Tell me about your background," he said.

Morgan had learned from Dashawna to be blunter about race. "Are you trying to figure out if I'm Black?" Morgan asked.

Kevin laughed. "If you are indeed Black, then yes."

Now it was Morgan's turn to laugh. "Yeah," she said. And told him a little about her family. That her grandfather was Black. That the other three of her grandparents were European-American. And one of her great-grandmothers was from Spain.

Kevin explained that he had been transracially adopted, and they had thought he was white and Korean. But a more recent DNA test had suggested that his nonwhite ancestry was from the Philippines. He'd bought a ticket to go visit for the first time, but the trip had been cancelled when the region had been hit by a super typhoon. But before that thought could sink their conversation, their entrées arrived. They dug in and were both pleased to find the food surprisingly good.

After dinner, they sat on one of the couches in the lobby.

"How did it get to be one in the morning?" Morgan asked. "We should turn in."

Kevin shrugged. "I don't know," he said. "I never sleep well in hotels."

Morgan smiled. "Me neither."

"You know what we need?" Kevin said. "That Jacuzzi they say they have."

"Yeah, but it closed at nine or something," Morgan said. "Before we even checked in."

Kevin's eyes glistened and he leaned forward. "Let's break in," he whispered.

Morgan grinned. "I've got a bathing suit," she whispered back.

Kevin shrugged. "I don't, but I'll just wear my boxers . . . unless that would offend you."

"Not at all," she said. "Meet you on the second floor outside the elevators."

Up in her room, Morgan opened the suitcase. Other than her two exercise outfits, it was all fancy clothes to look good for Sebastian. Even the swimsuit was Dilani Mara. She felt awkward in the luxury of it with Kevin. He was the type of guy you could wear your T-shirt and yoga pants with, and then dress up for an anniversary dinner, so you could watch his eyes pop out, seeing you all dolled up.

Why was she even thinking of him in those terms? Kevin was a nice guy providing her shelter in St. Louis.

She threw the sweats over her bathing suit and headed down in the elevator. Morgan looked in the mirror as she waited. She loved everything about the idea of being in a Jacuzzi with this lanky farm boy . . . except her hair. She'd had it blown out at a Dominican shop near Dashawna's place the day before she traveled. She rarely wore her hair natural these days, and certainly had not brought any of her curly hair care products. It would not do to be looking for

Black hair care products in Colorado. Without them, her hair tangled and frizzed. It was too unruly—not in keeping with her current sleek image. Sebastian had certainly never seen it in its natural state.

Occasionally, the heavy humidity would affect her hair, and she would pull it into a tight braid when she went out with Sebastian. Any tendrils around her face that curled more than usual constituted a level of detail that was much too subtle for his notice.

He had this ritual, though. Before they went out, he would sort of appraise her. It was as if he did a two-point inspection. Was she presentable? Check. Was she fuckable? Check. She always strove to be both.

Kevin was waiting for her on the second floor. His denim jacket was the only thing that stood out in the muted hallway.

"What's the plan to get into the Jacuzzi?" she asked.

"I thought you might know how to do this," he said.

"Me?" she asked. "I might know how to take a sewing machine apart. Nothing about breaking into hot tubs."

"But you're Black, right?" he said. "Aren't your people good at stealing?"

Morgan's mouth fell open. She wasn't sure whether to laugh or be offended.

"I'm Asian," he said with a shrug. "We're only good at helping white people find a deep inner peace and strength."

That was when Morgan knew to laugh. It echoed loudly in the empty hallway.

Kevin put a finger to his lips. "Worst Black thief ever."

Morgan stifled another giggle. She liked this guy. Not only could he tell she was Black, he was comfortable enough with Black people to joke about stereotypes with her.

They walked down the quiet hallway. Past the darkened fishbowl of a business center. Past the silent and empty meeting rooms. On the far end from the elevator was the pool and the Jacuzzi.

"You really don't know how to do this?" she asked.

He shook his head. "We'll have to improvise," he said.

A member of the staff exited one of the offices.

"Excuse me," Kevin said. "My wife misplaced her glasses earlier. We were thinking we might have left them in the Jacuzzi area?"

"I can't really—" the man said.

"I'm so sorry," Morgan said. "I just realized, and we leave before it opens in the morning."

The staffer sighed. "Okay," he said. "Can you look quickly? I've got to get back down to the front desk."

"Like lightning," Kevin said.

The staffer opened the door, and the lights came on. The two of them walked in, and Morgan did the thing she'd been practicing in recent months: walking into someplace she didn't belong and acting like she knew exactly what she was doing.

She strutted right over to the far end and looked down on the floor. There was only a silver bottle cap. She scooped it up and held it aloft, her hand facing away from the staffer, the curve of the cap just peeking out between her fingers.

"Found them!" she crowed. Did it look like a pair of glasses? Maybe. The staffer wasn't really paying much attention. Morgan walked back toward the door, pocketing the bottle cap.

"Thank you so much," Kevin said to the staffer. They all walked out, and Morgan slipped the cap between the door and the frame to stop it from closing. The three of them stood by the bank of elevators. Morgan pushed the Up button and the staffer pushed the Down button. They waited in awkward silence. Would the guy realize he hadn't heard the door click? Would he go back to check?

The Down triangle flashed red above one of the elevators.

The staffer stepped into it and murmured, "Have a good night."

The moment the door closed, Morgan and Kevin grinned at each other.

"You propped the door?" he asked.

Morgan nodded, and the two of them walked quickly back toward the Jacuzzi. "It came to me in a flash," Morgan said.

"What'd you use?" he asked.

Morgan pulled the door open and showed him the bottle cap. "Same thing I used for the glasses."

"You didn't mention that you're a genius," he said. "Remind me if I ever decide to pursue a life of crime to have you on my team."

"It's always good to have a fallback career plan," Morgan said.

They didn't dare turn on the lights, so they used their phones. Kevin's had a natural light app, so they selected the fireplace setting and stripped down. She put her hair up in a plastic clip. If she kept it up in the twist, she wouldn't have to straighten it again before she flew to Denver tomorrow.

Morgan was glad that Kevin wasn't seeing her designer suit in bright lighting. It seemed too flashy. His boxers were plain blue, the fabric itself unremarkable. But he had a really nice ass.

She admonished herself not to think about it. And when she slipped into the pool, the wonderfully hot water did temporarily take his ass, his long, muscled legs, those biceps, and his beautiful brown eyes, from her mind.

Morgan woke up in a barely lit room. She was still in the water. "Oh my God," she said. Her whole body was liquid from the heat.

"Kevin!" she said. She tried to lift her arm to shake him

awake, and her muscles took forever to respond. She could only jab him weakly.

Finally he woke, and the two of them stared at each other. His face was flushed and his sandy hair was dark and sodden.

"Shit, we could have drowned," she said.

"We need to get out of here," he said.

The two of them struggled to lift their bodies against the weight of the water with their lethargic limbs.

Morgan wiped her forehead. She had sweated out the blowout. She touched the crown and back of her head to find her curly hair was plastered to her scalp. And the tips of the hair that stuck out of the clip had also begun to frizz from the humidity. But she had bigger problems.

Five minutes later, the two of them were dragging down the hallway. Morgan had only managed to put on her sweatshirt and wrap her waist in a towel.

He had pulled on his T-shirt and done the same for his lower half. They carried their shoes and pants in their arms.

They slunk onto the empty elevator. His phone light had died. She checked her phone. It was 3:30 in the morning.

"We need to drink water," she said.

"There's a big bottle in the minibar," he said.

"Don't waste your money on that," she said. "I have a gallon bottle in my room. I filled it at the airport."

"I would definitely do crimes with you," he said.

They walked up to her room and drank half the gallon of water.

"I should go," he said.

"You could sleep on the other bed," she said.

"Really?" he asked. "That would be—amazing. I don't actually know if I can get up."

She laughed. "You probably can't, can you?"

"I can make it to the other bed," he said. "I know I can do it."

"Don't worry about it," she said. "I'll go."

"For the third time tonight," he said. "You're my hero."

A wake-up call jolted them up. It was seven and they were drowsy and disoriented. She was surrounded by beige walls and pale, sand-colored seaside paintings.

Morgan picked up the phone, blinking against the early light.

"Damn," Kevin said as he stumbled into his jeans. "We need to get to the airport."

Morgan's skin felt tender where the underwire of the bikini pressed into her skin. Her hair smelled of chlorine. She needed a shower.

"I'd better get my suitcase," Kevin said. "I'll meet you downstairs in ten minutes."

She nodded and stumbled into the shower. Just a quick rinse. No need to be careful with her hair today. It was beyond repair.

She blinked under the spray. Had they really spent all night together? Broken into the Jacuzzi of a Midwestern chain hotel? She had felt so at ease. Usually she couldn't sleep in hotels. Had they fallen asleep in each other's presence twice?

She smiled despite herself as she toweled off and blotted her hair. She looked longingly at the blow-dryer. No time. She braided it quickly so it wouldn't tangle. She'd have to improvise in Denver.

She dozed in the shuttle on the way to the airport. He dozed in the airport when they waited for their flight.

She looked over at him in the seat next to her. Those cheekbones.

At the gate, they learned that she had been bumped up to first class.

"Oh no . . ." she said.

"Take it," Kevin said. "One of us should get some sleep."

"The flight is completely full," the woman at the desk said. "You either fly first or you don't fly."

"I guess . . ." Morgan said.

"You can report back to the masses after we land," Kevin said.

Morgan laughed.

"Here are your boarding passes," the flight attendant said. "You and your husband need to board now, before they close the doors."

"He's not—" Morgan began.

"Thanks, ma'am," Kevin said and took Morgan's hand.

"We could swap," Morgan said as they hurried down the gangway. "You're so much taller. You could really use the legroom."

Kevin shook his head. "I'll crash out as easily in a middle economy seat as I will in first. Just don't get off the plane without saying goodbye."

"Of course," she said.

And then she was walking toward the front of the plane and he was walking toward the back.

Chapter 3

As she settled herself into the comfortable reclining seat, she got a text from Sebastian: **What time do you land? I'll send a car.**

A first-class plane seat. Sending a car. How else would she have gotten to the hotel with $7.53 in her wallet? Did Denver even have a subway? She knew she should be relieved, but she wasn't.

She had originally been booked into first class. Sebastian's travel agent had booked her on a last-minute nonstop from New York to Denver. The first class ticket was a fortune. She had called the airline directly to change the flight to economy. There was such a massive balance left over that she was able to get economy tickets to visit her great-aunt in San Diego for her birthday in April. Not only that, she had enough left over to fly her mother, her cousin, his wife, and their two kids. Usually balances weren't transferable to other travelers, but apparently Sebastian had a level of miles or clout or credit that those rules didn't apply to him. This year she was Santa Claus, delivering the whole family to her great-aunt.

So it wasn't just about first class and sending cars. It was what she could do for the people she loved. Besides, she had dated in New York City. Any guy could be charming during one night in a hotel away from home. But would he return calls? Pressure her for sex starting on the second date? Ghost after he finally got laid? Turn out to be married? She would not give up everything she'd been building with Sebastian for a pair of nice biceps.

But what could she say to Kevin when they parted ways? Should she take his number? Just in case "operation wife-up" (as Dashawna called it) didn't work out?

Morgan waited just inside the airport, and it was a good twenty minutes before Kevin came off the plane. First class had even more advantages than she'd realized.

Travelers bustled by, but then she saw him in the throng, his tall frame moving gracefully toward her.

"You waited," he said.

"Of course," she said. "When you do crimes with some-one, you really bond with them, you know?"

He laughed. "Maybe we could get dinner sometime in New York. I mean, if the lady at the counter thought we were married, maybe we should see if there's anything to it, right?"

She had hoped for a more noncommittal exchange of numbers. A sort of you're cool . . . let's stay in touch. But he was asking her out on a date.

She shrugged. "I don't know . . ."

He was right to be direct. She did have a really strong sense of attraction to him. A pull in her solar plexus that made her want to stand closer to him, touch him, feel those urban farm boy hands on her skin.

He looked at her for a long moment. "You have someone, don't you?"

She took a breath to speak, but he cut her off.

"I get it," he said. "Here's my number." He handed her an airport beverage service napkin with a 346 number on it. "Call me if it doesn't work out. Or—you know—you plan to do some crimes. Or need to plant some kale on a balcony."

She laughed, and it broke the tension a bit. "Thanks for everything," she said. Impulsively, she hugged him. His body felt exactly like she knew it would. Firm. Solid.

After she let go, he stepped back and blinked a few times. "I—I should go."

"See you . . . around," she said.

The moment was awkward now. He nodded and walked toward the baggage claim, his lone backpack on his back.

She stared after him, stuck in place.

But then he suddenly turned and made a phone hand, with a thumb near his ear and a pinky below his mouth. *Call me!* he mouthed.

She cracked up and wheeled her designer carry-on into the women's room to hide out. She didn't want Kevin to see her getting into the limo Sebastian would have waiting for her.

Why did she have this feeling of loss pressing on her chest? The last time she had felt this way was when she went away to college. She had cried saying goodbye to her high school sweetheart, Donnie, at the bus station. That was the last time she had been in love.

Morgan and Donnie had promised to stay together despite the distance. When they spoke on the phone, he was always sure she would find some big shot in New York and forget about him. Actually, it was the opposite. She looked forward to coming home to a guy who knew the real Morgan. She rode home on the bus for Thanksgiving, only to find out through friends that he had cheated on her with Amanda—his coworker at the hardware store.

After a miserable set of winter holidays that year, she always found a reason she couldn't make it home for vacation. Morgan stayed busy working one job or another during school breaks. She heard Amanda had gotten pregnant, and Donnie had broken up with her. Morgan settled into New York City feeling like she had dodged a bullet.

But that last good moment with Donnie at the bus station had felt like this goodbye with Kevin. Like she was full of hope and could promise anything. Morgan looked down at the name and number on the airline napkin: *Kevin Templeton*. Morgan shook her head. She wasn't eighteen anymore. Like Dashawna said, a girl needed to "be practical about this love shit."

Morgan crumpled up the napkin, tossed it in the toilet, and flushed. But she had a photographic memory, so she couldn't really forget it.

At noon, the limo dropped her off in front of a fancy hotel with a wide, U-shaped driveway. A bellboy hurried out to assist her. She waved him off, as she had nothing but a purse and a carry-on.

The lobby was huge and high-ceilinged, with marble floors, glittering fixtures, and tall, geometric sculptures of gleaming chrome. When she went to reception to check in, they told her Sebastian wasn't in his room. But he had left her name at the desk. Perfect! The room had dark, wooden furniture and was done in warm, rich shades of rust, bronze, and chocolate. She ordered room service, then showered and blow-dried her hair from 3B to 1B. She couldn't get it as flawlessly straight as the Dominicans, but it was straight enough that Sebastian wouldn't notice. She changed into one of the hotel robes, which felt like wearing a cloud. She sat in the luxurious fabric, eating lobster and watching a fashion-design reality TV show on demand. She was having what Dashawna called a "Morgan Markle moment."

"You gonna be the Black princess, girl!" her friend had said.

And Morgan was here for it. Sure, Kevin was hot, but this was the good life. She kept her eyes on the prize. Wife it up with Sebastian.

When Lourdes got her first marriage proposal, she was seventeen and in love. She had saved herself for marriage but had managed to slip away from her chaperone several times for stolen moments of passionate kissing. She confessed about it in church but felt more excitement than guilt. Rodrigo was strapping, handsome, and charismatic. He came from a good family. All the young women in town tried to get his attention. When Rodrigo went down on one knee and presented her with a ring, Lourdes was thrilled.

The women in her family were known for their sewing skills, and her aunt made her the most beautiful wedding dress she had ever seen. The day of her wedding, she looked in the mirror and felt like she was in a dream. It seemed she would have everything: the fulfillment of this deepest of desires, the blessing of the church, and a chance to spend the rest of her life with the man she loved.

But passion soon turned to pregnancy, and Lourdes had a hard one. She was sick. She was weak. Rodrigo's passion turned to contempt. He barely bothered to hide the evidence that he was having affairs. Lourdes was miserable. Lying in bed and blaming herself. Surely she should have been better, stronger, more responsive to his needs. After the first birth, she lay in bed for weeks, barely able to do more than nurse the newborn.

Eventually she rose from the bed, settled into her role as wife and mother, and had two more sons. And eventually the union that was supposed to guarantee her a lifetime of love became a threat to her life.

By the time the shy Colin Tehan proposed to her in

New York, Lourdes felt no sense of passion. Tehan was anything but charismatic. He was fine to look at, but not strapping and so handsome like Rodrigo had been. He had a limp, which probably explained why he was still in New York, working in a factory, not off fighting in World War II. But Tehan was kind. Steady. Helpful. Not the kind of man she had longed for as a young girl, but the kind she had longed for as a young mother. Someone who could partner in the raising of a family.

Tehan didn't sweep her away from a chaperone after church and go down on one knee to propose in front of everyone. He did it privately, in a moment of quiet conversation. His voice was steady. Would she want to get married? He didn't have the money to buy a ring because he was saving every penny to buy a house.

She knew he would eventually buy that house, and that the woman he married would be happy. Could she become that woman?

She had been keeping company with Mr. Tehan because he was such a comfortable companion. But she knew a moment like this would come, and that it would bring everything to an end. Like her, Mr. Tehan was Catholic. She was no virgin bride and couldn't pretend. The stretch marks on her belly would give her away. She dropped her eyes as she spoke: "I was married in Spain. Divorce was illegal in Spain. Marriage was supposed to be for life."

His eyebrows rose. "But your husband died, didn't he?" Tehan said, his eyes twinkling.

Her mouth flew open. Tehan wouldn't reject her? He would help her author a fiction that she was widowed?

Lourdes could barely suppress her smile. "Yes," she said. "It was quite tragic."

And so, for the second time in her twenty-nine years of life, Lourdes said yes to a man's proposal of marriage, and quietly became a bigamist.

At nine that evening, Sebastian entered the suite, followed by a waiter with a bottle of champagne in a standing ice tub. Morgan could tell by the furrow in Sebastian's brow that it had been a tough day.

As soon as the waiter left, Sebastian pulled her to him and kissed her firmly on the mouth. "You're a sight for sore eyes," he said. "Damn that delayed plane. I wanted to talk to you yesterday when I was in a better mood. These fucking, whiny—no, let me leave work at work."

He poured himself a scotch and walked back to the leather sofa, taking a long drink. "I wanted to ask you something, Morgan."

"Sure," she said, a bit taken aback. He never started a conversation that way. She sat down next to him.

"I realize I said our relationship would be casual, but I find I want something different now," he began. "I know you haven't been seeing anyone else. And I haven't been seeing anyone else."

Yes! This was it. The moment she had been waiting for. She could feel her heart beat hard in her chest.

"Move in with me," he said. It wasn't exactly a question. Not quite a command.

Move in? She hadn't expected him to propose or anything. Maybe not even say that he loved her. But something designed to make her feel even a little more special. "I want you to be my girlfriend"? Or "I really want it to be just the two of us"?

No one had ever asked her this before. She had expected it to feel more . . . romantic. But he wasn't that type.

What had Dashawna encouraged her to say? The next step was supposed to be sexual exclusivity. "Lock it down," Dashawna had said. Moving in was out of order. Would he still be free to see other women? She needed him to clarify what he was asking. But she needed to ask in some kind of way that wouldn't look desperate.

"How is that different from what we're doing now?" she asked with a shrug. It sounded perfect. Dashawna would've been proud. Nothing thirsty about that response.

"No need for you to be paying rent when you're practically living with me already," he said.

She nodded. "That's true." Actually, it wasn't true, but he didn't know that. She was sleeping on Dashawna's couch and not paying any rent. She was only saving money by having breakfasts and dinners with him. She mostly ate cereal for lunch.

She took a tiny sip of his scotch. It didn't burn like the stuff her grandmother used to drink. "That sounds nice," she said. "But I'm not interested in cohabitating if it's just casual. Are you saying I would be your girlfriend?"

"Yes," he said. "Absolutely."

"A committed and sexually exclusive relationship?" she asked.

"Yes," he said. Although not quite as emphatically.

Morgan frowned. Was he just lousy at communicating? Or was he ambivalent about what she was asking?

"I don't want to be just a convenience," she said. "Let's be clear: I'm not angling for a proposal. But I don't want to be on some sort of indefinite girlfriend track. I need to know this has the potential to become an engagement within five years. If things go well, obviously. But if you've already ruled it out, don't waste my time."

"Yes," he said, sounding relieved. "There's the definite possibility within that time frame. I appreciate a direct negotiation."

"It sounds good," she said, then had a brainstorm. "I need a room of my own, though. For my textile work."

"Certainly," he said. "Done."

"Then yes," she said with her highest-watt grin. "I'll move in."

"Let's celebrate," he said, and pulled out the champagne.

They toasted. They had sex. After he was asleep, she used her vibrator in the bathroom. At a critical moment, Kevin did cross her mind.

Sebastian was busy in meetings all the next morning. She had seen the signs in the lobby for the Green Executive Leadership Summit. Sebastian was apparently one of the highest-level participants.

Shortly after they began dating, she had looked him up online. She knew he was the head of an energy company. He'd been the subject of a finance magazine cover article: "Generation G: How Sebastian Reid Is Greening His Father's Company," about how Sebastian had taken a company that had been exclusively focused on fossil fuels and shifted to including renewables. "Reid's father, the company's founder, was always known as an 'oilman,' but the younger Reid is more of a Renaissance man, moving into the twenty-first century, with a much broader and greener vision." The article called him a "global leader" and a "voice of reason in the move toward renewable energy." No wonder he was part of this green summit.

They got a late checkout, and he called the room at noon to ask her to pack up and meet him in the lobby in half an hour.

She polished her toenails and hobbled around, talking on the cell phone to Dashawna.

"Fuck yeah!" her friend said. "Should I start calling you 'the future Mrs. Reid'?"

"That's definitely premature," Morgan said. "I don't know if I'd even say yes if he proposed." It wasn't just that she had thought of Kevin at that particular moment, but also that she hadn't fully envisioned her life as the wife of an unromantic billionaire.

"I gotta go pack," Morgan said, stumbling to the closet to get her clothes. "Don't want to be late for my first night living in sin."

Dashawna laughed. "I'll gather up all your shit here in the apartment."

"I think I left a paper bag under the couch," Morgan said. "That ought to be big enough."

When Morgan got down to the glittering marble lobby, Sebastian was standing around with a group of mostly middle-aged men in suits. They looked tense. Perhaps some of them were his colleagues? He didn't introduce her. The lone woman was even older.

Sebastian took her arm. "Do you have any sunglasses?" he asked.

"No," she said. Who carried shades in winter? Unless they were skiing, something Morgan had never done.

Sebastian motioned for the concierge, and within a minute, he was handing her a pair of shades.

The bellboy stepped out of the elevator with their bags on a cart.

Morgan always thought of Denver as a relatively quiet city, so she was surprised to hear a fair amount of noise outside the hotel as they prepared to exit.

"Some kind of protesters," Sebastian said. "Just ignore them."

Morgan nodded.

The hotel door opened as a bellboy walked in with a gold

luggage cart, and the sound was even louder. Then the door slid closed and it muted the noise outside.

Sebastian put on shades, and she did the same. They were a matching pair of wraparound sport sunglasses. They certainly looked awkward with her outfit.

She and Sebastian crossed the length of the lobby in the tight knot of suits. Another bellboy followed them with their luggage on another gold cart.

The doors opened as an older couple walked in, and an explosion of noise came in with them.

Morgan turned to Sebastian, worried. She couldn't see his eyes behind the glasses.

What was going on out there?

Sebastian's voice was tight. "I had hoped to spare you from this," he said. "These people are so childish. They have no idea what it takes to make the world go around. I used to be much more sympathetic, before I actually started running the company."

The doors slid shut again, and the noise dulled.

"Our whole way of life is built on fossil fuels," Sebastian went on. "You can't just yank out the foundation from under a house and expect it to still stand. Over the last five years I've made so many sweeping changes, and it's never enough for them. If a semitruck is going a hundred miles an hour, you can't turn it around on a dime."

Morgan realized she was nodding. Did she actually agree with him?

She got distracted as she passed the elderly couple who had just walked in. They both looked shaken, and the man's breathing was slightly labored.

Morgan, Sebastian, and their crew took the final few steps across the lobby floor. And then the hotel doors slid open again, and they walked out into the Colorado sunlight. On the far side, there was a cordon of press behind a rope at the edge of the U-shaped driveway. All the reporters began screaming, "Mr. Reid! Over here, Mr. Reid."

Behind another rope on the other side were hundreds of demonstrators. The protest spilled out into the parking lot.

Many protesters carried signs. The first one Morgan noticed had an image of the globe on fire. It said "ReidCorp= scorched earth policy." Another said, "GREEN SUMMIT IS GREENWASHING."

But her brain only dimly registered those visuals. She was completely taken aback by the swell of noise. Hundreds of voices yelling at the same time: "How does this sound? Leave it in the ground!"

A crew of students, maybe middle schoolers, pressed against the barricade. One caramel-skinned teen girl was dressed in what looked like a traditional Native American outfit. She held a sign that read: "SHAME ON THE GREEDY ADULTS WHO ARE STEALING OUR FUTURE!"

Sebastian had his arm tightly around Morgan's waist.

The protesters' faces were masks of fury. She hung on to Sebastian, her fist closing over the fabric of his lapel.

"Here's the limo, thank God," Sebastian muttered.

Ten more steps and they were at the curb. The police were holding back the crowds.

A chauffeur opened the door for her, and Sebastian released her waist. As she turned to enter the back seat of the vehicle, she looked up, and her heart stopped.

Kevin stood at the edge of the police barricade. Staring straight at her. His eyes were wide with bitter surprise, half angry, half hurt.

She heard his singular voice in all the noise. "Are you fucking serious?"

How had he recognized her? She had on shades and her hair was swept up. She grabbed the hem of her coat to swing it into the limo and realized it was the distinctive block blend of several fabrics that matched the dress she'd worn in the airport.

She didn't look back as she scooted over on the seat and Sebastian slid in next to her. The chauffeur closed the door and they pulled away from the curb.

"Did someone say something rude to you?" Sebastian asked.

"No," Morgan said. "Nobody said a thing."

Colin Tehan bought that house he promised to Lourdes. He moved them to Pennsylvania. So green. Not like home in Spain, but lush in the summertime. Alive.

Lourdes didn't miss the work at the factory, but she missed speaking Spanish to some of the women there. Her Pennsylvania neighbors were German and Dutch. They lacked a certain Mediterranean warmth—even more so than her quiet Irish husband. But then her daughters were born. And soon life was too full to miss anything.

Lourdes's youngest child was named Elizabeth, but growing up in the 1950s, everyone called her Betty. Her mother called her Betita, with a Spanish accent, and Betty was always both endeared and ashamed of it.

In the mid-60s, Betty married her college sweetheart, Tom Hayes. Tom was a nice, German Lutheran boy who wanted a big family. Betty had studied English, but Tom had studied business, and he was a catch. She was glad to settle down in a nice house in Pittsburgh and get ready for motherhood.

They started trying on their wedding night. Betty decorated the nursery in yellow, a sort of neutral color that could match with either pink or blue clothes, de-

pending on the sex of their firstborn. Besides, in a big family, they would likely be having both boys and girls. Who would have time to paint a nursery once the babies started coming?

She busied herself with nesting for the first six months, but every twenty-eight days the blood in her underwear would set off tears. She went to her mother to ask what to do. What was Betty doing wrong? Lourdes didn't know. She'd never had trouble getting pregnant on either side of the Atlantic Ocean. In the last decade before menopause, she was careful not to have sex with her husband when she thought she might be fertile. Her husband was one of twelve. No fertility trouble ran in their family.

Betty asked Tom if they could both go talk to a doctor. Tom refused, so Betty went alone. She went in hoping they would find something simple to cure. But the tests didn't find any obstructions or low hormone levels. "Almost no one gets pregnant the first time," the doctor said. "It's only been eight months. Relax. Keep trying."

After a year, Betty couldn't take it anymore. Too many uninterrupted hours of feeling like a failure. She wanted to get a job. What about raising a family? Tom wanted to know. Yes, Betty wanted that, but there was no family so far. Was she supposed to sit at home all day tending to children that didn't exist yet? She would quit when she got pregnant.

Tom resentfully agreed. She began working at the bookstore. She left by three every afternoon to make his dinner. She had it on the table by the time he got home. Nothing had really changed in his life, but somehow her working embittered him. He cooled toward her. They "tried" for a baby less and less.

On his birthday, she took off from work and went

to surprise him with a gift at his office. As she walked past the window, she saw him standing much too close to his secretary. The woman who had become inexplicably hostile toward her. In that moment it all crystalized. She felt a blaze of rage, of heartbreak, of panic.

She tried to call her mother, but she was out. Back at home, Betty opened the wine and began the party early. When Tom came home, she confronted him.

By then, she was too drunk to have a clear expectation of his response. However, even in her drunken state, it shocked her that he blamed her for his infidelity. She hadn't given him any children. She made sex seem like a chore. And with her job at the bookstore, she failed to put his needs first.

She stood there, in the immaculately clean house, with his favorite meal on the table. Hanging in the closet was the new negligee she had planned to wear to bed this weekend—before she learned about the affair. What more did he want from her?

In the morning he said he wanted a divorce. But by then her head had cooled. She begged him to stay. They could work it out. She would try harder. But he was adamant.

She moved from the nice house back to her parents' house in Lundberg.

By then, her dad had passed away. Her sister had moved out of town. It was just Lourdes living there now. Betty returned to her mother in shame, a divorcee, a failed wife.

The room smelled of patchouli and a sort of pungent herb Betty would later learn to identify as marijuana. But on this night—her first real hippie party—it was all new. Beaded curtains, incense and reefer, groovy music, and people making out right in front of her.

It was exciting, but also a little off-putting. Betty didn't know what she thought about free love, but shackled love hadn't worked out for her.

"Honey," her coworker from the bookstore said, "you should be thanking Tom for that divorce. He spared you from the square life. Now you can finally experience freedom."

Later that night, she did feel free when, armed with a contact high, she was dancing with a guy who had a wild Afro. Which led to making out with him. Which led to a sexual encounter. It was everything she wasn't supposed to be doing: sex without marriage, with a Black guy? She was both more excited and more relaxed than ever before and had her first orgasm. She never really knew his name.

Walking home, she felt buzzed, loose-hipped. Had she really just done that? She had been raised to be a good Catholic girl, but a new generation was saying no to all the rules.

Over the next few months, she smoked weed in earnest, dropped acid, and had sex with several more guys.

None of them bothered to ask if she was on the pill, but she knew from her time with Tom that she couldn't get pregnant.

Lourdes was the first one to suspect. Betty had gotten home from working at the bookstore one evening unexpectedly. She had planned to go to a party but was too exhausted.

Her mother frowned. A face Lourdes had made

often lately. Betty stayed out late, sometimes all night. But what could she say about it? Betty had been married, lived on her own, and now was back in a sort of limbo. Not a child, but not quite living an adult life. It was as if being a wife had not actually prepared her for adulthood, but rather an adult child role.

"When did you last have your monthly?" Lourdes asked.

"My . . . ?" Betty asked, and found herself standing still, trying to remember. With Tom, she had counted so carefully. Clocked everything and tried to be ready on her most fertile days. But since the divorce, she hadn't paid attention at all.

The next day, a urine test at the doctor's confirmed it.

Betty didn't know what to do. Abortion was still illegal, but some of her hippie friends knew doctors you could go see in New York. As a Catholic, she didn't exactly believe. Still, abortion seemed out of the question. But did she really want a baby now? Now that she was just sort of finding her way in the world as a woman with more freedom? But after all that infertility, it seemed like a miracle. What if this was her only chance to become a mother? God had given her this opportunity. And Lourdes had offered to help her raise the baby. They had the house— bought and paid for. They had her dad's pension. She wouldn't keep working at the bookstore; Pittsburgh was too far away. But she could find a local job.

A decade before, she would never have considered a baby out of wedlock. But a decade before, she wouldn't have expected her own self being out of wedlock.

It wasn't so much that she decided to have the baby, more that she never mustered the courage to call the friends who knew who to contact in New York. By the time she was showing, she realized that the decision had been made without her. It wasn't going to be the life she had dreamed of with Tom, but maybe it would be a fine life.

Her mother pressed her for the name of the father. Shouldn't Betty tell him? Wouldn't he want to know?

Lourdes had no idea about the scene these days. Betty wasn't even sure of the guys' names, let alone how to contact them. There was Dan, Steve, Rob (or was it Bob?), Keith, and another white guy who had changed his name to a Hindu name she couldn't quite pronounce. There was also the Black guy from the first party—whose name she never knew—but that was before the doctor estimated her pregnancy began.

So imagine everyone's surprise when the baby came three weeks early. The doctors and nurses were worried that the baby was so premature. But in defiance of all their expectations, the baby girl was born perfectly to term. And with a tawny skin and full head of curly hair that hinted at the fact that she was Black.

At first, Betty was just so out of it from the epidural. And then so in awe of the perfectly formed little face. The ten tiny fingers and toes. It wasn't until she was discharged and saw a white couple with their baby and a Black couple with their baby. Her daughter—whom she had named Elaine—looked like the Black baby.

And so, starting on the ride home, she had begun to worry.

By the time they got into the house, she was sinking into a swamp of panic and despair. What if the baby was Black? Would get more Black over time? Could she handle raising a Black baby?

She had her mother hold Elaine when she got home, and she went into the bathroom and cried.

"I think the baby wants to nurse, querida," Lourdes said, tapping on the door of the bathroom.

She walked in to find Betty slumped down on the toilet, sobbing silently.

"Oh Betita! What's wrong?"

Betty stood up and tried to wipe her face. "What if the baby's Black?" she blurted out.

"If she's—?" Lourdes asked. "I don't care. We'll raise her just the same as if she's white."

Betty leaned onto her mother and sobbed openly then. And baby Elaine cried along with her. Lourdes leaned back onto the bathroom wall and rocked both of them.

Chapter 4

The first time Morgan went to Sebastian's apartment, it was to redo his living-room furniture and assist with upholstering his walls in fabric. It didn't make sense to her to call the place an apartment. It took up three floors of an Upper East Side luxury building. Sebastian had also inherited the family home Upstate, but he chose to live in their "city place." The apartment had high ceilings with chandeliers, glossy wooden parquet floors, and fine antiques.

She didn't see the bedroom until later, with its king-size bed and huge windows that overlooked the East River. Downstairs, his rec room had a full complement of workout equipment, including a state-of-the-art treadmill.

A friend had hooked Morgan up with the interior design gig. It paid a couple thousand for maybe fifteen hours of work. Usually she would live off that money for a few months while she made quilts. But after she and Sebastian started dating, his fees became her stash to pretend that she didn't need him to pay for anything.

The first time they went out, she told him: "Look, I'm only comfortable going out if I can pay my own way. I consider sharing finances to be intimate. More so than physical intimacy in some ways." Dashawna had coached her from the beginning to act like she didn't give a damn about his money.

So that first night, she had eaten a pricey seafood dish, drank an expensive wine by the glass, and had a fancy dessert. Then asked the waiter for separate checks, and she paid her own. She swallowed the lump in her throat at the bill—that could have been her food money for weeks. They had continued this way for a few dates.

"I'm gonna go broke if I keep this up," she told Dashawna.

"No, girl, just until you have sex for the first time," Dashawna said. "If you only do it once, he'll think it's a fluke. Just do it until the first time you take him to bed. Most of these guys aren't great lays." She laughed. "They wanna offer you something to keep you around."

Dashawna had been right. After they had sex, Sebastian asked if she would spend the night and if he could take her out to brunch. He was hoping they had gotten to the place where she would let him spoil her.

She shrugged, lying in bed feeling a different kind of satisfaction.

"I guess so," she said.

The next morning he had taken her to a staggeringly expensive restaurant. She had ordered modestly, and he had been happy to pay.

"You're on your way," Dashawna had said.

From then on, he paid for everything.

When Morgan moved to New York, she had reversed the journey of her great-grandmother. This was the part of the family lore that she had been told. How Lourdes had sought to escape the teeming metropolis, to find something quieter, closer to the Spanish city in which she'd been raised. Small-town Pennsylvania wasn't really what she had wanted, but three generations of her family had figured out how to patch together a life there.

Morgan had cut those threads. She—like her great-grandmother—was stunned by New York City's dirt and crowding. But also dazzled by its diversity and vibrance. And both had lived in marginal parts of the city. Lourdes in a Lower East Side tenement as a garment worker. Morgan in an overcrowded Brooklyn apartment as a fashion student.

Now, she was getting to know a different New York. The day she moved in with Sebastian, she paced in front of his building, waiting for the moving truck. It was her first time standing in front of the building. She usually just walked in from a cab or limo at the curb. She'd noticed from the beginning that the building was fancy, but for the first time, she took in how nice the sidewalk was, too. Where was the broken glass? The junk food wrappers? The used condoms in the gutter? Was this really the same city?

She knew that oil money paid for the apartment and that fossil fuels were destroying the planet. But how could she blame Sebastian for what his father had done? He was trying to change the company for the better.

"Now remember," Dashawna said over the phone. "Don't carry any of your things. Just sit on the living room couch and flip through a magazine. My friends will do everything."

"That feels so weird," Morgan said.

"You're paying them to move your stuff," Dashawna said.

"It's not really my stuff," Morgan said. "Some stuff I bought off Craigslist to act like I have stuff."

"You want to walk into his place with nothing but your paper bag?" Dashawna asked.

Morgan did not. She reclined on the couch and flipped through a quilting magazine as two tall, Puerto Rican guys carried a queen-size futon and frame that converted into a couch and a bureau she had bought from a student leaving town. Two hundred dollars had bought the contents of an entire apartment. She didn't need the guy's desk and left it on the street with a "FREE" sign. She got his sheets. A comforter. Pillows. A few kitchen utensils. The pretense of a life. After that, the two guys brought up the one significant possession she actually owned—a sewing machine with a little folding table and stool.

They moved it all into what was now her room. It had been a former guest room, and it was nearly as big as Dashawna's studio apartment. After the guys finished moving everything in, she paid them—including a large tip—and thanked them.

"Anytime," one of them said.

"Ya doin' good," the other one murmured to her with a thumbs-up.

Morgan had exaggerated. All her possessions didn't fit into one paper bag. They fit into two large rolling suitcases and a carry-on. Plus the sewing machine.

The paper bag was filled with fabric. She didn't feel at home until she was able to lay out all the panels onto a clothes-drying rack. Then she sat at the little stool and set up her sewing machine.

That was her reason for doing all this. Sebastian would be the patron of her arts. Even if they never got married. She would let him support her for long enough to get her career off the ground.

Dashawna was a genius who knew how to exploit her assets. Dashawna had the world's smoothest brown skin, the color of a pecan. Large eyes, full lips, and an hourglass shape. Men were always following her down the street. Next to her, Morgan was plain, with her medium brown hair and slender figure.

"When you dress up, you have a Manhattan look," Dashawna said. "I'm built for the boroughs."

Dashawna was a sugar baby, and she had several older gentlemen friends in Manhattan who had committed to spoiling her. One paid her rent. Two gave her money monthly. She stashed most of it away.

"I'm retiring when I'm forty," Dashawna said.

After Morgan had arranged all her stuff in Sebastian's house, she called Dashawna. "Thank you so much!" she said.

"This is not all altruism," Dashawna said. "You're the one, Morgan. Look at you. You can live the Black princess dream. And I'm gonna make sure that if you marry him, you not gonna leave any of your people behind. First off, you gotta let me do the wedding. A destination in the Caribbean. I'll do the dress, the catering, the decorations, the travel, the hotel, the cake, the rehearsal dinners. I'll outfit everyone. I got hustles. I'll charge him full price and get everything at deep discount. With a multimillion-dollar wedding, I could retire at thirty-five. Trust me, honey, this is not charity. I got skin in this game."

Three years earlier, Morgan, Dashawna, and Vivian had graduated from the Fashion Institute of Technology. They had squeezed into a one-bedroom together during their final year. Morgan and Dashawna shared the bedroom and Vivian slept on the couch. As they prepared to graduate, their paths diverged. Vivian had connections through her father and took an unpaid internship at Dilani Mara, while her family supported her. Morgan got an entry-level job at a fashion house but could barely make rent. Dashawna didn't even get any interviews. She sent out a second round of résumés with Shawna on it instead of Dashawna and got a couple of callbacks but was always determined to be "not right for the position."

During school, Dashawna had occasionally gone out with guys because they had money. After she graduated and was unemployed, she tipped over from dating to sugar babying. Morgan crashed on Dashawna's couch whenever her housing situations fell apart. Morgan also acted as a bodyguard when Dashawna met a prospective sugar daddy. Morgan dressed down, looking like a local college student. Morgan arrived shortly after Dashawna and sat at a nearby table. The two women had such different appearances and personal styles that no one ever put them together. Including the one creepy guy who grabbed Dashawna and jammed his tongue down her throat in a dark bar. Dashawna pulled back and tried to leave, but he wouldn't let go. He didn't anticipate an attack from the slender, white-looking girl at the table behind him. Morgan whacked him in the back of the head with her hard-cover book. He staggered, letting Dashawna go, and the two women fled onto the street. They hailed a cab, tumbling into the back and closing the door. Dashawna burst out crying, and Morgan put her arms around her.

"I should have known," Dashawna said. "He came on too strong on the phone." She wiped her face. "Just the way he talked about Black women. But I thought . . . I don't know what I thought. I guess I thought, 'fuck it, rent is due.' I should have been more careful."

"Don't blame yourself, honey," Morgan said. "That's why you have me for backup. You're not responsible for these entitled, rich assholes who don't respect women."

Dashawna pulled out a handkerchief and blew her nose. "Thank God you were there," she said to Morgan. "And I'll bet that motherfucker isn't even rich. The rich ones don't use brute force. They get you on the hook with the money and then act like they own you."

That was one of the bad days. On Dashawna's good days, Morgan trooped out to an entry-level job at a boutique and

Dashawna slept in. While Morgan dealt with entitled Manhattan women, Dashawna lay in bed reading a novel.

The morning after Morgan moved in with Sebastian she felt . . . lonely. After the sex, he fell asleep and she texted Dashawna. Usually, she said **"See you in the morning,"** but not this time. She was used to comparing dates with her bestie and laughing about how clueless men could be. But Morgan was all the way uptown now. It didn't make sense to trek out to Brooklyn just to compare notes. They could do it on the phone, but it wasn't the same. Still, she had a workspace. She buried herself in fabric and let the muse keep her company.

Morgan had given notice on her boutique job. For the first time since . . . ever . . . she didn't have to worry about making money. She could focus solely on her art, a luxury she hadn't even had in college.

Morgan spent the morning sketching and then began to sew. She had a pile of special textiles she'd been hanging on to for years. Waiting for the right moment to make something out of them. The previous week she got a perfect bolt of fabric to use as a background. She'd found it at a going-out-of-business sale—one of her favorite neighborhood fabric stores in Queens was closing. The owner had brought out all of their inventory, and there was this strange, shimmering, blue-black silk. It was perfect.

When Sebastian came home, she was still working—utterly caught up in her quilting.

He looked at the fabric laid out on the futon, blinked twice, and looked back up at her. "Have a drink with me, babe," he said.

Morgan looked from him to the quilt. "Of course," she said.

* * *

Sebastian complained about work in a monologue she couldn't follow. He hated whiners. So many whiners out there. They didn't like this. They didn't like that. What did they expect from him? She didn't exactly know who these ReidCorp whiners were, but she wasn't going to learn from this diatribe.

She put on a face of listening and ran her hands back and forth on the rich fabric of the chenille sofa.

"Chinese?" he asked.

Was there an issue with his corporation's trade with Asia?

"Morgan," he said. "Babe. Do you want Chinese food?"

"Sure," she said. "Whatever you like."

"You seem far away tonight," he said.

"Sorry," she said. "Long day in the studio."

"You might need to call it quits a little earlier," he said. "Do something to unwind before I get home. I hate talking to myself."

Morgan smiled. "Of course, sweetheart," she said. "Let's get mu shu." Internally, she did a double take: Did he really just say I need to stop working earlier to get ready for him to come home?

Be careful, Dashawna had said. The sugar daddy thinks he owns you.

"I'm not so hot on mu shu," Sebastian said. "I think General Tso's chicken. With a shrimp dish. Would you like wine?"

"No," Morgan said. "I'll just have whatever you're having."

The next day, Dashawna happened to be uptown, and she came over to Sebastian's apartment.

"Damn, girl," she said, looking around. "This is what I'm talking about."

Morgan gave her a tour that ended up in her studio. She showed off the quilt pieces she had laid out.

Dashawna shrieked, "Morgan, this is amazing! And just in time. You need to enter it into that contest."

"What contest?"

"CFI?"

Morgan looked blank.

"Keep up, girl," Dashawna said. "Contemporary Fabric Intersections: Fine Art, Folk Art, and Fashion. It's a collaboration between the American Folk Art Museum, the Glenmore Gallery, and Dilani Mara. The winner's design will get to be a textile in Dilani Mara's fall fashion line."

"Oh yeah," Morgan said. "I remember Vivian telling us about that. I thought I'd never have time to make something."

"You got time now," Dashawna said. "You need to let me take some photos to submit it day after tomorrow."

"It's not sewn properly," Morgan said. "Just tacked down."

"So what?" Dashawna said. "It's just a photo. What's gonna draw them in is these colors." She ran her hand across the fabric. "You don't have to submit the final for a while."

"Okay, yeah," Morgan said, brightening. "Hell yeah."

The two of them set up the photo shoot.

Dashawna pulled a selfie stick out of her bag and secured her phone on it. Then she set the whole thing up on a chair like a tripod and pointed it at the bed.

"The light in here is amazing," Dashawna said, looking at the bright November afternoon sunlight streaming in through the large bay windows. "Hey, after I shoot this, hook me up with some boudoir photos."

"You have on cute underwear?" Morgan asked.

"Girl," Dashawna said. "I don't leave the house without my best shit. You never know who'll call."

They shot some photos of the quilt, and then Dashawna stripped down to a black lace Merry Widow and thong with an old-school garter belt.

"Damn," Morgan said. "You really do leave the house prepared."

"You don't know the half of it," Dashawna said, and pulled a pair of stiletto pumps out of her bag. As Morgan recalled, she had walked into the apartment in low-heeled boots.

Dashawna lay down on the bed with her ass in the air.

"Start the photo shoot with my good side," she said and laughed.

Morgan took a hundred photos, but the first one was the best, with Dashawna laughing, ass out in the afternoon sunlight.

Within two weeks Morgan got into a groove. First thing in the morning she ran on Sebastian's treadmill. She still couldn't believe he had a whole gym he never used. He had another one in his office.

After a four-mile run, she showered and ate scrambled eggs and toast for breakfast. Then she worked on her textiles until midafternoon. When Dashawna was free, they simultaneously streamed a TV show and watched it over the phone to wind down in the afternoon. The combination of creativity and talking trash with her bestie filled her with joy. By the time Sebastian came home, she felt elated. Even he noticed.

"Have you been working out?" he asked. "You seem like you're full of endorphins or something."

It wasn't the jogging. It was the economic freedom. "Joie de vivre," she said.

She felt passionate, randy, even. She often initiated sex, and he was pleased.

By the third Thursday she was living with him, she begged off her date with Dashawna.

"Sebastian's birthday is this weekend and I need to go shopping downtown," Morgan said. "Wanna come?"

"Hell no," Dashawna said. "Shopping for a boring white man is work."

And it was. Morgan wandered around the men's departments at a few downtown stores. What would he like? What would send the right message? How much should she spend? Was a tie too predictable? Were body products too intimate? Would sex toys send the wrong message? She sent Dashawna a string of texts. Did you name a star after a guy like Sebastian? Was there any jewelry that was expensive enough not to seem cheap but cheap enough that she could afford it? She wasn't working now, so she had no new money coming in. Just a fixed amount of savings that didn't dwindle on the daily with him supporting her. But still, she might need to find something part-time.

Dashawna didn't answer any of the texts. Morgan tried calling but got voice mail. She hung up and didn't leave a message.

And then it hit her. The one thing she knew about that he didn't. Art. He had said that he was interested in becoming a collector, but he didn't know where to start. She should lead the way. He didn't need to like the piece, just to know that it was valuable. He might even put it on the wall, which would make her feel more like she belonged in his apartment.

She took the subway downtown to an art supply store where a friend of hers worked.

She looked around at the bright displays. She used to walk into this place counting her pennies.

"I want something by an up-and-coming artist," she said. "Someone who would sell for pennies on the dollar of what it's gonna be worth."

"Pennies on the dollar?" he asked. "You been hanging out with investment bankers? Mafia guys?"

Morgan laughed. "My boyfriend is a corporate type. I guess his money talk is rubbing off on me."

"I know just the guy," her friend said. "This new, incredibly hot artist at school. But he's not a painter. He's a sculptor. Does these huge pieces in wire. He planes the wire in spots so it glistens like a gem. And he's amazingly productive. He's the one to buy. You can get it for a couple hundred, but I think they'll end up being worth a hundred thousand."

Sculpture? Morgan had envisioned a painting she could easily slip under her bed.

"Are they fragile?"

"Yes, honey," her friend said. "You need to get a ride share to take this home. It'd get crushed on the subway. But they're amazingly light. You can carry it by yourself."

After she agreed, her friend made the call. She took the train to a studio in the Bronx, where a Panamanian guy with dreadlocks was working on a huge sculpture out of chain link and barbed wire. Inside of it was a human figure made of a lighter wire, painted red.

"Wow," she said.

"It's my senior project," he said. "Border Patrol."

Morgan nodded. "I can see that."

"Let me show you the ones I have for sale."

Morgan selected a tree. It was beautiful and halfway as tall as she was. Just over a hundred dollars.

"How do people usually display these?" she asked.

"You can put it on an end table," he said. "Some people hang them. But the tree kind of demands to be rooted, you know? I'd set it on the floor. Better juju. But not everybody has floor space."

Morgan nodded. The apartment had plenty of space. Hopefully Sebastian would like it. Or at least see value in it. She paid the artist and called a ride share.

*   *   *

When the driver dropped her off in front of her building, she asked the doorman, Carl, not to mention the sculpture. "It's a birthday surprise," she said.

Carl put a finger to his lips and called the elevator for her.

When she got up to the apartment, she wasn't sure where to put it. The sculpture wouldn't fit under her bed, and the guest-room closet wasn't really big enough. Her fabrics were jammed in there.

Sebastian had been nice enough to allow her to stash some of her extra fabrics in a storage space off his study. That storage space had a Japanese screen and a dark corner where she could hide the sculpture. On her way to the study, she admired her upholstery work. She loved to touch the walls she'd done in the world's softest leather. It made the hall womblike. The entire house had thick, wooden doors and carpets that muffled sound.

She set the sculpture down in the hallway and tried the door to Sebastian's study. The door swung open into a small entryway, so Sebastian—who had his back to the door—didn't hear her. Morgan caught sight of a stranger through a reflection in the mirror. He was middle-aged, balding, and had on a pair of tortoise shell glasses. When the stranger saw her reflection in the doorway, his eyes flew open.

Sebastian turned, his eyes suspicious. "Who's there?"

Morgan stepped back. "It's just me, sweetheart."

"What are you doing up here?" He stood and blocked her view of the stranger.

"I just—" Morgan stammered. "I just wanted to put something in the storage—"

"It's not a good time," Sebastian snapped and closed the door.

Morgan stood in the hallway, the tree sculpture glinting beside her.

Okay, she thought. Bedroom closet it is.

* * *

"Darling," Sebastian said that evening at dinner. "I'm sorry I snapped. I was so startled."

"I apologize for not knocking," Morgan said. "I wanted to store a few things in the space off your study, but I should've checked with you first."

"No, no," he said. "I offered you that space, and I need to keep the study door locked if I have a sensitive meeting."

"As long as you're not cheating on me with a faceless, middle-aged man, I'm fine."

Sebastian looked at her for a moment, then laughed.

"I had a flash picture in my mind of it," he said. "And then my mind quickly erased it. We might need to have sex tonight to permanently remove the image."

"Sounds good," she said.

In the middle of the night, Morgan woke up. Sebastian's face. The anger in his face. Her father had had that same expression sometimes. Her father. Barely ever around but had made a few indelible appearances with that face.

"Keeping my daughter away from me?" he had demanded. But didn't actually ever focus on Morgan. It was all about how her mother had done him wrong. Each time he had stood there and ignored Morgan, with his focus riveted on her mother. Ignoring the baby, then toddler, then kindergartener he was supposedly so upset to be banished from. He had barely looked at her.

And later it was her stepfather, Brian. She didn't recall his rage, only her mother's stories about him.

Morgan shuddered. Climbed out of bed and went down to her studio. She worked for a couple of hours and then felt tired again. She wanted to fold out the futon and slide under one of her quilts. But she didn't want it to look like she was upset. Was she upset? He hadn't meant to be so sharp with her. It was an honest mistake. And he had apologized. She wasn't sure if she was still hurt by it or just shaken by the memories it triggered of her father and stepfather.

She climbed the stairs to the bedroom, sliding her hands along the leather walls for comfort.

Elaine was one of two Black kids in her middle school. "Biracial" was the term people were using, but she didn't like the word. It sounded so meticulously divided at fifty percent. She didn't know her dad. Was he just one race? Was her mother just one race? Elaine had curls only slightly tighter than her grandmother's. Lourdes was Spanish from Spain but didn't look that different from some of the Puerto Rican kids who lived a few towns over. People sometimes called Elaine half and half, but was she really an exact fraction?

Besides, as some of the boys at school pointed out to her horror, some things about her seemed to be all Black. From the beginning, the problem had been her hair. Her mother had no clue how to take care of it. But Grandma Lourdes knew. She taught Elaine what type of brush to use, how to comb it wet, with a little olive oil. Elaine liked the way it looked wet, but when it dried, it was too puffy. She kept it braided. By high school she learned to let it dry overnight in four big, thick braids, then take the braids out. It would be wavy and long.

Yet there were other ways she looked Black that she never figured out how to tame. Like her butt. No matter how baggy the jeans she wore were, it stuck out like a shelf. She stopped eating for a while in ninth grade, hoping to starve it down. Maybe it got a little smaller, but overall, her butt just looked bigger, with the rest of her so slim.

From the time she was little, everyone asked her if she was adopted when they saw her with her mother.

Less so when she was with her grandmother. Starting in sixth grade, she dreamed of leaving this crappy town.

Until high school, when suddenly rap music became cool. And some of the white boys were interested in her. Well . . . they had always been curious about her—had whispered obscene suggestions in her ear. But now, some of the boys were hinting that they might even want her as their actual girlfriend. A sort of trophy to go with their Beastie Boys' "(You Gotta) Fight for Your Right (to Party)" anthem. Okay. Sure. She could dance on tables while all the boys at the party admired her.

Her best friend wasn't so impressed.

"I don't know why you're acting like such a slut," the best friend said.

"A slut?" Elaine asked. "You've gone further than me. I've never even done more than make out with a boy."

Elaine didn't say what they both knew: Her friend had let the boyfriend put his hands under her shirt and into her underwear. Elaine had made out with a few boys, hoping that it would lead to a boyfriend, but it hadn't.

"You don't get it," her friend had said. "If people see you making out with boys at a party, they'll think you're doing more."

Sure enough, by Monday it was all over school that she had given four blow jobs at the party.

Elaine and her friend fell out when the friend didn't defend her. The harassment got so bad that she dropped out in her junior year.

After moping around the house for a few weeks, her mother insisted that she needed to get a job if she wasn't going to school.

Betty worked as a manager at a pizza restaurant and got Elaine a job there, working the counter. Those same idiots came in from the school, and Elaine fantasized about putting a dab of piss in their pizza. She never did it, but it made her feel better to know she could.

Once, a family came in, and her mom had a particularly broad smile for them. Her mom addressed the husband as "Tom." He was older than the wife, and the three kids were all Asian.

"Did you know them?" Elaine asked.

"Just the guy," Betty had said. "From a long time ago."

Yet Betty had been depressed all the following week.

After a series of dead-end jobs, Elaine had gone back to school to get her GED at the local community college. She was still the only Black student in any of her classes. There, she had met Joey, a white guy who dealt speed but was taking business classes. He had visions of himself as a future mogul. He had wooed Elaine with promises of a much better life. Speed was just to get some money together so he could build a legit business. She fell hard, and within the first year and—despite using the pill—she got pregnant.

Elaine was shocked when her mother, Betty, begged her to get an abortion, "even though it would kill your grandmother if she knew. So don't tell her."

Elaine wasn't sure what to do. She and Joey wanted kids. She had already told Joey, and he said he would take care of her. She really hadn't wanted to get pregnant just yet. He was so romantic. After all those

*years of being the unlovable, undatable girl, she
wanted a little more of that for herself.*

*Her mother pressed. "Tell Joey you had a miscar-
riage."*

*But Elaine would feel too guilty. It was her own
fault. She had misplaced her birth control pills. And
then Joey had surprised her with a weekend getaway.
It was such a luxurious gift. What was she supposed
to do? Tell him no? Tell him that she needed to make
an appointment with the gynecologist before they
could go? It was a delicious, sex-soaked weekend. She
prayed for the best. She got knocked up.*

*Joey moved them into a beautiful apartment a few
towns away from her mother's house. He would be
out doing business most of the time, but she was free
to shop and decorate with her mother. One day, when
she was about six months pregnant, his former room-
mate was moving out of their old apartment. He came
by with the last box of Joey's leftover stuff.*

*Elaine was determined to get it all put away. She
pulled various familiar items out of the box. Some of
Joey's clothes—T-shirts, a couple of old plaid button-
ups, some out-of-date magazines, and some bathroom
items. She put the clothes in the laundry and put the
magazines for kindling in the fireplace. Joey had a
fireplace.*

*She took the rest to the bathroom. Mostly hair
products. Some shampoo and conditioner, plus a few
jars of hair gel. And in the bottom of the box was a
small beige item. A compact of pills.*

*Elaine's breath caught. It was her pills. Her "lost"
birth control pills.*

Elaine swayed as her knees felt weak. She leaned

against the wall and made her way to the couch. It took a while for the thought to put itself together, but she had the emotional sensation first.

Sabotage.

He had sabotaged her birth control. She hadn't lost her pills. He had taken them. Hidden them. Then offered her a long weekend to keep her off them for several days. It was so sinister. But what was he always saying? "I'm a businessman. I know how to get what I want. I gotta think three, four steps ahead."

Did that mean tracking her cycle? Knowing when to plan the weekend? When to hide her pills? Elaine could barely breathe. Her heart was racing and her chest felt tight.

Suddenly, she wished she had taken her mother's advice and gotten the abortion. Now it was too late. She would be tethered to him forever through this child.

No. She refused. They weren't married. She didn't owe him anything. She called her mother to pick her up. Elaine and Lourdes protected her from Joey's angry visits. At first daily, then weekly, then they trailed off. When the baby was born, they were four generations under one roof. The baby was a girl, and they named her Morgan.

Sebastian loved the sculpture Morgan gave him for his birthday. He set it in the entryway, just inside the door. He turned one of the track lights onto it so it gleamed.

Morgan went back to blissful days of quilting. She started running on the treadmill for a second hour at the end of the workday.

On Thanksgiving afternoon she was running and listening to NPR. Now that she didn't have to go to a job, the days all blended together in a swirl of quilting and Sebastian, who worked seven days a week, even holidays.

Morgan was half listening when she heard his name in a news segment they were rerunning from earlier that day.

"In business news," the male announcer said, "fossil fuel mogul Sebastian Reid of ReidCorp has come under fire from environmental watchdog groups when it came to light that ReidCorp will be bidding on Green Fuel Contracts with the Department of Energy early next year. NPR spoke with Yolanda Vance, an attorney who represents several climate action groups."

"There are two areas of concern," Yolanda said. "Reid-Corp has been a fossil fuel company benefitting from government subsidies for half a century. They've made a few recent moves toward renewables, but to many of us in the climate movement, it seems like more of a public relations move than a genuine change."

Yolanda continued, "But the thing that's even more troubling is that the chief of sustainable energy transition in the Department of Energy, Mitchell Brightwell, is Sebastian Reid's godfather. Brightwell has tons of sensitive information on multibillion-dollar contracts ReidCorp will be bidding on. Who's to say that he won't let something slip at the Thanksgiving dinner table? It's a clear conflict of interest. Or a potential case of nepotism. ReidCorp should drop out, or Brightwell should resign as chief of sustainable energy transition."

"Sebastian Reid spoke with us from his New York offices," the reporter said.

Sebastian's voice came through her earbuds, familiar but cool, with his business voice: "People just don't understand. Changing from one form of energy to another takes time. We are overhauling a massive company infrastructure and also need to retrain our workforce. We don't want loyal employees to lose jobs. And we need to keep making money to keep paying them."

His voice was even, and she could imagine the slight frown of concern between his eyebrows.

"Also," he went on, "there are rules against family members bidding on these contracts, and that makes sense. But people are wrong to call my relationship to Mitchell Brightwell a family connection. We're not blood relatives. Just because he had a social friendship with my father doesn't mean we have one. Any allegations otherwise are ludicrous," Morgan heard the dismissive tone in Sebastian's voice. "I haven't seen him for at least six months. We won't be sitting together at any Thanksgiving table."

Sebastian shifted into his cool business voice again: "Mitchell Brightwell is a seasoned professional in the energy industry with a fifty-year history. That's why he makes a great chief of sustainable energy transition. He knows the field. But that also means he's gonna know some of the players and, in my case, some of their sons. It's naïve to think he wouldn't. But he's an honest and ethical man, and I have no doubt he will run a fair bidding process. And the whole time, there'll be a Chinese Wall between us. No contact. So there can be no question of malfeasance."

The treadmill began to rise to create a greater incline. Morgan was focused on the interview and nearly lost her stride. It was dangerous to slip on a treadmill going this fast. She turned off the radio and kept running.

She had heard Sebastian complain a few times about living in his father's shadow, about people unfairly holding the sins of the father against the son. She finished her workout and prepared herself to hear him complain about it at dinner. Thanksgiving was at his sister's house in Darien, Connecticut. Mitchell Brightwell was definitely not going to be there. Ever since his parents died, the brother and sister had a quiet meal together, ordering in from a local catering service.

Morgan took a quick shower and checked email while she blow-dried her hair. A news thread popped up on her email website. There it was again, the same story about Sebastian. But this time there were photographs. Which was how Morgan realized that Mitchell Brightwell, the CEO of Brightwell Industries, was the man Morgan had seen in Sebastian's study.

Chapter 5

Morgan sat there, stunned, staring at the picture. The photo of Brightwell wasn't current. He looked younger, thinner. Maybe she was wrong. Maybe they just looked similar. She stared at the features of the man's face on her phone. She compared it to the image in her mind. She focused until her vision blurred. She had only seen him briefly. But the sinking feeling in her stomach told her she was right.

She googled a more current photo and her breath caught. It was definitely the same guy.

Sebastian had lied. Sebastian was trying to rig a bid on a Department of Energy contract. Billions of dollars were at stake. Not to mention the potential impact on the environment.

And then Morgan did something she hadn't done since just after she returned from Colorado. She put a new name into her google search: Kevin Templeton.

There were a ton of hits. She added "Iowa" and "farm." Still too many. She googled "Kevin Templeton," "Iowa," "farm," and "climate change." And there he was. Those deep brown eyes. The long-muscled arms. The chiseled cheekbones. He was standing on stage holding a microphone. Behind him were people of various colors with signs that read "There Is No Plan(et) B" and "Save the Earth."

He was the only person she could imagine giving this information. He was probably pissed at her. She had thrown away his number. But her photographic memory meant she remembered it just as clearly as Mitchell Brightwell's face.

"I can't call him," Morgan told Dashawna.

"Excuse me?" Dashawna asked. "You have to fucking call him. The goddamn planet is burning. These motherfuckers are the ones burning it down. You got some dirt on ReidCorp? You need to give it to someone who can do something with it."

"I know you're right," Morgan said, biting her lip.

"I thought your man was just some random rich guy named Sebastian," Dashawna said. "You never told me your boo was Sebastian *Reid* of ReidCorp."

"I didn't realize everything that ReidCorp was doing," Morgan said.

Dashawna sucked her teeth. "Please," she said. "Get your head out of the sand. While we still have sand. Climate justice is racial justice."

"What does that even mean?" Morgan asked.

"Girl, I'm from Houston," Dashawna said. "Half my neighborhood washed away in Hurricane Harvey."

"I'm sorry," Morgan said, feeling a bit mortified at her cluelessness. "I didn't realize."

"My mama was lucky," Dashawna said. "Because climate change comes home to us Black and brown people first. But it's coming for Sebastian's ass, too. Open your eyes. The least you can do is call the cowboy and tell him what you saw."

"Farm boy."

"Call the boy and tell him," Dashawna said.

"I will," Morgan said. "As soon as I get off the phone with you."

But she didn't. It was Thanksgiving. She promised herself she would call him tomorrow.

Thanksgiving dinner was awkward. Sebastian's car dropped them off in front of a huge, white house with a wraparound deck and a sweeping lawn. It was located next to a pond that stretched out next to them, moonlight glittering off its smooth surface.

Sebastian's sister, Neve, was a bone-thin platinum blonde who flitted around the large dining room, arranging and re-arranging everything on the massive, wooden table. Her husband, Warren, was bland and quiet. Their twin boys were engrossed in their iPads throughout the meal and then asked to be excused. The food was too abundant and too fancy. Neve carried most of the conversation with an incessant stream of chatter. Sebastian seemed sunk in melancholia. Warren chimed in occasionally with small talk, and Morgan made conversation by asking about the art on the walls. A series of black-and-white photographs of a wet day in New York City—studies in water on different surfaces. She had been interested in the content of the work, but Neve and Warren talked about them mostly like they were financial investments.

On the ride home Sebastian was quiet and moody.

"Neve seems nice," Morgan said. "How often do you all see each other?"

The limo sped down the interstate.

Sebastian shrugged. "Thanksgiving," he said. "The odd lunch when she comes into the city. And we make an annual pilgrimage to our parents' graves on the anniversary of their deaths."

They rode for a while in silence. Outside the window, Morgan watched as the limo's headlights illuminated a shadowy view of spindly trees without leaves.

The whole day began to feel surreal. The image of Mitchell Brightwell. Did that really happen? Did she really see him in Sebastian's office? Catch him in a massive lie on the radio? Then she went with him to a holiday dinner that didn't feel like a holiday?

He and his sister were so . . . not . . . not warm. So different from the raucous Thanksgiving dinners her mom used to host with a couple of older single women friends from work. After the meal, they'd all get to drinking and laughing until late.

The strange dinner with Neve and Warren and the twins made her feel as if she were in a dream or an episode of a TV show. Right down to being so certain he was lying.

But whatever his faults in his work life, he was her boyfriend. And she could see he was hurting. Did holidays ever stop being hard after someone lost their parents?

She reached for his hand.

"No need to baby me," he said. "I'll be fine by tomorrow."

"I'm not—" she began, recalling her grief when her grandmother died. "I'm not trying to baby you. I just—when people lose someone, they deserve comfort."

"I don't need comfort," he said. "I just need to get home and get to bed." He leaned away from her in the limo.

It wasn't easy to find a phone booth in New York City these days. Morgan went to Grand Central Station. Not only did she want the untraceability of a booth, she wanted the anonymity of a bustling area. In the wide space with commuters rushing by, she felt strangely private.

She closed her eyes, dropped in the coins, and visualized the phone number from the airline napkin. Even though she was certain of the numbers, she dialed slowly.

Her heart beat hard as she listened to it ring.

"You've reached Kevin," his voice mail said and gave the date. "If you're calling about today's Black Friday action, we'll be outside Amazon's Midtown headquarters from noon to five. Join us!" He gave the address and cross street. Then the recorded voice came on, telling her how to leave a message. As if she didn't know. She hung up.

Amazon's headquarters weren't far. She could get there on foot.

Her legs began walking before she had even made a decision to go. She wouldn't need to actually decide anything yet. She could just go and check it out. See what the protest looked like. Maybe he'd be chained to the building. Maybe getting arrested or something. Unavailable. She could tell Dashawna she had tried.

She walked the fifteen blocks to where he was, the chilly wind whipping her hair in and out of her face. She expected loud chants, people blocking traffic. But instead, there was a sweet, mournful sound. A group of street musicians playing nearby? A sort of melodic, harmonic, a cappella vocal.

As she got closer, the sound got louder, and she saw it was the protest making the sound. A humming. An intense, melancholic tune.

When she rounded the corner, there were about seventy-five people, all in black, humming. They were pressed back against the building on either side of the entrance. Not blocking the sidewalk. Just standing there.

She crossed the street so she could look at them without being noticed. In the center of the group, to the left of the doors, was a coffin. She expected to find a picture of the Earth, but instead there were several white chalk outlines of different animals and insects. "EXTINCT," the sign said.

It took a moment to pick Kevin out from the crowd. There were several women on stilts who dwarfed him. But there he stood, humming, eyes closed. He wore a T-shirt that demanded "CLIMATE REPARATIONS FOR THE PACIFIC ISLANDS."

There were no words, no exact melody to their music, just melancholy minor harmonies. The sound suddenly took hold of her and she started crying. She had to put a hand on her own chest to press on a sharp pain. She didn't sob, she just stood there, transfixed, crying for something she hadn't even realized had been lost. And just beside the coffin was a man she hadn't realized how much she had missed.

The group, on some subtle signal she hadn't seen, slowly brought their final note to a close. The subsequent street noise was strange, abrupt, the spell broken. The group opened their eyes.

Across four lanes of cars and taxicabs, Kevin's eyes widened in surprise at her.

Morgan blinked and wiped her face. It was now or never. She ran across the street, weaving in between the stopped traffic.

Kevin's brow was knit.

She felt offensive in her brightly colored dress among the mourners. But she had to talk to him.

"We are here today," a woman began in a megaphone. "To mourn what has been lost and talk about what can still be saved. Saved if we act now and act boldly." She had long, pink extension braids like Dashawna wore when they were in school.

Another woman handed out leaflets. Morgan took one and stepped up to Kevin.

"Excuse me," she said. "Could I please speak to you for a minute?"

Kevin looked over at the speaker, talking about endangered species, particularly pollinators critical for maintaining our food supply.

Kevin handed his end of the EXTINCT banner to the woman beside him.

He stepped forward. "You happened to be walking by?" he asked. "Or were you coming to Amazon?"

"No," she said. "I came to find you."

"How did you know I'd be here?"

"Your voice mail."

He nodded. "Okay," he said. "Well, it's not like my offer still stands. I know who your boyfriend is. Or was. Did you break up? You're looking for a little activist action after the fact? Forget it."

Morgan's mouth contracted into a tight circle. "No, that's not it," she said. "This isn't about you. Or you and me. I came to find you because I—" She leaned forward toward him. "I found something out. Something your movement should know."

His face changed from wary to concern. He looked around and saw a few cameras setting up. "Let's go somewhere we can talk," he said. He gave her the name and address of a nearby bar. "Meet me there in ten minutes?" he asked.

Morgan ordered a vodka. She didn't usually drink, but she felt shook, jittery. The swell of emotion at seeing Kevin and thinking about the impact of ReidCorp. She had googled more articles about Sebastian on the subway to Grand Central. There were over a dozen takedown pieces of the "Generation Green" profile she had read.

Under Sebastian's leadership, ReidCorp was still making record profits from the fossil fuels that were causing the climate crisis. These weren't conspiracy websites but leading news outlets. How had she been so naïve?

And now that she knew, how could she stay in his house? Eat his food? Share his bed?

She looked around the bar. They did live music at night. She saw signed artist photos on the walls. Nobody she recognized.

Kevin walked in, still in black. He sat down beside her. When the bartender came over, Kevin leaned across the bar and hugged him. Kevin asked for a bottle of EarthBound. His friend said they were out. Kevin asked for water.

"I didn't know," Morgan said. "I mean, I didn't dig that deep. I didn't want to know. I read that "Generation Green" profile. I thought he was—" She shook her head. "I grew up with nothing. It just seemed like rich people had something I needed. And that they were the ones doing everything right. I just—I didn't look the gift horse in the mouth."

"I don't need your confession," he said. "What did you find out?"

Morgan looked up and down the bar. It was quiet. A guy at a far table was writing on a laptop.

"Hang on," Kevin said. He walked over and talked to the bartender.

Kevin walked back. It was painful to watch him change from the smile for his friend to the expressionless face he offered to Morgan. "My buddy says we can talk in the storage room," Kevin said.

They walked through a narrow back hallway, past a pair of restrooms, and through a door marked "Employees Only."

It was a tightly packed room, and there was nowhere to sit. Morgan leaned back against a row of kegs. Kevin leaned against a tower of liquor boxes.

"So what's up?" Kevin asked.

"The DOE guy," Morgan said. "Mitchell Brightwell. I saw them together. At Sebastian's apartment. Just for a second. But it was him."

Kevin leaned forward. "You're sure?"

Morgan nodded. "I saw him before I knew who he was. But then I saw him later, in the news."

"If you're certain," Kevin said. "That's huge. You're sure?"

"I have a photographic memory," Morgan said. "That's how I remembered your phone number."

"You threw it away after you saw me at the protest?" he asked.

Morgan shook her head. "I threw it away in the airport," she said. "I didn't want to be tempted when I was involved with . . ."

"Sebastian Reid," Kevin said. "A one-man army of planetary destruction. Whose company—"

"I need to leave him," Morgan said. "I can't be with him anymore now that I know what his company is doing."

"Hold on," Kevin said. "We need to make sure your testimony will be admissible in court."

"Court?"

"Yeah," Kevin said. "Let me call our attorney."

Morgan went to the bar and got another drink.

When she got back to the storage room, he handed Morgan his phone. "Our attorney," he said. "Yolanda Vance."

Morgan recalled the name from the NPR segment. She took the phone. "Hi, Morgan," Yolanda said. "What exactly did you see?"

"Sebastian Reid and Mitchell Brightwell were talking in Sebastian's study," Morgan said. "I only saw Brightwell at a quick glance, but I know it was him."

"You recognized him?"

"I did later," Morgan said. "When I saw a photo of him on television. Then a few video clips after that."

"What was the date you saw them together?"

"Two Thursdays before Thanksgiving," Morgan said, and looked up the exact date.

"You were looking directly at his face?"

"There was a mirror," Morgan said.

"You saw the reflection of his face?"

"Yes."

"Did you hear Sebastian say anything to him? Call him by name?"

"No," Morgan said.

Morgan heard a keyboard clicking in the background.

"Look," Yolanda said. "This is a great lead, thank you for coming to us, but it won't hold up in court. You saw his reflection. You identified him two weeks after the fact."

"I have a photographic memory."

"It won't matter," Yolanda said. "They'd tear you apart on cross-examination. We need more evidence if we're going against Sebastian Reid. Thanks again. Does Kevin know how to contact you?"

"I'll give him my information."

They signed off, and she handed Kevin back his phone.

"It's not enough," Morgan said.

Kevin nodded.

"Here's my number," Morgan said. "In case you need me."

She pulled out a twenty and handed it to him. "Please give this to your friend the bartender," she said.

He waved the money away. As much as she needed to conserve her cash, she hated to feel indebted. She turned the knob on the storage-room door.

"Is your conscience clear now?" Kevin asked.

"Is my—?" Morgan shook her head. "Goodbye, Kevin."

She hiked her purse up higher on her shoulder and walked out the door into the incongruous sunshine.

If only she had called Kevin from Denver, or when she had gotten back to New York. She should have told him she'd had no idea what Sebastian did for a living. How it impacted the world. She should have told him she would leave

Sebastian. That it didn't matter how much money he had. Maybe if she had, she would still have that connection with the Kevin she found so appealing. The warm Kevin. The one who lit up when he saw her. But, of course, she hadn't done that. She had moved right on in with Sebastian and kept her head in the sand. And now she would end up with neither of them.

Chapter 6

At the apartment, she stood in the room where she had been keeping her stuff. She hadn't ever really begun to think of it as her room. Her studio, sometimes. But never her room. "Room" was too intimate. Too much about belonging in a house. A studio was a space you could rent or share or maybe just sign up to use sometimes at a school.

She picked up the phone to call Dashawna, to tell her she had failed. To ask if she could come back to crashing on her couch. But maybe it was time to call that off, too. Stop fantasizing about all this make-it-as-an-artist-in-the-big-city bullshit. Maybe it was time to get a job waitressing. Or move back to Pennsylvania. Or maybe . . . maybe she could become a sugar baby, like Dashawna.

At first she had liked Sebastian. She had never been repulsed by him. At first there was real attraction. At least she was flattered that *he* seemed attracted. It was exciting to think that a man like that could like *her*. But maybe it was never any more than that. Whatever it had been, it was over. She began to pack. How could she get anyone to move her things out? She didn't have cash to spare. But maybe she didn't need any of this stuff. The furniture was just pieces she was pretending to own. All her real stuff fit in a couple of suit-cases. She could drag it across town on the subway later tonight.

Sebastian's dining room had always been too big for just two people. The high ceiling. The table for eight. Morgan and Sebastian always sat together at one end, but that night it felt cavernous.

He arrived home, oblivious to her mood. She smiled and made all the right noises. She was mustering up her courage to tell him she was leaving. But then she heard something that caught her attention.

". . . making trouble . . ."

He was talking about people making trouble for his company. Protesters? She had heard him say it before. But he had left it vague, and she didn't ask. She had assumed it was competitors or disgruntled employees. But maybe it was people who were concerned about warming planets and melting ice and rising sea levels.

"It's just so absurd," he was saying. "I have to account to my stockholders. I can't just stop everything just because of some conspiracy theory."

Yes, he had always spoken in these euphemisms. But now she knew what he meant. He meant scientists. He meant climate change. He meant that he wasn't going to stop or even slow down making money simply because there was massive scientific evidence that his company was destroying . . . everything.

"Sebastian," she said. "About that."

He looked up, startled. He hadn't expected her to speak. "About what?"

"About your company," she began.

"ReidCorp?" he asked.

"Yeah," she asked. "What exactly do you all do?"

"We provide energy," he said. "We research and develop new products to better serve the energy needs of today and tomorrow." It was a slogan. Their slogan. He rattled it off the tongue like he had just come up with it in the moment. As if he was the one to come up with it, instead of a Madison Avenue ad company, who had focus-group-tested each word.

"What kind of energy?" she asked.

"We lean to green," he said. "We have a contemporary, mixed portfolio."

This was what the protesters had meant about greenwashing. Anyone could say the word "green." Or run commercials for their company with pictures of forests and rivers. Or add some ethanol or solar panels to their products. But they hadn't actually stopped extracting fossil fuels to burn. They hadn't dumped coal. They hadn't stopped fracking. She smiled, feeling less guilty for not having known what he did. Here she was, finally asking, and she wasn't learning anything. He wasn't answering her direct questions. Just giving her the runaround.

"How is it that people are making trouble for you?" she asked. "For your company?"

His brow furrowed. "These conspiracy theorists. They're like children. They have totally unrealistic expectations of what can be done. They think this is Harry Potter and we can wave a wand and change everything."

Morgan was ready to tell him that maybe he should listen. Maybe they weren't conspiracy theorists. Maybe they had science on their side. Maybe if we could put a man on the moon, we could put sun and wind power in everyone's houses. Maybe he should go fuck himself. She was leaving. But just as she opened her mouth to speak, her phone rang. There was no name, just a number. Kevin's number.

Instead of the challenge that had been sitting on her tongue, she decided to play along. She smiled as she spoke. "Fair enough," she said. "You've been heading up the company for a while. I'm sure you have some of the best people working for you. You would know what is and isn't feasible."

He smiled. "Exactly," he said. "You get it."

Morgan smiled back, a genuine smile. Maybe she really did get it. And he had no idea how very much she saw. And maybe Kevin had called because the lawyer had found a way to use what she knew. Or maybe Kevin was calling to apologize for being such an ass earlier that day. Whatever it was, she wanted to find out before she let Sebastian know she was moving out.

Sebastian wanted to sit on the couch with her and listen to jazz. A sort of sterile type jazz. He had taken her to a concert once. All the musicians were young white guys. Clean-cut. They didn't have much soul. Nothing like the basement jazz club Dashawna had taken her to.

He sat with his arm around her. His eyes half closed. She was a prop in his unwinding. They had sat here like this at other times, but she hadn't noticed. Maybe it was the expensive wine. Or the luxurious fabric of the chenille couch. Or the newness of the relationship.

No, it was her own work. Those other days she had sat there and the colors of her own work had filled her head. The syrupy jazz wasn't a problem because her mind had been filled with her own creative plans. But tonight she didn't have any of that. Only the knowledge that he was a . . . a . . . a denier. He was a climate-change denier. A profiteer. And her own creative work would have to take a back seat to the work of figuring out what, if anything, she could do about that.

His hand was traveling down toward her breast. She yawned and slid out from under his arm. "Babe, I didn't realize how late it was," she said. "I have an early dentist appointment. I should really get to bed."

"Oh." He looked up, startled. Like it had never crossed his mind that she went to the dentist. "Of course."

"Are you coming to bed?"

"Not yet," he said. "I'll be up in half an hour."

"Okay," she said and kissed him on the forehead before walking up the stairs.

She closed the bedroom door and walked through to the huge bathroom. She pulled the door mostly closed so she would see if Sebastian came in.

She dialed Kevin's number.

"Look," he said. "I'm sorry I was a dick today. It took guts for you to come to me, to the protest, and I really want to apologize. I spoke to Yolanda again, and we have a proposal for you. What if you could find some evidence?"

"Evidence of what?"

"Anything that could help us," he said. "Any documentation of a conversation with Mitchell Brightwell. Maybe there's something else. There are so many possibilities."

"I could look around before I move out tonight," she said.

"What?" he asked. "You were living with him, but now you're gonna move out?"

"Yeah," she said. "I don't see how I could stay."

"Oh," he said. "That sort of changes things."

"What do you mean?"

"I was just thinking," he said. "It just seems like—"

"What?"

"Maybe you shouldn't move out," he said. "Yolanda says you don't have enough information. Maybe you could get more."

She blinked at the phone. "Are you asking me to spy on my—on Sebastian?"

"Am I asking you to spy on a man who is lying to the public and the authorities and is part of a tiny group risking the entire fucking planet to enrich themselves?" he asked. "Yes, Morgan. That is exactly what I'm asking."

"I'm not the cleaning woman," she said. "Kevin! I'm his *girlfriend*. I'd have to pretend to still be together."

"He hasn't changed," Kevin said. "He's the same man you walked out of a Denver hotel with, in shades. You think he gave them to you because of the Colorado glare? Some part of you always knew. Don't act so shocked."

"I thought there was only one asshole in my life," she said. "But I can see there are two. I'm not spying for you or your movement or whatever. I didn't get it about Sebastian. And now I get it. I'll be acting accordingly." With the touch of a red button, she ended the call.

She felt exhausted. More exhausted than she had felt in ages. And then she just walked out into the bedroom, took off her jeans, and got into bed. It was sort of a reflex. She didn't want to make a scene. She could more easily pack everything and leave in the morning. She could leave a note. She was still composing it in her head when he came in. She pretended to sleep.

Dear Sebastian,

Not "Dear"—

Sebastian,

It has come to my attention that—

No, she didn't need a declaration.

This just isn't working out for me.

He would need some type of reason, though.

Or maybe not. Maybe she would just leave.

He went into the bathroom and brushed his teeth. Before he came back to the bedroom she had fallen asleep.

Chapter 7

The next thing she knew, she felt movement in the bed. It was morning—six, maybe—and Sebastian was getting up. She pretended to be asleep, looking out at him from under her nearly closed lids. She watched him go into the bathroom. Heard his shower. She realized she *was* spying. It was just an extension of what she usually did. Tracking him. His moods. His movements.

She tiptoed over to his phone and looked at the texts on the lock screen and anything she could see without knowing the code. Could she get the code? She probably could. What would she find? Phone calls to Mitchell Brightwell? No, they could easily subpoena the phone records for that.

Could she do this? She was doing it. She watched him get dressed. But this was the easy part. She could pretend to sleep. Could she pretend through dinner? Could she pretend through sex? More than she had been pretending, anyway. She didn't know. Then he was gone for the day. And she could lean out the window high over the East River and smoke a cigarette—something she hadn't done since college—wondering if she could be a spy.

* * *

She went to Sebastian's study and the door was locked.

She walked around the house, trying different doors. She walked into different closets. Another guest room. Several bathrooms. But Sebastian's study was locked, and that meant she also had no access to the storage room that led off of it.

Morgan arranged to meet Dashawna at her studio apartment in Bed-Stuy.

"Do you know how to pick a lock?" she asked her friend when she got there.

"Nope," Dashawna said. "You tryna get some cash on top of the room and board?"

"Something like that," Morgan said.

"You better be careful," Dashawna said. "Men like to be generous. They want to give things to women. They don't want women to take them."

"I know," Morgan said.

"Besides," Dashawna said. "Men like Sebastian don't keep their money lying around. They have wall safes."

Morgan nodded. "That makes sense. Do you know how to crack a safe?" she asked.

"Can't do that either," Dashawna said. "But I'll ask around. This guy I'm seeing today probably has a wall safe."

"How do you do it, Dashawna?" Morgan asked. "Have sex with a guy you don't really . . . find attractive?"

"There are different kinds of sex," Dashawna said. "Sex is hot for me when I'm feeling someone and it's mutual. Especially if he has that dangerous energy. That's the best sex. It's great if it's after he pays for a nice dinner or we do it at a fancy hotel and get room service. But some guys are just great lays and I'd fuck them in a crappy apartment and then get pizza delivered."

"Even if you're not in love?" Morgan asked.

"I've been in love," Dashawna said. "I'm sure I'll be in

love again at some point. That sex wasn't always hotter, and it was definitely the best when it was love and it was really hot. But you can't always have that. Or at least . . . you can't always keep a relationship hot. Or you can't always keep a hot relationship going."

"But how do you pretend, day after day?" Morgan asked.

"I don't know," Dashawna said. "I've never lived with anyone. I'm just a part-time pretender. I can keep it up for about sixteen hours, if I get a good night's sleep in the middle. I don't know how kept women do it. Or wives. You know my goal is to retire. But I thought you wanted to marry Sebastian."

"I did," Morgan said. "Or I thought I did."

"Did he do anything fucked up to you?" Dashawna asked. "Or is it just the climate shit?"

"Just the climate," Morgan said. "Plus it's just . . . so . . . transactional." Morgan ran her hand back and forth across the smooth leather of Dashawna's couch. "He used to ask about my day, or what I was reading, or something. Now he doesn't even do that. He just moves through a series of choreographed moves. Evening. Dinner. Sitting around. Sex."

"Let me give you a tip," Dashawna said. "This is what another girl told me. Ask him ahead of time when you should keep your schedule open on Saturday and Sunday. Then book up with friends for the rest of the time. Otherwise you won't be able to do anything over the weekend. I think she checked in with her sugar daddy on Wednesdays. If he had a party or a special event over the weekend, she would know ahead of time. And then she would have an excuse to get her hair done before. She'd hang out for hours at the salon with her friends. Hair and nails were part of it, but mostly she was just hanging out."

"I don't know if I'm gonna be able to do it," Morgan said.

"To be honest," Dashawna said, "I do drink a little more

when I'm gonna be fucking someone I'm not really feeling. I like the way it makes me feel kind of like I'm in a movie or a music video. I always play music while we fuck. Sometimes a little cannabis. But when you think about it, not that much time is spent having sex. Sometimes I like to act all hot about it, so I can get it over with and enjoy the meal or whatever."

Morgan started to cry. "Dashawna, I don't think I can do this."

Dashawna's eyes got wide. "Oh, honey," she said. "You don't have to do anything you don't want to. I thought it was just a learning curve."

"I just—when he's gone, I feel so free. Like, those hours of the day where I get to work and time just flies by. It's amazing. I didn't realize how many hours of the day I spent worrying about money until I didn't have to anymore."

"Look, Morgan," Dashawna said. "Girls like us don't get to live the life of leisure. We gotta work. Either a daily hustle, or you fuck a guy a couple of days a week. You decide what's gonna work best for you."

"If I could only keep it up for a few months and get some work completed. Have something to show. Something to sell."

"That's good," Dashawna said. "That's a goal. He can be a temporary patron."

Morgan dried her eyes. "I like that," she said. "A temporary patron."

On her way back into Manhattan, she got a phone call from a 212 number she didn't recognize. Could it be Kevin calling from a landline? Yolanda? Someone connected to their movement?

She picked it up.

"Hello," a woman's voice said. "I'm calling from CFI."

"What?" Morgan asked. Was this one of Kevin's organizations?

"Contemporary Fashion Intersections," she said. "The Folk Arts, Fine Arts and Fashion competition."

"Oh yes!" Morgan said. "Of course."

"Congratulations. You've been selected as a finalist. We're looking forward to your final product at the end of the month!"

Morgan was too stunned to be excited. But she wrote down the information and thanked the woman for letting her know.

And that sealed it. It was some kind of sign. She wasn't just going to be a spy. She was going to have Sebastian as her patron. At the end of the month she would turn in her finished quilt. If she had found evidence to incriminate Sebastian, great. If not, she would move out, regardless.

She texted Kevin to say she would do it.

She called Dashawna to give her the good news about the contest.

Kevin texted back: **Thank you so much. I realize it's a big ask. I'll call later tonight to check in.**

She texted, **No, let's talk tomorrow. Can we meet at that same bar?**

He wrote: **Sure. Noon?**

She wanted to get some work done on her quilt first, before the day got away from her. She texted: **Can we make it later? Like 4?**

He wrote: **Of course. Whatever you say.**

She was three drinks in when Sebastian got home.

"I have something to celebrate," she said. "I'm a finalist in CFI."

She expected him to ask what it was but wasn't really surprised when he didn't. "Well, congratulations, babe," he said.

"Have a drink with me," she said.

"I see you've already gotten started," he said, pouring his usual scotch. "Let's make it a toast."

She raised her glass. "To fabric," she said. "The fabric of life and the world and everything around us."

He raised his scotch. "To fabric," he said, and they clinked glasses.

"And to you, Morgan," he said. "You've brought so much color and beauty into my home. Our home."

They clinked glasses and he smiled at her. She could see something authentic in him. Something human and warm. With the disinhibition of the alcohol and the connection in the moment, she didn't want to squander the opportunity. She lunged at him and kissed him.

He laughed. "Wow, looks like we really are going to celebrate."

In the moment she could forget about Kevin, about the climate crisis, about trying to find evidence. She could just hold on to the taste of the vodka in the back of her mouth, the kind words he'd spoken, and the colors of the quilt she'd been working on.

And the alcohol did her another favor—it removed her verbal filter. So this time, when they were having sex, she said aloud the thing she had always thought.

"Don't pull on my hair," she said. "It's killing the mood."

He looked startled for a second but let her hair go.

Something about letting herself be authentic—letting herself ask for what she wanted—emboldened her.

"Let's go back to that other position," she said. "When I was on top."

"Okay," he said.

While still inside her, he rolled onto his back, and she rode him hard, her body flushed from the alcohol and the new sense of herself. She climaxed that night. For the first time with him.

* * *

She woke up late and hungover. Sebastian had left for work. She texted Dashawna for a hangover cure. Her friend prescribed a smoothie of milk, orange juice, ginger, and banana. The consistency was a little gross, but it tasted okay. She took it with a little hair of the dog and shuffled into her studio.

In three weeks she needed to finish this quilt. She had a goal now: to be a contender for this goddamn prize. Besides, she needed to focus on something other than these men. She wouldn't see Kevin until this afternoon. Let her get four solid hours of work done first.

Sunlight streamed in through the windows of her workroom, illuminating the wide table that held her latest project. It was phenomenal to work in Sebastian's apartment and have so much room. When she'd been a student, she had to compete for space in a community studio. She could lay her project out on a table and work for a few hours, but then she'd have to pack everything up when she was done. Or she could see half of the quilt at a time in her apartment by laying it out on her single bed. But she could only stand a foot or so back, because the room was so small. And then she'd have to disassemble it and fold it all up when she went to sleep.

But her space at Sebastian's was a totally different experience. She had a worktable all to herself, where she got to lay out the fabric and view the entire quilt before she sewed a single stitch. She could leave the work out on the table overnight and come back the next day to see it with fresh eyes. And beyond that, the apartment also had high ceilings, so after she'd sewn the quilt, she could hang it up. When she looked at it from across the large room, she would notice different things, different patterns, what worked and what didn't.

The quilt she was working on used images of money. In graduate school one of their instructors had given them an opportunity to make their own textiles, and she had made fabric with different images of oversize paper currency from all over the world. Each was the size of a large shoebox, and all the currency displayed images of women. She had Nanny of the Maroons from Jamaica. Maria Montessori from Italy. She had a 1000 franc note from "French Equatorial Africa" while that region was still a colony—an idealized image of African women at market. She had Indira Gandhi from India, Eva Perón from Argentina, and Kate Sheppard from New Zealand. From the United States, she had an old Martha Washington dollar bill and, in the center, she had a round panel onto which she'd embroidered the 2000 US Sacajawea dollar coin in metallic thread. The light from the window danced off the golden strands.

But the positioning of the panels didn't feel right. She moved things around so that the women from the Global South were on top. The queen of the UK was in the bottom right-hand corner. Right. That was better. She wanted to up-lift the women of color.

She looked at the quilt laid out on the table with navy blue borders. Yes. This was it. She put the quilt together with basting stitches and hung it up on the wall.

She stepped back to the far end of the room and stared at her work for several minutes. She liked it. She wanted to love it. But she didn't. Now, as she squinted at it, she loved everything but the borders. She liked the dark blue, but there was something missing.

She lay on the floor and gazed up at it. She let her eyes un-focus, the colors and shapes blurring in her vision. Then she focused again. All the women smiled down at her from the money.

No. There was no tension. No counterpoint. It looked too benign, too easy. Money wasn't actually so friendly. It needed something more . . . edgy.

She flipped through her mental file cabinet of fabrics. With her photographic memory, she could envision the different patterns in her collection. She liked the navy, but she wanted something with texture. Maybe a print. Nothing she already owned was right. She went online to look at her favorite fabric store for something different . . . more dangerous.

A pinstripe? Or a different direction entirely? A sequin? No. She needed something more graphic. And then she found it. A rayon textile that had a black background with barbed wire tangling across it. From a distance it looked a bit like fireworks, but as you got closer . . . Yes! It was perfect. She began to rip out the seams to redo the quilt. Did she have time to take it apart? No. When she checked the time, she realized how late it had gotten. She would just have time to pick up a few yards of this new fabric on her way to see Kevin.

The end of worktime was a letdown. She felt a tightening of her chest. The anxiety rose again. Her freedom would soon be revoked. Working in the studio that day was like wearing a bulletproof vest. It protected her from everything. But when she left the workroom, it was like taking it off. She felt exposed, vulnerable. She pulled on her jacket and rushed out to the subway.

An hour and a half later, she walked into the bar with a bag of fabric under her arm. Kevin hadn't arrived yet. She used the bathroom—which was surprisingly clean. It also had a coin-operated dispenser with tampons and condoms. She went back to the bar and ordered a virgin margarita. She didn't want any more alcohol today.

She took a swig of her drink and wondered if he wasn't coming. She was about to text him and ask when he texted her: **walking up from the subway now.**

* * *

She had finished her margarita and was chewing the lime when he came in. The two of them walked silently to the back room.

"Thanks for coming," he said. "For everything, really."

"I made it through the first thirty-six hours," she said. "I think I can do it."

He nodded and pulled an EarthBound beer from one of the cases, twisting off the top. "The first thing you should probably do is get some basic background info about climate," he said. He set down the bottle on the case and reached into his messenger bag. Of the two books he handed her, the first one had a brightly illustrated cover. It was called *This Book Will Save the Planet: A Climate-Justice Primer for Activists and Changemakers* by Dany Sigwalt.

"This one is written for all ages," Kevin said. "So I recommend it to folks who are new to the movement. They break everything down. Then I say read this one next." The second book was *All We Can Save: Truth, Courage, and Solutions for the Climate Crisis.* A collection edited by Dr. Ayana Elizabeth Johnson and Dr. Katharine K. Wilkinson. She set the books on top of her bag of fabric.

"Have you seen that short video that Naomi Klein did with Alexandria Ocasio-Cortez and Molly Crabapple?" Kevin asked.

"No," Morgan said.

"Google it," he said. "It's by The Intercept. I'll text you some other links as well. About particular stuff that has to do with ReidCorp. You need to know what to look for."

"He has a locked study," Morgan said. "I've looked around the rest of the house. Nothing work-related anywhere."

"There's also his office downtown," Kevin said.

"I've never been there," Morgan said.

"They have a big Christmas party every year," he said. "You'll be going soon enough. He hasn't said anything to you about it?" Kevin took a long swig of beer.

"The sort of unspoken agreement is that I'm free during the days," Morgan said. "But at night, I'm sort of on call. I'm sure he'll tell me about it a few days before."

"We've been working for over a year now to infiltrate that event," Kevin said. "We have movement folks who never show their faces at demonstrations who've started working for the catering companies they're likely to hire. Just so we have some eyes and ears in there."

"Wow. Good to know I won't be strictly on my own," Morgan said.

"Listen," he said. "I seriously am sorry I was such an ass. I do care about you, and not just your safety. I really—"

This was the thing she had been hoping for him to say, but now that he was saying it, she couldn't bear to hear it. Not when she had weeks of pretending with Sebastian ahead of her.

"Listen, Kevin," she said. "We both know there's something here. But I've got a role to play. And I can't be distracted by whatever this is. You can see that, can't you? I mean, you get to leave here and be yourself, but I've got to pretend to be the girl who is willfully ignoring the climate crisis and is buying my boyfriend's greenwashed image."

"Of course," he said. "I'm sorry. Just wanted you to know."

She couldn't look at him, but she nodded. "Duly noted."

"I should go," he said. "But if you need anything, anything at all. Call me, Yolanda, or this number for our movement tip hotline."

"Thanks," she said.

He patted her hand and walked out. The gesture was awkward, but her hand tingled where he had touched it.

* * *

On her way back uptown, she stopped at a bookstore. She found a book by Sebastian's dad, the one who built Reid-Corp. It was from the nineties and called *Fueling My Way to the Top*. They had a 99-cent section, and she picked a campy thriller that had been on the top of the best-seller list a year before. It was the perfect size. After she bought it, she took off the cover and put it on the book of essays. She dumped the coverless thriller in the donation box for the local library.

That night, she read about climate tipping points and what could be done to avoid climate collapse. Sebastian sat in bed next to her, working on some spreadsheet. She tipped the book away from him, not wanting him to see the illustrations—it would betray the fact that she wasn't reading a novel at all, but an all-ages climate book. As a visual artist, she loved the bright illustrations. She looked up from time to time to make sure Sebastian couldn't see her book. She also stole occasional glances at his laptop screen, but there was nothing she could understand, either about the numbers or the initials at the tops of the columns. She fell asleep dreaming of brightly colored illustrated people demanding change.

Chapter 8

The next morning, right after he woke, Sebastian was on his phone for a half hour. Morgan pretended to be asleep, even as he cursed and tossed the phone down, heading into the bathroom to shower.

She picked up his phone and looked at it before it could lock. She used her phone to carefully photograph the page he had left it on so she could put it back exactly.

She scanned through the apps he had running open. Mostly the usual: email, web browser, and productivity apps. She took another photo of the order of them. She didn't want to leave anything changed.

She glanced at the bathroom door. The shower was still running.

She looked at the web pages he was browsing. Mostly news outlets. Nothing interesting.

She used her phone to photograph his list of texts. Apparently, he deleted them pretty quickly. He only had a few days' worth. She also photographed his call log, which was similarly short. She pulled up his email, which included both work and personal. She photographed a couple of screens of the inboxes for each.

One email caught her eye. The sender was "Security."

She didn't take the time to read the text of the message; she just photographed it.

She heard the shower shut off. Quickly, she worked her way backward, opening each app in reverse order, so they'd be exactly the way he'd left them. She shut off the phone and put it exactly where he'd dropped it. She pretended to wake when he walked in.

"Hey, babe," she said. "You headed into the office?"

"Yeah," he said, putting on his boxers and undershirt. He only kept underwear and casual clothes in the bedroom. His suits, dress shirts, ties, and shoes were in another closet across the hall. "There's a Christmas party week after next at the office. I'd like to have you there."

That was exactly what she hadn't liked when they were just dating, even before she knew all about him. He didn't ask when he wanted something. He didn't exactly command, but the way he phrased it, as far as the tone and language, it was the way you spoke to an employee. You told them what you wanted with the expectation they'd do it.

"Of course," she said. "I love parties."

With a quick kiss on her forehead, he was gone.

Chapter 9

Later that morning, Lena, the housekeeper, came in. She was a Polish woman in her fifties, with brassy blond hair piled up on top of her head.

Morgan was sitting on the couch reading *All We Can Save,* under the cover of the discarded thriller.

"That's a great book," Lena said. "I won't spoil the ending, but it's got a good twist. How far are you?" She peered over Morgan's shoulder to see how far she had gotten into the book. "You passed the part where she finds out her mother isn't her mother? That was really a shocker, right?"

Morgan closed the book over her finger holding the place.

"Actually," she told Lena, "I'm reading that book by Sebastian's dad, *Fueling My Way to the Top.* I put this other cover on it. I didn't want him to—I don't know. It makes me look—"

"Honey," Lena said, "you don't have to explain nothing to me. I just clean and stay out of everybody's business."

"Thanks," Morgan said.

"And you should read that other book when you get a chance," Lena said. She lifted the family photograph from the mantel to dust. It was a posed portrait from when Sebastian was maybe twelve, with a mouth full of braces and a forced-looking smile. Behind him, his parents' smiles didn't look fake, but they didn't look warm, either. His brunette father looked smug. His mother had platinum-blonde hair that matched her children, but dark lashes and eyebrows that matched her husband. She had the practiced expression of a beauty contestant. His younger sister was the only one whose smile looked genuine.

Lena set down the photograph and picked up the next one—of the family skiing when Sebastian was in his teens.

"Do you want me to clean the room you're staying in?" Lena asked. "I know he's very particular about certain rooms. Doesn't ever want me to clean his study except when he's here. How about you?"

"Oh no," Morgan said. "I can clean it myself."

"Not even to empty the wastebasket?"

"Sure," Morgan said. "I guess."

"Okay," Lena said. "I'll finish vacuuming and then start in the kitchen. Though there's never much to clean in there, because he always has takeout. Just keep the dishwasher door closed, it'll wash automatically midweek."

Funny that she'd never heard the dishwasher. But when she got into a groove with her quilting, she learned to block out everything else.

"Thank you so much," Morgan gushed at the housekeeper. It felt strange to sit on the couch while someone else cleaned. Besides, she was grateful for the distraction. She was anxiously waiting for a text from Kevin.

Morgan had texted him as soon as Sebastian left and hadn't yet heard back. She had tried to work on her quilt, but she couldn't focus. She felt too unsettled by what she had seen in Sebastian's email.

It was the one titled "Security." It had been brief but ominous. **"Chief, moving forward on all fronts. Our inside operator is finally getting some traction with the whiners. Keep you posted."**

"The whiners." Didn't that mean the protesters? And "inside operator"? Did that mean she wasn't the only spy in this equation—that ReidCorp had some, too? Now that she thought about it, she imagined they probably had corporate spies—operatives who kept an eye on their competitors. But it hadn't occurred to her that they might plant someone in one of the climate justice organizations, maybe the one Kevin was in. And did Kevin know? Was he right now saying something about Morgan that could compromise her to Sebastian? Why wasn't he texting her back?

Lena turned off the vacuum cleaner and Morgan checked her phone again. She had missed five texts from Kevin, must not have heard them. The final one was the most cryptic of all.

Turn your phone off. Meet me at our spot. I'll wait.

Morgan could feel her heart beating hard. She turned her phone off and grabbed a jacket. She yelled a goodbye to Lena, who was carrying the vacuum cleaner back to the closet.

Morgan waited for the elevator, but it was slow today. The anxiety had her edgy, jangled. She couldn't abide just standing there. She trotted down the stairs and headed out to the subway.

Sitting on the train, she couldn't do any of the things she usually did. Check email. Read the headlines. Text Dashawna. Having her phone off increased her anxiety and sense of foreboding.

When she finally walked into the bar, she felt frantic. She didn't see Kevin anywhere, so she crossed straight to the storage room.

When she opened the door, she saw Kevin had a margarita waiting for her. Not a virgin.

"What the hell is going on?" she asked, then took a big swallow.

"I'm sorry," he said. "I didn't want to say anymore. It's probably fine. But if you took pictures on your phone, you need to be careful they don't get uploaded into the cloud. Does your phone have an auto-backup setup?"

"I think so," she said. "But it usually backs up at night."

"It's probably safe, then," he said. "Let's see. Can you turn on your phone? But put it on airplane mode, just to be safe."

Morgan did as he asked, then opened to her camera roll.

"Holy shit," Kevin whispered when he got to the "security" email.

"Do you think he means they have some kind of infiltrators in your organization?" Morgan asked.

"I always assumed the FBI or . . . maybe the police . . . but a private spy?" he said. "One that reports to Reid. That's just so . . ."

"Like something out of a movie," Morgan said.

It was helpful that Kevin called him "Reid." Sebastian was the man she lived with. Reid was the enemy.

"If I can't send them to you," Morgan asked, "should I airdrop them?"

"No," Kevin said. "Nothing on my phone. Let's just do it totally old-school."

He pulled a digital camera from his backpack and used it to snap pictures of the relevant photographs on her phone.

The lines of his third-generation photos had lost much of their sharpness, but they were clearly legible.

Kevin's phone pinged an alert. He pulled it out and looked at it. Then he sighed and put it away.

"Listen," he said. "Given all this, I don't want you to call the hotline. Just me."

"What about Yolanda?" Morgan asked.

"She's not very accessible," Kevin said.

"Neither are you," Morgan said. "I tried you this morning and it was hours before you got back to me."

"I know," he said. "I got a burner phone. Just for you. Put in this number. Take mine out. Delete all the calls and texts to my personal phone. And let's delete these photos."

"I already did," Morgan said.

"Did you erase them from the 'recently deleted' file?"

"I didn't know that was a thing," Morgan said.

"Yes," Kevin said. "Otherwise they'll get backed up in the cloud anyway."

"Got it," Morgan said. She searched for the recently deleted file. When she deleted the photos from there, she got a message that this would be deleting them permanently.

Kevin's phone pinged again, but he ignored it this time. He pulled a tiny disc out of the digital camera and replaced it. "Here," he said. "You take this. And here's an extra disc. We can go old-school. Photograph anything you think is worth investigating. I'll download whatever is on the discs to a secure server, and we can keep swapping back and forth. There's a little bit of room on the camera. Make sure you have some decoy photos on there. But when you take pictures of his stuff, make sure it's saving them to the disk."

Morgan nodded. "You've done this before?"

"No," Kevin said. "I'm just sorta making this shit up as I go along."

She let out a bark of laughter in recognition. "Me, too."

He suddenly hugged her. "Be careful," he said.

She squeezed back. "I will," she said. "You, too."

He began to lean toward her, and she thought for a moment he might kiss her. But then his phone pinged again.

He closed his eyes. "I gotta go," he whispered.

He pulled back from the embrace and headed out the door.

Morgan felt even more jittery than when she'd arrived. She drained the margarita and brought it to the bar. She rummaged in her pocket to pay the bartender, but he waved her away. "Your money's no good here," he said. "Kevin's got you."

She smiled, grateful not to have to give him any of her precious cash. She handed him the empty glass and headed out into the cold.

At noon Morgan got a call from Dashawna.

"You still interested in learning to pick a lock?" her friend asked.

"Yeah," Morgan said. "You learned how and wanna teach me?"

"No, but I met someone who can do it," Dashawna said.

"Why would a complete stranger be willing to teach me to pick a lock?" Morgan asked.

"She's Greek," Dashawna said.

"Um," Morgan said. "I don't get it. Is that some sort of sexual thing? What does it have to do with locks?"

Dashawna laughed. "No, girl," she said. "It's a climate crisis thing. Greece is heavily threatened by sea-level rise."

"Oh right!" Morgan said. "So when can I meet her?"

"She doesn't live too far from me," Dashawna said. "She can meet at my house tomorrow in the early afternoon."

"Great," Morgan said. "See you then."

When Morgan arrived at Dashawna's apartment, it felt a little odd to have someone else there. Usually it was just her and D in the tight studio. They had their own little best friend world, and they saw other friends out in Manhattan or Brooklyn.

Dashawna and the other woman were on the couch, so Morgan pulled up a kitchen chair from across the room. On and around the kitchenette table were various white mesh bags and boxes of wedding favors: miniature white plastic pairs of doves, gold-wrapped chocolates, disposable cameras, little white plastic bottles of bubbles, and tiny, tinkling bells. Apparently, Dashawna's side business had another wedding gig.

The friend wasn't at all what Morgan expected. Serena was petite and angular, with sandy, flyaway hair and bright pink lipstick that matched her dress.

"It's good to meet you," Serena said.

"Thanks so much for helping me," Morgan replied. She realized she really was incredibly grateful and relieved to have someone else helping them out.

Serena shrugged. "Dashawna said you were dating someone in the fossil fuel industry," Serena said. "This is the least of what I'll teach you. If you need a pipe bomb, I'm your girl."

Morgan's eyes flew open. Whoa. Wait. Had it been a mistake to invite this woman on board?

"Serena is kidding," Dashawna said. "We're just here to learn how to pick locks."

Morgan still felt a bit uneasy. She wasn't sure if Serena was kidding or not.

Serena handed Morgan a ring of slender metal pieces.

"You know how a key works," Serena said. "There are tumblers. If you can get the right-shaped pieces into the right parts of the lock at the same time, you can replicate the action of a key."

Serena worked on a lock made of clear plastic outside the metal tumblers. You could see what was happening.

Morgan found the methodical work of the lock to be fascinating. As she watched, Morgan relaxed. She saw the sinewy muscle of Serena's arm flexing. It reminded her of Kevin's arm that first time she'd looked at it on the plane. You rarely saw these type of muscles on a woman unless she was an Olympic athlete. Morgan began to wonder if Serena was transgender.

"Did you see how I did that?" Serena asked.

Morgan blinked. She felt stupid, worrying about this woman's gender identity, when there were much larger issues at hand. Besides, it wasn't any of Morgan's business. Trans women were women.

"Sorry," Morgan said. "I got distracted."

"Focus, girl," Dashawna said. "Serena has to get back to her job."

Morgan focused. She watched closely as Serena manipulated the lockpicks in a few of Dashawna's interior doors.

"Now you try it," Serena said.

At first Morgan couldn't get the feel of it at all. She kept expecting it to work like a key. But it wasn't like a key, it was about the angles. About listening. About getting each of the tumblers to move separately.

But after a while she was able to transfer some of her other skills. The precise angle at which you aimed a needle. The slow way you guided fabric through a sewing machine. The precision of removing stitches. After about ten tries, she felt the first tumbler click in the first lock. Then, eventually, the second. Then the third.

She tried again on the second lock. Then, finally, Serena announced they would try the front door lock on the apartment.

"It'll make you a little more nervous and conscious of time," Serena said. "Replicate field conditions."

Morgan did feel nervous as she knelt before the lock on

Dashawna's door. And when they heard someone come up the stairs, she quickly stood up.

"Hey, girl," Dashawna said to the neighbor as she pulled out her key and opened the door. But after the woman went into her apartment, Dashawna closed the door again. Morgan got back to work.

After what felt like forever, Morgan opened the lock.

She couldn't help but grin as the three of them trooped back into Dashawna's apartment.

"Seven minutes," Serena said. "Not bad. If the lock is interior, you'll be fine. On the street you'll get arrested. Breaking into an apartment? Depends how busy the building is."

"Thank you so much," Morgan said.

"Don't mention it," Serena said and handed Morgan the lockpicks. "Merry Christmas."

"Thank you," Morgan said.

"Oh wait," Serena said and took them back for a moment. She wiped the lockpicks on the hip of her sweater dress. "Just in case you do get arrested. Fingerprints."

She handed the picks back to Morgan.

"Don't worry, girl, you'll be fine," Serena said. "I just don't believe in taking any chances."

And then, in a swish of pink, she was gone.

"You gotta hustle back to Manhattan and pick a lock?" Dashawna asked.

"No rush," Morgan said. "Looks like you could use some help with those gift bags on the table."

Dashawna let out her breath in a sigh of relief. "I was just about to ask," she said. "Yes, girl. I'm way behind on this wedding."

The two of them sat down on opposite sides of the small table and Dashawna showed Morgan what belonged in each bag.

"Don't worry, honey," Dashawna said. "This is the

bargain-basement gift bag for the bargain-price clients. If you had married Sebastian, I would have gotten the designer shit."

"These are cute," Morgan said.

"I'm just saying," Dashawna said. "If you ever get married, I'm gonna hook you up with something really nice."

"Thanks in advance," Morgan said. "But at this point I can say with certainty there's no risk I'll marry Sebastian."

Chapter 10

The next morning when Sebastian left for work, Morgan was up and around. "Have a good day, honey," she said. "When does Lena come next? She was hilarious."

"Lena?" Sebastian asked.

"The woman who cleans?" Morgan said.

"Oh right," Sebastian said. "I don't think I ever knew her name. My assistant handles all that. I'm not sure. Maybe every week. I only see her on the second Saturday, when she cleans my study."

"This Saturday?" Morgan asked.

"I guess," Sebastian said. "Like I told you. My assistant keeps the calendar. I just show up. Bye, babe." He gave her a quick kiss on the cheek and walked out.

The assistant—Dawn—sent a car for him every morning with his breakfast and coffee in it. Dawn had the takeout delivered right when he walked in the door after work. It was like Dawn did part of the wifely duties and Morgan was supposed to do the rest. Sex. Escorting him to events. A warm body beside him on the couch and in the bed. Someone to keep the house from being empty.

Morgan had never asked Sebastian if he wanted kids. Dawn the assistant probably couldn't really make that happen. He would need a wife and a nanny for that. And he was probably expected to have kids. Correction—to have sons. To take over the family business. As he had done, and his father before him had built a fossil fuel empire out of Sebastian's grandfather's gas station. Well, if he ever had children, it certainly wouldn't be with her.

Morgan drained her coffee cup and realized she was procrastinating. Sitting alone in the breakfast nook, she listened to the empty apartment. Silent. Only muted traffic noise outside and the barely audible hum of the fridge. Morgan ran her fingers across the lockpicks in her pocket. Why not break into the study now?

Slowly, she got up from the stool and put her coffee cup in the dishwasher. As she walked down the hall, she wondered for the first time if Sebastian had any security cameras. She looked carefully around at the walls and ceilings. And at the moldings. She certainly didn't see anything that looked like it could be a camera. Besides, he probably wouldn't want to be recorded; it might be incriminating for him.

Still, as she knelt in front of the study door, she felt her anxiety spike.

"Field conditions," she mumbled to herself.

The lockpicks slipped several times. She had to stop twice and sit down in the hallway, pressing a hand against her chest and breathing deeply. But eventually she got it. The lock turned and the door opened.

That first time she had been in the study, she had just passed through to store her fabric in the next room. Sebastian had opened the storage room for her and stood holding the door. And she had gone in quickly and deposited her stuff in the corner. The second time she had barely stood inside the doorway, maybe for just a few seconds before Sebastian sent her out. But now she took her time.

There was a small entryway, then the room opened out to look like something out of the movies. Dark wood paneling.

When she had come to decorate the apartment, he had said it was the one room that didn't need anything because it was done in wood. But her quick glance hadn't allowed her to appreciate it fully. The wood was gorgeous. A deep brown, with undulating darker rings in it. Polished to a sheen but not varnished. The chairs and desk were also dark wood. If it had been a movie, there would have been a deer or a lion head on the wall. Instead, there was just a large oil painting of a rustic lake at sunset. Ironic. Wasn't his company destroying all those kinds of places? On a whim, Morgan pushed the painting slightly to the side. Sure enough, there was a safe behind it. On the far wall was the mirror where she had seen Mitchell Brightwell's reflection. On the wall in between was a huge flat-screen TV.

Carefully, she looked through all the papers on top of the desk. She used the lockpicks to open the drawers. The top ones had only pens, sticky notes, and other random office supplies. In the second drawer he had a few bricks of cash and a receipt book that didn't have many used pages. She photographed them all with the digital camera. In the bottom drawer she found a handgun and a ledger book. She photographed all the pages of the ledger, but she had no idea what it could be. It had only written initials at the top. But it definitely looked like his handwriting.

There was no computer on the desk. He used a laptop, and he had taken that with him. Occasionally he left it on the nightstand at night, but it had a complicated password.

It didn't look like he did a lot of work at home. Although she wondered what might be in the safe.

She made her way through the study and into the storage room. The overhead light illuminated a lot of miscellaneous items. Skis. Other sports equipment. An old trunk of what looked like random family heirlooms. An ostentatious oil portrait of Sebastian's family with both of the kids as young adults. Boxes of what seemed to be clothes. One box had childhood stuff of Sebastian's. Morgan was surprised to see that he had gone to public school for the first few grades of elementary. He looked so normal. Just like any blond kid with crooked teeth.

But then she found a series of prep-school photos. The teeth straightened with braces. The upscale outfits. The prestigious crests. She even found a paper he had written about the environment and social justice. She felt herself tearing up. The boxes told a story. About a boy who had loved kickball and comic books and had a best friend named David. About a teen who cared about the world around him. But he had become a young man who played polo and turned his back on the entire planet.

And he didn't seem to have any friends anymore. She never saw him with anyone but business associates. Suddenly, she felt sorry for him. He obviously hadn't started out wanting to be this guy. Who listened to sterile jazz and didn't know how to connect with anyone. Yet this was exactly who he had become.

She looked at her phone for the time. Damn. It was already almost 1 p.m. How had she let herself get so lost in here? It was rare, but every now and then Sebastian came home early.

She had been careful to lock the study door behind her. She had also turned off the study light and put a piece of fabric at the foot of the storage room door. In the very unlikely event he did come home and came into the study, he wouldn't know she had been in there—was still in there. Getting trapped in the storage room like this would be a nightmare. But eventually he'd have to leave, and she'd be able to get out. Eventually.

She listened for a moment before lifting the fabric from the foot of the storage-room door and putting it away. She opened up the door and stepped back into the study. Everything was exactly as she had left it.

The one thing she noticed now was a feature of the wood. A dark knothole in the wall that was on the side of the study that shared a wall with the storage room. Maybe they could figure out how to put a camera there.

She smiled. Had she really thought of that? Maybe she was becoming a good spy.

Chapter 11

After Morgan started taking photos with the camera, it made everything real. Now Sebastian's apartment felt like living behind enemy lines. Any time they were in separate rooms of the apartment, she expected him to suddenly appear, tower over her, camera in hand. *What is the meaning of this?*

Except when she did her textile work. While Morgan quilted, the experience transported her. She wasn't a kept woman, wasn't spying on anyone, wasn't in any danger. There was no climate crisis and she didn't have to brace herself for any sex she didn't want. She was free. Colors and patterns spooled in her head and the space was a playground where she could run freely.

"I think I need another camera," Morgan said to Kevin when they met at the bar the next day.

"What happened to the one I gave you?" Kevin said. "We don't just have money like that."

"No," Morgan said. "I mean a video camera. I found a possible spot to put one in his study. We'd have to drill a hole in the wall and cut a panel out of the other side of the wall.

Cover over any red light that showed we were filming. We'd need some type of one-way, reflective material to film through, and we'd need to figure out how to put a matte finish on it. Gloss would be a dead giveaway. But I really think we could do it."

"Piece of cake," Kevin said, surveying her skeptically. He leaned back against a tower of beer cases in the bar storage room. When he crossed his arms, the fabric of his shirt pulled against the muscles in his arms. Morgan looked away, but her eyes landed on a package of condoms. Refills for the dispenser in the restrooms.

"This isn't the FBI," he went on. "We don't just have unlimited access to high-tech equipment. You're not James Bond. I'm not Q, outfitting you with the latest stuff that hasn't even hit the market."

"Bullshit," Morgan said. "You got me reading these books about how urgent the situation is. I got access to one of the top fossil-fuel CEO's private study and you're like, 'that's not in the budget'? Make it happen. Reach out to your network. Hack it. If this could bring ReidCorp down, don't you think it would be worth someone putting a few thousand on their credit card? I doubt I'll need to use the equipment for thirty days. We could probably return it."

Kevin looked at her with a frown. "You know what?" he said. "You're totally fucking right." He smiled suddenly. "Damn, you're thinking more like an activist than me. Get it done. We can make it happen. I like this new Morgan. You're turning into kind of a badass."

"How do you think I managed to get from a tiny, shit town in Pennsylvania to New York City?" she asked. "I had to hustle, and hack things, and figure out workarounds, and make it happen."

"Okay," Kevin said, nodding. "Let me see what we can figure out. Will you draw me a sketch of the setup?"

The two of them huddled over an unfolded cocktail napkin. Morgan leaned it up against the boxes beside him and sketched with a pencil. She tried to ignore the fresh smell of his soap or shampoo or whatever as she sketched the floor plan of the study and the storage room in Sebastian's apartment.

"It's such a weird layout," Kevin said. "Why is there a storage space behind the study?"

"I have a theory," Morgan said. "I think it's because this used to be a staircase that led up to servant quarters. And maybe there was a little prep room where the servants used to wait and keep some supplies. Could be that what's now the study was like a drawing room or something. There's a regular staircase in the front of the house, and those rooms are big. Then, in the back of the house, the rooms are much smaller. I think when they stopped having those type of live-in servants, they must have remodeled and repurposed what had been the servants' quarters. There seem to be these small spaces on each floor. Just big enough for like a staircase and a little room."

"You're not telling me that Sebastian Reid doesn't have an army of staff doing all his domestic work, are you?"

"Not at all," Morgan said. "But it's all takeout. A cleaning woman once a week. And his assistant, Dawn. She handles everything virtually."

"Well, this is great," Kevin said, holding up the sketch she had done. "You'll need to get in there and do some measurements. The exact depth dimension of the wall. Anything you can find out about the thickness of the paneling on the study side and the Sheetrock or whatever the material is on the storage-room side. How high up is the knot in the wood. How far in from the door frame. Everything you can possibly measure."

"I can do that," Morgan said.

"I worked construction a couple of summers," Kevin said. "We need to come up with some ruse to get me in the building and I can help you install it."

"Doesn't he know your face?" Morgan asked.

"Worse than that," Kevin said. "He has a restraining order against me."

"For what?" Morgan asked.

"I might have thrown some rotting seaweed on him at a protest once," Kevin said.

"You what?" Morgan asked.

"It was early in my activist career. I was overly zealous."

"Then we need someone else to do it," Morgan said. "In case he recognizes you. Or he might have given your picture to the doorman."

"We just need to figure out how to disguise me . . . somehow," he said. "Do you know any makeup artists?"

"No," Morgan said. "But I know someone who might."

On her way back to Sebastian, she texted Dashawna: **U know anyone who does makeup?**

On the train, she got a reply: **My friend Lily's sister, I think.**

At seven p.m. Morgan was sitting around the apartment living room. She couldn't focus. She couldn't settle. After six p.m. Sebastian might come home at any minute. There were two tiny scratch marks around the keyhole of his study door. She regarded them like bloodstains. He would see. He would know. Of course he wouldn't. That was ridiculous. The minutes ticked away: six fifteen; six thirty. Why wasn't he home yet? Did he suspect something? Finally, at seven fifteen she got a text from Sebastian's assistant, Dawn, that he was stuck in a meeting. He wouldn't be home until nine at the earliest. Did she want anything for dinner? Morgan declined.

Knowing Sebastian wouldn't be home for the next few

hours, she relaxed a bit. She could focus on getting a few things done. First, she took all the measurements Kevin requested. Then she ate leftovers.

At nine fifteen Sebastian still wasn't home. Morgan had finished the climate books and all the articles Kevin had sent. She didn't usually work in the evenings, but then, she was usually "on" with Sebastian in the evenings.

The night was clear and a bluish light streamed into the studio, a combination of moonlight and all the city's light pollution.

From across the room, the Sacajawea dollar glinted at her, not just darker but cooler than in the daylight. In the dimmer light, the quilt still worked. She couldn't see all the detail in the barbed wire, but she also couldn't make out the expressions on the faces of most of the women. Their heads and torsos towered over her, not quite menacing but not smiling, either. She liked the way it read in dim illumination.

Then she turned on the light and it still worked. The barbed wire fabric was perfect. Yes. This was it. Time to sew. She switched on her sewing machine.

First, she did the large, basting stitches to hold the quilt top together; then, she started the final stitching that connected all the panels, making sure they were all perfectly straight and flat.

She was so deep in work that she didn't hear Sebastian come in at first. Only as he moved around the apartment did she realize he was home.

She checked the clock and saw it was after midnight. Her heart began to race, the way it does when an alarm wakes you from a heavy sleep.

She took a deep breath. Everything was gonna be okay. It was late. He wouldn't want anything from her. He wouldn't be looking around the apartment, noticing scratch marks on locks. He would soon go to bed.

As she felt her body calming, she realized she had unconsciously been rubbing the smooth silk of the fabric in the Sacajawea dollar. She put a hand on the quilt to ground herself. She looked at the faces of the women, as if reassuring them that she would be back soon.

She came out of her studio with a huge smile. "Hello, sweetheart! I'm in the middle of a project, but I wanted to welcome you home."

He looked tired. "You off to bed?" she asked.

He nodded and mumbled something affirmative.

"Good night," she said and gave him a quick kiss. "Don't wait up. I'll probably be at it all night."

Then she went back to her fabric. When she finally finished up for the night, it was nearly seven in the morning. When she was dragging herself to bed, Sebastian was already getting up to go to the office.

She woke after just a few hours' sleep. Bleary-eyed and jangled, she went to the kitchen to get coffee. Then she went back to her studio. She hadn't worked a marathon like this since college.

Having finished the top, she needed to add the batting and the backing. So much stitching to finish the entire project.

She was exhausted, but who knew what spying would demand of her in the next couple of weeks? She needed to keep her eye on the prize. Maybe she would get evidence on Sebastian and maybe not. But she was determined to leave this house in a better position as a fabric artist, one way or another.

She got a text from Kevin that he had found a camera. So that afternoon she coordinated with Dashawna, Kevin, and the friend's sister who Dashawna had mentioned.

By dinnertime it was dark. She'd finished the quilt but was too tired to feel triumphant. She just felt ready to crash. She was falling asleep when Sebastian came home.

"Come on, babe, wake up," he said. "I brought Indian food for you."

Morgan was too tired to say anything—let alone correct him. He hadn't brought anything. His assistant had ordered it, someone else had cooked it, and yet another person had delivered it to his door. And he had brought it for himself. Just brought extra of what he was having. He hadn't even asked her what dish she wanted.

But she got up and joined him. Throughout dinner she wore her exhaustion like a shield, protecting herself from the anxiety that usually spiked in his presence. After they ate, she went back to bed and slept straight through to eight the next morning.

She woke with a start. All the anxiety flooding back. But when she got up to look around the apartment, Sebastian was gone, and the dampness of the bathroom let her know that she had only just missed him.

She would need to get going herself if she planned on meeting Kevin at the makeup artist's house. She went to take a shower of her own. Inexplicably, she felt the need to lock the bathroom door to protect herself from the empty apartment.

Violet's place was a one-bedroom in Brooklyn. She was in her late twenties, with skin the same dark color as the wood paneling in Sebastian's study. She had the large-eyed, full-lipped face of a model, though she didn't seem to be wearing any makeup.

Morgan looked around. There were photographs on the wall that had a sort of Caribbean circus theme. Black people in bright costumes on trapezes and tightropes. The photos had been retouched, with deeply saturated colors. Morgan loved them.

Violet sat Morgan and Kevin down at the kitchen table

and got to work. Violet brushed a fine, dark hair into Kevin's short mustache. He had sandy coloring, but Violet had already put a dark wash in his hair. The mustache would disguise him effectively from anyone who didn't know him well or wasn't looking too closely.

She also gave him a pair of glasses with clear lenses.

By the time she was done, he really looked like someone else.

Chapter 12

Around noon, Morgan was back at the apartment. She called Sebastian's assistant, Dawn.

"Sebastian Reid's office," the assistant answered brightly.

Morgan identified herself. "I'm so sorry to bother you," Morgan said. "But the kitchen sink tap seems to be stuck. I can't turn it off."

"Okay," the assistant said. "Let me call someone."

"Thank you so—" Morgan began. "Wait, it looks like there might be a plumbing truck in front of the building. Should I ask the guy to take a look if he's already here?"

"Sure," Dawn said. "That would be amazing."

"Okay," Morgan said. "I'll call if I need anything."

And that was that. She buzzed Kevin in and he came upstairs.

"Please," Morgan said. "Don't say anything about the place."

"Which way to the leaky faucet, ma'am?" he asked.

"Smart-ass," Morgan said. "Right this way."

She had already taken time to pick the locks of the study and storage room. Kevin came in with a large toolbox and a small camera.

*   *   *

They made a pretty good team. While Kevin used the power drill to carve out the knothole, Morgan experimented with different clear matte finishing for the dark film the camera would look through.

Then, while he set up the camera, she covered the hole with the film and made sure the edges were perfect.

In the study itself, she installed an audio-recording device. He had gotten one that was voice-activated. She taped it behind a bookshelf and they checked it.

"Testing. One, two," she said, sitting in the swivel chair at Sebastian's desk.

"Levels look good," Kevin said.

But then Morgan heard a hissing sound from somewhere in the apartment.

Kevin started to say something else, but she shushed him.

"What is that?" Kevin whispered.

The hissing was coming from downstairs.

Morgan threw up her hands in an I-don't-know gesture.

Wait here, she mouthed to Kevin, then thought better of it. Quickly, they got him and all the gear into the storage room and she closed both doors behind her.

She put on a cheerful face, in case she walked right into Sebastian. Internally, however, she was trying to figure out how the hell she would ever be able to smuggle Kevin back out of the apartment. Or explain why the plumber had been in the wrong part of the apartment.

She walked down the stairs and followed the hissing sound. It was coming from the kitchen.

She put on her highest-watt grin and walked in. The hissing was louder, but there was nobody there.

Then she heard the gurgle of the dishwasher, changing from Wash to Rinse cycle.

She let her breath out. Right. Lena set it to run automati-

cally every week. Men like Sebastian didn't even have to remember to turn on their appliances.

She jogged back upstairs to the study and gave Kevin the
all clear.

"Where'd you get the camera?" she asked as they went
back to work.

"I did like you told me," Kevin said. "I got a friend to put
it on his credit card."

She nodded. He had started sawing a hole in the Sheetrock to put the camera inside the storage-room wall.

"The equipment wouldn't have cost that much," he said.
"It's the remote control on the camera and the voice-activated
trigger on the audio recorder that really drove the price up."

"Let's hope he'll be able to return it all," she said.

Kevin nodded. "He kept all the boxes."

After they had installed everything, he spackled over the
seams in the wall where they had cut out the square of
Sheetrock to hide the camera.

"It's not invisible, but it wouldn't be noticeable to a casual
observer," he said.

"Like you," she said.

He turned to her, his face puzzled.

"I mean, the fact that it's you under that disguise," she
said, reaching up and touching the fake hair of his beard.

Then, without warning, he grabbed her hand and kissed it.

Morgan snatched her hand from his mouth, concerned
more about the possibility of mussing his disguise than the
press of his lips against her palm. Lips that had been warm
and delicious.

"I'm—I'm sorry," he said. "I—seeing you here. It just brings
home to me how much of a risk you're taking. I really care
about you. Seriously, if anything ever happened to you—"

She raised her index finger and put it back on his lips.

Gently. Careful not to muss the disguise. "It won't," she said. "Let's get you packed up and out of here."

Kevin put the drill back in the toolbox and put his fake glasses back on as Morgan called the assistant again.

"Sebastian Reid's office."

"Hey, it's Morgan," she said. "The guy was so nice. He said it was just loose and he adjusted it. He won't even charge Sebastian."

"That's great," Dawn said. "Sebastian's on his way home to get a different suit. These ridiculous protesters threw blood at him. He should be there any minute."

Morgan could feel the panic rise in her chest.

"Great," Morgan said. "I'll get this guy's card in case we want to use him in the future."

She hung up quickly and rushed to where Kevin stood looking out at the river.

"Sebastian is on his way," she said. "You need to hurry."

Kevin nodded and picked up the toolbox.

Morgan opened the front door and was prepared to show Kevin out when she caught sight of his mustache hanging slightly askew.

She pushed him back into the apartment and straightened it. Then she opened the door and showed him out.

"Thank you so much," she said, careful to keep her face polite and cool.

"Morgan," Sebastian called from down the hall. He was stepping out of the elevator.

It took everything in Morgan's power to make her face light up. "Hey, honey!" she said. "Here's our miracle worker. What did you say your name was? Ron?"

"Shawn," Kevin said, using the name from the fake card he had made. Just in case Sebastian or anyone else caught them. He was determined to look legit.

"Thanks, Shawn."

Kevin walked toward the elevator. Sebastian leaned in toward her, and Morgan kissed him.

"I missed you," Sebastian said. "Two nights without you is too long."

Over Sebastian's shoulder, Morgan saw Kevin in the elevator, his eyes locked on them.

"Let's get inside," Morgan said.

"These assholes ruined one of my favorite Armanis," Sebastian complained. It was then she could see the dark stain on the lapel of the suit. There was another stain on the pants.

"You have so many," Morgan said.

"Well, maybe it's worth it, if I get to come home in the middle of the day to take off my clothes," he said, pulling her closer.

Morgan could feel her stomach clench. Was it the sight of blood? The smell of it? The fact that she wasn't drunk this time? Knowing that Kevin was still in the elevator, descending to street level.

But she couldn't put Sebastian off forever. She needed him to trust that Kevin was Shawn. She needed to be the girl he had asked to move in. The eager, accommodating girl who didn't care about ReidCorp.

She gave a laugh that sounded brittle in her ears and pulled him down onto the couch. "Let's get these pants off."

She couldn't stomach the idea of sex with him—of intercourse. So she went down on him, leaving all her clothes and his shirt and tie on.

As she did, she visualized the camera in the wall, the app on her phone—so carefully installed that it wouldn't have any connection to the cloud. She thought of everything she could, except where her body was, what it was doing, who it was touching. And throughout it all, her palm burned where Kevin's lips had touched it.

* * *

The next morning Morgan couldn't get out of bed. She'd had a drink after her sexual tryst with Sebastian. And then another and another. She'd slept straight through his departure. At ten she woke with a nasty hangover, a half-empty tumbler of liquor on the nightstand beside her.

She was desperate to pee. She felt glad she hadn't wet the bed. But after emptying her bladder, she decided against making Dashawna's hangover cure. Instead, she reached for one of Sebastian's sleeping pills. She drank it with a leftover swig of vodka and crashed again.

It was afternoon when she finally woke up. She felt like shit. She considered taking another one of Sebastian's pills. She didn't want to be awake. She didn't want to be in this fucking house. Goddamn spying. On this planet that was fucking burning. She couldn't talk to Dashawna about it, not really. The only person she could confide in was Kevin. And she couldn't tell him anything right now.

She picked up her phone to see what time it was. Had Sebastian texted her? How soon would he be home? She couldn't do it. She couldn't do it one more goddamn day.

Sebastian hadn't texted. But he had apparently made some noise in his study. Because the recording device had been activated.

Morgan jolted up.

Two hours ago. She needed to know what had been said. And what the fuck? What if it had been another visit from Mitchell Brightwell? What if she had been too out of it to activate the camera? Had she really endured all this miserable fucking spying to miss the most important moment?

She sat there, staring at the phone, feeling like she might cry. But then she had stared so long that her phone went dark, snapping her out of the moment.

Okay. Deep breath. She needed to get herself together. She

couldn't wallow in self-pity; she needed to decide. Was she a spy or was she done here? She could call Dashawna right now and get the hell out. She had finished her quilt. She could deliver it to the Folk Museum today. The only thing keeping her here was the spy operation. Was she going to do it or not?

She couldn't stand the thought that she might have missed her chance to get some real evidence and be done. It sickened her. Or was that just the hangover? But she needed to know what she had missed. She had to get into the storage room and listen to the audio recording. She sat on the edge of the bed and rubbed her eyes. She sent a quick text to Sebastian's assistant: **Do you know his schedule for tonight?**

They never used Sebastian's name. His pronouns were he/him/his. They knew who they were talking about.

Morgan changed her mind about Dashawna's hangover cure. She made a batch and drank it down. Then she took a swig directly out of the vodka bottle, drank a cup of coffee, and took a shower.

The coffee was a mistake. In combination with the alcohol, it had her jittery. Or maybe all of it was a mistake. Maybe she needed to be drug-free for the rest of this operation. Or maybe she just needed to have the right drugs at the right time. This get-blackout-drunk-after-blow-job plan was not the way to go. That was for sure.

Eventually, she was able to open the study and the storage room. She used the remote control to play the audio from the digital recorder. Because they had it Sheetrocked into the wall, she had to be close to make the remote work.

"It's Sebastian Reid," the recording began, then a long silence.

Yes! Morgan thought. A phone call. She hadn't missed the big moment of evidence. "I can't get away this week . . . Maybe Friday . . . But these protesters follow me wherever I go. It's fucking insane. . . . No, it's too risky for you to come to the holiday party. . . . Skip's company party? . . . I suppose that could work. But how do we keep from being seen together? . . . You really think that'll work? . . . Well, I'm willing to try it. We can't meet here since my girlfriend almost saw you last time. . . . She's an artist. Mostly works at home . . . Yeah, things are fine with her. . . . Marriage? I don't know . . . She's a little hot and cool . . . I hadn't thought of it that way. We'll see if nuptials are in order . . . Okay, then. See you at Skip's."

And that was it. She downloaded the recording and reset the recorder.

"Who the hell is Skip?" she asked Kevin when they met at the bar storage room.

No mention of her hand to his lips or the kiss with Sebastian he'd witnessed afterward. All business. They also ignored the word "marriage."

"I don't know who Skip is, but you've got to get to that party," Kevin said. "Can you get him to bring you along?"

"He won't want to," she said. "Not if he's meeting Brightwell."

"Can't you do some feminine wiles thing?" Kevin asked.

"Excuse me?"

"No," Kevin said. "You know what I mean. There are those things women—some women—do to get their way. Manipulate him."

"That's not my strong suit," Morgan said, thinking of the blow job disaster.

"Don't you have magazine articles that tell you how to do it or something?" Kevin asked.

"No," Morgan said. "But I know who I can ask."

"Good," Kevin said. "I'll work on figuring out who Skip is."

* * *

On the way back uptown, Morgan texted Dashawna. She hoped to catch her at home, to find a reason to go over there. She dreaded going to the apartment, especially now that her quilt was done and she didn't have a big project to distract her.

The train was moving slowly, then ground to a stop. According to the conductor, there was a disabled train up ahead. Morgan tried to check messages on her phone, but they had stopped in a spot where reception wasn't good. She went back to reading the article on climate work on the website of the Movement for Black Lives. *We will not sacrifice Black Lives or accept false solutions that perpetuate unjust social and economic systems*. That was exactly it. Sebastian Reid and his company had been offering false solutions that were really about sacrificing human lives to make more money.

She went back to the website. *Climate Justice is Racial Justice*. Dashawna had said the same thing. Morgan understood it now. But the implications were so big. How were they going to fix everything?

It just made her more agitated. The situation felt so big, so urgent, and she was stuck. Finally she played a few rounds of Tetris. Colored blocks soothed her. Even if they were falling fast.

By the time she got home, Dashawna was calling back. "How do you get someone to invite you to a party?" Morgan asked.

"I'll show you," Dashawna said. "Can you get me into the ReidCorp holiday party?"

"I doubt it," Morgan said. "I don't think I'm a plus-one who can have her own plus-one."

"Well then, I can't give you advice on how to get invited to another party," Dashawna said.

Morgan laughed. "Okay, I get it. Hold something hostage."

Dashawna laughed, too. "Just get a little pouty with him. 'You never take me out. Waah waah.'"

"That's so not me," Morgan said.

"Get yourself a new dress. Ask him where you can wear it."

"He'll say to his holiday party," Morgan said.

"Get two dresses," Dashawna said. "You went and got one for his party, but they had a second one. He just has to take you somewhere else. Pout if he says no. Sleep in your room. Throw a fit about being a kept woman. Something. See what he does. You already finished your quilt. You got nothing to lose."

"You're right," Morgan said. "Not a thing."

Only the fate of the entire planet.

The next day Morgan and Kevin met in the bar storage room again. "I've narrowed Skip down to a few different people," Kevin said. "It was a college nickname for Byron MacQuoid of MCM. His company is having a holiday party this weekend. Side note, MCM stands for MacQuoid Coal Management, but they use initials now so as not to be associated with coal."

"Who are the other Skips?" Morgan asked.

"It could also be Kim Simmons, whose holiday party is next week. There's some inside joke about his yacht and calling him the Skipper, but it's a stretch. The obvious choice would be Skip Tatum. But his company's holiday party was last week."

"How the hell am I supposed to get invited to something when I have no idea when or where it is?"

"Did you talk to your feminine wiles source?"

"Please stop calling it that," Morgan said.

"Did you?"

"She said to buy a dress and demand he take me to a party," Morgan said. "It won't work."

"Why won't it work?" Kevin said.

"He'd just take me out someplace fancy or to another party," she said. "I need to know where I'm trying to go before I put on the pressure."

Kevin sighed. "Okay," he said. "I'll keep trying.

After her meeting with Kevin, Morgan sat at a café with her quilt for CFI on the chair across from her. CFI was on the way back to the apartment and she didn't want to go back yet.

She drank coffee and searched the internet on her phone. She looked up Byron MacQuoid, Kim Simmons, and Skip Tatum. A "Skip MacQuoid," "holiday," and "party" internet search yielded only eight entries. One was the word "skip," not the nickname. This one seemed like the furthest reach. Kevin was right. Simmons was occasionally referred to as "the Skipper" on social media. but if close friends called him Skip, there was so mention of it on the internet.

She looked at the online photos from Skip Tatum's holiday party. Celebrities. Local politicians. Tons of businessmen. A photo of Skip and his wife with champagne glasses raised. Skip in a tux with a green tie. The wife in a glittering red dress, with a decorated pine tree behind them. They called it a holiday party, but they were a Christmas cliché.

"Skip Tatum and his wife, Chelsea Tatum, at New Fuel Enterprises' holiday party last night. Tatum was named CEO this year. His wife is executive director of the Tatum/Dean Foundation."

Morgan blinked at the screen.

She had heard of the Tatum/Dean Foundation. They were big in New York City. Definitely big enough to have a holiday party of their own.

She searched longer and found several articles that were critical of Skip being the major donor to his wife's foundation, getting a tax write-off to pay her salary and essentially support her as a socialite, while the foundation's supposed good works were quite lackluster. Their attorney had been quoted as saying it was certainly all legal.

Morgan went to the company's website and found that they were throwing a party the following night—a holiday fundraising gala. Five thousand dollars per person. Of course. Skip would invite all his cronies and they would donate to his wife's organization, which was really just a trinket he'd given her to play with.

What did the foundation even do? She searched around. Looked like they threw a lot of parties to raise money. It took fifteen minutes to find the actual causes they supported. Some outfit that rescued women in Asia from sex trafficking? Right. She had heard about these folks. They were in the news a while back, a scandal that some of their projects in Mexico involved wealthy men having some of the "rescued" women sent to their hotel rooms. They were acquitted, but they shut down the Mexico operations. Now they only operated in Asia. Ugh. This reeked of bullshit. Start to finish.

Skip's party. It wasn't one that his company was throwing. It was one that his wife's organization was throwing but he was paying for. Yes. That would certainly qualify.

She sent Kevin a text on the burner phone and grabbed the bag with her quilt. She was going dress shopping.

The Dilani Mara showroom was a big square room with white walls and a dark wooden floor. Sunlight streamed in through the wide windows, and it also had abundant track lighting to illuminate everything. But when Morgan walked in, she looked around with her hands, as usual. Her fingers dazzled by the delicious fabric textures.

She spent the first five minutes touching some of the different silk dresses before she even tried anything on. Soon she had a growing pile of garments slung over her arm, a rainbow of colors luscious to the touch.

An hour later she had picked a little black cocktail dress for the ReidCorp holiday party, and another cream-colored, floor-length gown for the Tatum/Dean Foundation gala.

She snapped photos of herself in both.

Went shopping at Dilani Mara and got this cocktail dress for your holiday party. But they also had this gorgeous gown, and it would be perfect for the Tatum/Dean gala tomorrow night. Please say you'll take me? I'm buying them both!

She took her purchases to the register and asked for Vivian.

"She's not in today."

Morgan blinked. "She said she'd be here."

"She was supposed to be," the salesgirl said, "but they had a snafu at a fashion show downtown; she had to take some dresses. She'll be back day after tomorrow."

Morgan pasted on a smile. "Sure," she said. "Just give me a minute."

What the hell was she going to do? Dilani Mara dresses cost thousands. They didn't even have price tags. Dashawna didn't have that kind of money to lend. She certainly couldn't ask Sebastian. The whole point was her telling him she was buying these gorgeous dresses and he needed to take her out to show them off. If she'd known Vivian wasn't going to be in, she might have borrowed something from Dashawna or gone into her own designs. She could still do that. No. She couldn't. She had already sent the photos to Sebastian. Now she had to get the dresses.

The balance in her checking account was $237.92. She went outside and called the bank where she had one of her credit cards. If she bought them today, Vivian would make sure she could take them back.

She waited on hold for five minutes. Most of her cards were maxed out, but there was one she had kept up payments.

A young woman came up to her and asked for spare change. Her pale face was all anxious lines. Morgan fished a couple of quarters out of her wallet and set them in the woman's hand.

When someone from the bank finally came on the line, Morgan asked if they could increase her credit line. She waited on hold some more. No, sorry, they'd checked her credit score and it was too low.

Shit. Morgan took a breath. She had no choice.

She texted Kevin: **Got a minute?**

He responded right away: **What's up? Running between meetings in midtown.**

She texted back: **My friend was supposed to hook me up at this dress shop, but she's not here. The dress is supposed to be my reason for going to the party. Need a credit card with a few thousand on it. It'll all get refunded. Any chance you can help?**

He texted back: **A FEW THOUSAND??!!**

She felt the irritation rise: **Can you or can't you? Feminine wiles are expensive. Here's the address. Make it or break it. LMK.**

She watched the ellipsis of him typing.

See you in 30 min.

A pair of men in suits walked by eating falafel. As the smell of spices drifted past, Morgan realized she hadn't eaten. Except the hangover cure. She could feel her blood sugar drop. She needed food. Damn, why hadn't she brought something from home? Or eaten before she left? She looked around at all the nearby corners but couldn't find the vendor. She went into a convenience store, but in this neighborhood even the markets were upscale. She spent six dollars on some almonds, bringing her balance to $231.92.

She walked back into Dilani Mara chewing the first mouthful.

"Oh good," the woman said. "There you are. Did you want the size eight in the cream? There's another young woman interested."

Morgan smiled. "Absolutely."

"Wonderful," the salesclerk said. "Would you like to purchase it now?"

"Not just yet," Morgan said. "My boyfriend's on his way over to check it out."

The clerk smiled. "Of course," she said. "You can try it on for him."

Morgan didn't have the energy to refuse. Besides, in the dressing room she could finish the almonds. "What a great idea," Morgan said. She carefully brushed the oil and salt from her fingers before she took the gown.

In the dressing room she finished the bag of nuts and texted Kevin: **Long story. You're posing as my boyfriend checking out the gown before I buy it. Got it?**

Kevin replied: **Got it.**

Morgan sat on a satin upholstered bench in the cream-colored dress, waiting for Kevin. It was a beautiful gown. She'd wear it to the party with a better bra, and her hair up, and some kind of jewelry, but it did look great on her.

When Kevin walked in, he looked all wrong for the place. Faded jeans, but not distressed in the fashionable way, a little grubby. Worn sneakers. Old T-shirt with a slight fraying at the neckline. And a worn peacoat. The dark wash had faded from his hair and he had a half-hearted goatee. But he was incredibly handsome in that rugged farm guy kind of way.

And when he walked in, Morgan stood up and smiled. He froze for a moment. Then ground back into action.

"Hey, honey," he said. "You look great."

He leaned in to hug her and pressed his lips to her temple. He lingered a moment. There was that soap smell she loved. He stepped back and held her hands.

"Wow," he said. "Look at you. Just wow."

"Should we get it?" she asked.

"Definitely," Kevin said. "It'll be perfect for the party."

It was the most contact they had had since their goodbye hug. Morgan could barely catch her breath.

Kevin fumbled in his pocket for his wallet.

"Here you go," he said to the salesclerk, and handed over a personal credit card.

"That'll be five thousand two hundred and seventy-three with tax," she said.

"Sounds good," Kevin said, but Morgan could see the lines around his mouth tighten.

He walked over to where she stood.

"You have a plan to get my money back, right?" he murmured.

"Definitely," she said. "As early as tomorrow. Next week at the latest."

"Good," he said.

"May I see your ID, Mr. Templeton?" the salesclerk asked.

"Of course," Kevin said, and flipped open his wallet.

Morgan slipped into the dressing room and out of the dress. She came out a few minutes later, and the salesclerk was returning Kevin's credit card.

"Well," Kevin said. "I've got to get back to work."

"Okay, honey," Morgan said. "Thanks so much for coming by."

"Of course," he said. "My pleasure."

The salesclerk smiled as she hung the dresses.

"See you at home," Morgan said, and leaned forward for what was supposed to be a quick kiss on the lips. But they both felt it. The split second when they slipped from the pretense of a kiss to the real thing. Kevin's lips were soft and he tasted vaguely of peppermint. She leaned her whole body forward and he slid an arm around her waist. The two of them locked together for a delicious second, then she was the first to pull away.

Kevin's eyes were still closed as she pulled back. Then they opened and he gazed at her for a moment before he stepped back. He could only nod before he walked out. Morgan felt almost drunk again, her face and neck flushed.

"Do you need a garment bag?" the clerk asked.

"Sure," Morgan stammered, feeling suddenly exposed. She ducked her face down to check her phone. Sebastian had texted: **Darling, you look amazing. Of course I'll take you.**

Mission accomplished! She looked back up from the phone.

The bag the clerk handed her was a thick plastic. When Vivian hooked her up with clothes, she got them in a thin sheet of plastic like you get from the dry cleaner. But when you paid full price, apparently you got a garment bag that might protect your dress if you were embedded in a war zone.

"Thanks so much," Morgan said. "Sorry for the delay."

"Honey," the clerk said. "Any guy who looked at me the way that guy looked at you is worth waiting for. Hang on to him."

Morgan smiled at her. "I will," she said.

"Oh," the clerk said. "And here's the bag you checked."

Morgan blinked. In all the drama, she had practically forgotten her entry for CFI.

Morgan had her hands full. Over one arm was the Dilani Mara garment bag. Over the other arm was a separate garment bag that held her quilt. She was determined to drop it off today. She didn't know how long she could keep up this charade with Sebastian. The deadline wasn't for a few days, but she didn't want to leave anything to the last minute. What if she was heading to drop off the quilt on the day it was due and Mitchell Brightwell showed up? Or God forbid she got busted and Sebastian threw her out? Or just had a total meltdown and had to abandon ship? She would feel like an idiot if, after all this, she didn't get her quilt turned in. Eyes on the goal. Always.

The gallery was lit so differently from the designer showroom. Instead of illuminating everything, these lights guided your eye to look certain places. Morgan was captivated by the jewel-tone colors in a textile sculpture of a pregnant woman, life-size. The textile was a translucent yarn in patches of cranberry, royal blue, and amethyst. It was one of several sculptures that showed female figures doing various tasks. One had a woolen broom and was sweeping. Another was drying a dish. Yet another was stirring a pot that hovered in midair.

"So amazing, right?" the clerk said. She was a thickset brunette whose hair was held up in a messy bun with a chopstick. "I love her work. She's been in the game for decades. So glad she's finally getting some recognition. Can I help you with anything?"

Morgan shook her head to clear it. "Wow. I almost forgot why I was here," she said, and lifted her quilt bag. "I'm dropping off a submission for CFI."

"You're a finalist?" The young woman's eyes lit up. "Can I see?"

"Sure," Morgan said as they walked over to the counter.

Morgan opened the bag and smoothed out the quilt on the glass surface.

The young woman sucked in her breath. "It's stunning," she whispered.

"Thank you," Morgan said. And then—without warning—started crying.

"Don't get it wet!" the woman said, fumbling behind the counter for a tissue.

"I'm sorry!" Morgan said.

"No, I just—" the woman said, handing the tissue to Morgan. "I know this particular silk is so delicate—" She fingered the fabric of the Sacajawea dollar.

Morgan wiped her face and regained control. "Wow," she said again with a shaky laugh. "You know your fabrics."

The woman shrugged. "It's my job."

"Well," Morgan said. "So awkward. Anyway, I'm Morgan Faraday, and this is my official submission."

"Got it," the woman said. "Let me give you an official receipt."

The woman filled out a piece of paper and handed it to her. "That's it," she said. "You're official."

"Thanks," Morgan said.

"I'm not supposed to say this," the woman said. "But I really love it. I hope you win."

"Thanks," Morgan said. "That means a lot." She began to tear up again. She shook her head and walked out quickly, carrying the Dilani Mara bag in front of her chest like armor.

The next thing she knew, she was sitting at a bus stop down the street from the gallery, crying into the garment bag. After the wave of tears washed over her, she expected to feel refreshed. But why didn't she? She knew, but she didn't want to say it. Not even to herself.

Kevin.

Oh God. That kiss. But even before that. His hug hello. Him holding her hands and pretending to admire the dress. Or really admiring it. The salesclerk seemed so sure he had looked at her with adoration. But had he? Or was he just faking it? Yes, he was attracted to her, but these days he had plenty of contempt, as well. But maybe now that she was spying . . . maybe now that they were on the same side . . . maybe after it was all over . . .

Don't think about that right now. She needed to prep for the party. She needed to look at as many pictures as she could of Sebastian's associates. And review a list Kevin had given her of fossil-fuel industry honchos. When she walked into that party, she needed her photographic memory to be full of faces.

* * *

Morgan had had a few shots of vodka by the time Sebastian got home.

He kissed her hello. "Didn't you look delicious in that dress?" he whispered in her ear.

She could tell what he wanted. For her to put the dress on, so he could take it off her. She couldn't do it. Not after the kiss with Kevin. She could wear it to the party, but not in the house, in this intimate moment. Not really intimate. In this sexual moment. She just couldn't.

"I have something else on for you," she said. "Something special."

She undid her robe to reveal some lingerie—a matching red bra and underwear. This was separate from Kevin, part of the costume.

"Ooooh," he said. "I like."

She drank champagne and threw back her head and laughed. "Well, come here, then," she said.

She imagined herself the femme fatale. Poison in her ring. Novocain in her lipstick. Danger between her legs. As he pressed into her, she dared not let her mind wander. Didn't want to think of Kevin. Not under these circumstances. She thought of redwood trees, crashing waves, tropical beaches. Then it was time to put on her performance. She faked a huge orgasm, and then he came, too.

"Wow," Sebastian said. "Things seem to go better for you when you have a little drink to loosen you up."

"Definitely," Morgan said. "So much better."

The next evening, when she was getting ready, Morgan dug into her suitcase for Spanx. She didn't usually wear anything like that. She liked her body. She wasn't an hourglass like Dashawna, or svelte like Vivian. Her build was a little tomboyish. But she wanted the Spanx so she could be . . . contained. She would have worn a girdle or a corset if she had one. She wanted to be locked down. Sexually unavailable.

She put the dress on over the Spanx. It looked about the same. Her cleavage was more prominent, but if Sebastian tried to feel her up, her nipples would have no sensation from his touch.

Sure enough, he ran a hand down the front of her dress in the limo. Had it always been like this when they went out? Him pawing at her? It hadn't quite felt like pawing before, but it did now.

She realized it was an opportunity. There was going to be an exchange tonight with Brightwell. Did Sebastian have anything on him? She felt in all of his pockets, coat, and pants. She felt only his wallet, phone, and erection.

His groping felt even more tedious. Maybe if she got what she needed tonight, she could invent a pretense to dump him. Pretend to get really drunk and say something unforgivable. One way or another, she was counting the hours.

The gala was held at Le Fleur Hotel in Midtown. Despite the French name, it had been taken over by a US hotel corporation. Morgan had come as an undergraduate to see the upholstery fabric, a delicate, imported silk that needed to be redone every few years. But now they had reupholstered in a synthetic American fabric with a similar design. Morgan could see and feel the difference. She noticed other subtle touches of corporate cost cutting. They used to be known for their towering arrangements of fresh flowers and now they had very upscale fabric flowers.

What a shame. The natural fabrics and fresh flowers had been so lovely.

Sebastian undoubtedly didn't notice any of it as they crossed through the lobby and into the grand ballroom.

"Let me get us some drinks," he said, and left her standing by herself at one of the ballroom's tall tables. Morgan looked around, trying to recognize faces from her research. Across the room she spotted a man who might be the CEO of Exxon. And the woman in the burgundy gown was Chelsea Tatum, the hostess.

Thank goodness these were corporate guys. All of them were clean shaven. No wonder Dashawna's friend had used Kevin's mustache to disguise him. With facial hair, you could hide anyone.

Sebastian appeared at her side. "Vodka cran for you, my dear," he said, and handed her a drink. She'd need to be careful not to spill any on herself in this unaffordable dress. If he had asked for her drink order, she'd have requested a vodka and soda. But that was Sebastian. He didn't ask.

Not that he had ordered for her when they first went out. But once she had ordered something and he knew she liked it, he just assumed she would want it every time. Which bothered her. He didn't always get the same food from any given restaurant. Why would he assume that she would? But perhaps for him, the smugness of knowing was its own reward. Or maybe, as the kept girlfriend, she could only expect that he would buy her food that was generally to her liking, not take the time to find out what she might actually be desiring at that moment.

Desire, it turned out, was only his provenance. She was the object of desire. The object to satisfy his desire.

A woman walked by in a cloud of perfume that clashed with the fake scent of the flowers. Suddenly, Morgan felt like she was choking. She reached for her drink but couldn't risk taking a swig while she felt so shaky. She grabbed Sebastian's drink instead. A paler scotch and soda.

"You like scotch?"

"I don't drink anything red when I'm in a pale dress," she said.

He looked startled, as if it had never occurred to him.

She felt better having said something. The choking feeling started to subside. Maybe she needed to speak her mind more.

"You know," she said. "You could ask me before you get me a drink. What I want, you know? It would be nice to be asked."

"Most people just have a regular drink," he said, a touch of defensiveness in his voice.

"It's not just the drinks," Morgan said. She knew she should stop, but somehow she couldn't. "You order food for me at restaurants."

"If you don't like what I order, why don't you say something?"

"If you expect me to say something, why don't you let me order for myself?"

"Are you really going to do this here?" he asked, his mouth tight.

"I'm just saying, I'm right here, Sebastian," Morgan said. "Would it kill you to ask what I'd like to drink?" Or if I want you to touch my breast, she thought, but didn't say.

"This is ridiculous," he said.

"Look," she said. "It's just a drink. Let's drop it. We can still have a good time."

Sebastian seemed to be considering it.

Both of them were looking toward the door when Mitchell Brightwell walked in. Morgan almost didn't notice him because his wife's dress was so elaborate. A custom couture piece designed to get attention. It had a swirling black-and-white pattern and jeweled seams, on a wife who would've gotten attention in a burlap bag. She looked like a runway model. She was at least three decades younger than Mitchell.

Sebastian looked from the Brightwells to Morgan. "You know what?" Sebastian said. "This evening isn't really fun anymore. Let's call it. I should talk to a few business contacts. I'll see you at home." He drained his glass and left the table.

Morgan was stunned. She stood stuck for a moment as he walked toward the far end of the ballroom. Brightwell was headed in the same direction.

Shit. This might be the big meetup. She was missing it? She had pissed Sebastian off at the exact wrong time?

He walked quickly through the crowd. She hurried to catch up, but it was tough in six-inch heels, with an ankle-length gown.

Brightwell posted up at the bar in the back for a moment as Sebastian approached. Brightwell slipped into the hallway that led to the restroom.

Seriously? They were going to meet in the men's room?

Morgan hustled across the ballroom floor. Fortunately, a couple stopped Sebastian and engaged him in conversation. No one was stopping Morgan. She knew no one else. She kept out of sight as he smiled at the couple and excused himself.

She slipped into the restroom hallway before Sebastian could see her. It was empty. Brightwell must have already entered the men's room.

That wasn't good. If she photographed them together in the men's room, it would have plausible deniability. They could say it was just a coincidence. Two billionaires at a billionaire event in New York City. Happening to be in the bathroom at the same time. It was possible. Not the same firewall breach as a visit to Sebastian's house.

Whatever it was that they were going to exchange or hand off, she needed to keep it from happening tonight.

Would she be able to delay Sebastian?

She sent Kevin a text. **If you have anyone at this party, send them into the restroom hallway. Preferably a man. I think the meetup is in the men's room.**

She had just finished hitting Send, when Sebastian came around the corner and saw her. He was surprised. Like, didn't I send you home?

"Morgan," he said. "What are you still doing here?"

"Baby," Morgan said. "I couldn't leave things like that. From the table, I mean. I just—this is our first big event, and I can't be that awkward newcomer with a red stain on her dress. I totally overreacted. Can you forgive me?"

"Can I—? Sure," Sebastian said. "I forgive you, sweetheart. Let's talk about it at the apartment later."

"Please don't send me home," she pouted. "It's my first big party since we got together."

"Fine," he said. "I'll meet you back at the table, okay?"

"Really?" she said. "Okay, good. In fact, to show my gratitude, I'm gonna make you one happy boy."

She yanked open the doors to the men's bathroom and pushed Sebastian inside.

"I don't think this is the time—" he said, then broke off. Mitchell Brightwell was standing at the sink, washing his hands.

Morgan realized that the loud shushing sound of the faucet had been a quieter shushing sound from the hallway. Brightwell had been standing at the sink, pretending to wash his hands, for a long time. He had definitely been waiting for Sebastian.

Morgan giggled. "Excuse us."

The men exchanged looks.

Brightwell dried his hands and walked toward the door.

But before he could open it, a young man walked into the restroom. Morgan recognized him from a photo Kevin had shown her. He was the environment reporter from the daily paper.

"Wow," he said. "I thought I was just going to pee, but maybe I'm getting a scoop."

"What would that be?" Brightwell asked. "Two men at a party with an open bar both need to use the restroom? Good luck pitching that."

"Please," the reporter said. "And what is she supposed to be? The firewall?"

"Oops, wrong restroom," Morgan said, and backed out.

A moment later, Brightwell came out. The reporter followed him. "While I happen to have your attention, can I get a comment on the latest fires in Southern California? Your family is from that area, right?"

"Run along, junior," Brightwell said. "Didn't you need to tinkle?"

The reporter trailed after him into the main ballroom.

When Sebastian came out, Morgan walked over to him. "So much for our tryst," she said.

"I have a headache," Sebastian said. "Let's go."

"Okay," Morgan said, halfway pouty.

As the two of them passed Brightwell, she pulled out her phone. "Let's get a selfie before we leave."

She pulled up the phone and snapped the shot with Brightwell in the background.

Sebastian's jaw was tight as they walked out through the lobby.

When they got into the car, Morgan put up the partition. "I'm glad we finally got out of there and can be alone."

She leaned into kiss Sebastian, but he pulled back. "I told you, I have a headache."

"Oh," Morgan said. "I thought that was code for 'Let's go somewhere private.'"

They rode the rest of the way home in silence, and Morgan was grateful that Sebastian was in a bad mood. The last thing she wanted was for him to get amorous. She hadn't had nearly enough to drink.

* * *

Morgan woke up early with a plan.

When Sebastian stirred, she rolled over and kissed him on the cheek, but he pulled away.

"I'm late for a meeting," he muttered.

"I'm so sorry, love," Morgan said, following him to his closet. "I promise not to be such a brat at your holiday party. Please say you forgive me."

He pulled a suit out of the closet. "I don't have time for this," he said.

"Please, honey," she said. "I'll make it up to you." She ran her fingers down across the fly of his pajamas.

He hesitated for a moment. She meant it this time. Not that she was turned on, but she was prepared to do whatever it would take to finish this assignment.

His face was still cold as he went to untie his pajama pants.

Morgan took a deep breath and steeled herself to go down on him.

But just then, his phone sounded. It was the special ring for his assistant, Dawn.

Sebastian stepped back and grabbed the suit. "Another time," he said, and walked toward the master bathroom.

On the way, he stabbed several buttons on the phone. "I'm on my way," he said, and closed the door behind him.

Morgan took her laptop and charger to an uptown café. She spent the day reviewing images of people to look for at the ReidCorp holiday party, which was only two days away.

She was home by six for dinner, but the apartment was quiet. Morgan couldn't stand it. She put on an old sitcom she used to watch with her mom. It calmed her nerves.

She wasn't sure if she'd get a text from Sebastian, or maybe his assistant, but she heard nothing until he walked in the door at eight o'clock.

"I've got a lot of work," he said curtly. "You're on your own for dinner."

She had eaten leftovers an hour before. She went back to binge-watching the sitcom with headphones.

Later that evening, Morgan's phone alerted her to sound in Sebastian's study. She crept down the hall and listened at the door. Her heartbeat seemed so loud in her ears, he might be able to hear it through the thick wood. But how could he? She could barely hear him talking. His voice was muffled, but from the long pauses, it definitely sounded like a one-sided phone call. Damn, she wished she knew how to tap a phone. Wasn't the FBI or someone supposed to care about these things? Yeah, good luck with that. Sebastian wasn't even suspected of a crime yet.

The phone call seemed to end, and her anxiety spiked. She retreated back down the hallway.

He was still in his study at midnight. She guessed this was how he handled conflict. Just retreated. Fine with her. She was bleary-eyed from the sitcom marathon. Morgan turned out the light and went to sleep.

When she woke at four to use the bathroom, Sebastian was asleep on the other side of the bed. While in the bathroom, she checked her phone and saw it hadn't alerted her to any more sound from the study. Good.

She finished her business and slipped back into bed. Not that she was able to fall back asleep right away. She lay there. Listening to him breathe. Worrying about the climate crisis. Wondering if she would find the evidence she needed. If the movement would be able to generate enough pressure, enough power, to make the changes they needed to make to avoid ecological catastrophe. But then she recalled one of the climate books she'd been reading. Any time in history when a nonviolent movement got 3.5 percent of the population active in demanding change, it had succeeded. They just needed to get the climate movement in the US to 3.5 percent. That seemed doable. But it also meant that her getting this evidence could be a huge tipping point. And now Sebastian was mad at her. Would she be able to pull this off? The pressure felt like a stone on her chest. For a moment she could barely breathe. Then she drew in a ragged breath and shuddered.

She fumbled for her phone and played another episode of the sitcom. She lay on her side and put an earbud in the ear that was facing up. She turned the volume way down and fell asleep to the sound of distant, canned laughter.

The following morning Sebastian was withdrawn again. When he headed to work, Morgan waited a good fifteen minutes. Then she picked the lock on the study and storage room to retrieve and switch the audio card.

She met up with Kevin at their bar. He had a margarita waiting for her.

His face looked different today. Open. Warm.

Morgan swallowed. It wouldn't do to get her hopes up. She needed to just focus on the assignment. Get it over with. Then they could see what might be possible.

They went into the bar's storage room and she handed him the cream-colored dress.

"I'll get the black dress to you tomorrow," she said. And then they listened to the recording together.

"I know," Sebastian was saying. "Just fucking bad luck . . . Any trouble with the reporter? . . . Good . . . Well, we've answered the wife material question . . . I'll start fresh in the new year. . . . What's our play? . . . Are you serious? . . . Isn't the party too public? . . . Well, who do you trust to send it with? . . . Oh, I can see that. . . . Good idea."

"It's gotta be Brightwell," Morgan said. "A reporter came into the men's room."

"How do you think he got there?" Kevin asked.

"You sent him in after you got my text?" Morgan said.

"Bingo," Kevin said. "You think this other handoff is gonna happen at the ReidCorp holiday party?"

"That's what it sounds like," Morgan said. "I've been studying faces of different guys in the industry, overall. Should I look at the staff at Brightwell Industries?"

"I think so," Kevin said. "I'll forward you some files."

"Okay," Morgan said, and stood to leave.

"Wait," Kevin said, taking her hand. "I just—I have to tell you. You're doing an amazing job. I'm sorry for every way I've ever doubted you. I'm so deep in this. Some nights I don't sleep. I'm a little crazy. Look, I'm just saying . . . maybe when this is over, we could see about . . ."

"Yes," she said. "I think—I mean, I'm hoping it'll be over soon. Really soon. Maybe day after tomorrow."

That was the moment when Morgan should have left. She almost did. She put one foot in front of the other until she reached the doorknob. But the storage room was so small. Kevin still held her other hand. It was that choice in that moment. She should have turned the doorknob. Should have kept walking out through the doorway. Should have continued out through the bar onto the cold street. But instead, she pressed in the button in the knob and locked the door.

The metallic click seemed to release them both from whatever restraint that held them. Suddenly Kevin's fingers weren't just tangled in hers, they were in her hair, pressed between her shoulder blades, pulling her to him. And she was kissing him. Finally tasting those lips, the spice of beer on his tongue. Running her fingers across the muscles in his back, down along his firm ass.

His own hands were climbing up under her shirt, and then they hit the underwire of her bra.

He shook his head for a second. "Wait," he said. "Is this okay? Are we—? Do you agree—?"

"Yes!" Morgan gasped. "Yes! Yes, to all of it."

"All of it?" Kevin asked.

"Yes," Morgan said. She turned and reached for one of the condoms for the machine in the restroom.

Kevin's mouth fell open.

"All of it," she breathed.

The two of them stood, suspended for a moment, not touching. Kevin with his palms wide. Morgan's mouth slightly open, never having closed it after the s-sound in yes.

They locked eyes. He had asked. Had checked. She had gotten the condom.

Yes. Yes. Yes.

And then, having made the decision, having given themselves and each other permission, they couldn't stand to wait another second.

Morgan was unbuckling his jeans, with the condom in her teeth. Kevin was pulling up her shirt, pulling off her bra.

She was pulling off her own yoga pants, her underwear—white and plain and boring—the pants tangling in her shoes for a moment until she pressed them off, toe to heel.

She took the condom from her mouth and Kevin kissed her; they were each ravenous for the taste of the other. As she pulled down his jeans, he fumbled with the condom behind her back, tearing open the packet.

Then she pulled back from him.

His eyes flew open. "Are you okay?" he asked.

Morgan smiled and nodded. Breathed slowly, in spite of her elevated heartbeat. She took the condom from him. Pinched the tip of it and rolled it onto him.

Kevin made a strangled moan. Then he carefully set his jacket on a case of EarthBound beer and lifted Morgan up onto it. They made love against the clink of bottles carrying "the best the planet has to offer."

She wanted every bit of him—had wanted this for so long. As a lover, he was intense but stayed connected. Kept looking in her eyes. He didn't rush. When she could feel herself getting close to orgasm, she bit down on the sleeve of his jacket to keep from making too much noise. He was kissing her neck, her shoulder. Finally she spat out the jacket and kissed him desperately as she climaxed, letting him swallow her moans of pleasure, her hips pressing against the jacket and the beer, feeling anything but earthbound.

After he had climaxed as well, the two of them lay slumped against each other. Quiet. Just breathing each other in.

Morgan could feel the condom starting to slip. She was the first to move, and he pulled out.

The moment was awkward. Him tying the condom and neither of them sure where to put it.

"Morgan," Kevin murmured. "I'm falling—"

Morgan put a hand over his mouth.

"Please don't," she said. She couldn't do this. Not if she had another forty-eight hours with Sebastian.

She leaned in and kissed him, hard. "Soon," she said. She pulled her clothes back on and fled out the door.

Chapter 13

Unlike the previous party, ReidCorp held their holiday bash at their own headquarters. The second floor of the building had a dining room that doubled as a ballroom and a full kitchen. Mostly it produced cafeteria food for employees and fine dining for executives, but a few times a year a catering company came in and provided food for a great party.

During Sebastian's father's era, they consistently had fossil-fuel themes. They often used caviar in their hors d'oeuvres, mixing it with olive oil and black food coloring and drizzling it over crab puffs or lobster quiche. They always had a sundae bar, in which an engineer created a working miniature oil well that pumped black hot fudge out of a fake mountain onto the ice cream.

They brought in cooks who knew just the right amount of charcoal to add to sauces to make them black without having a medicinal effect. They hired a specialty pastry chef who made all their desserts with molasses.

Since the climate crisis had escalated, Sebastian had abandoned these traditions. But the sundae bar had originally happened on his tenth birthday. The kids liked it, but the adults had loved it so much that his father had replicated it at the holiday party.

The ballroom was really just a huge box on the second level, with a wall of windows and a lacquered wooden floor. Morgan walked in, wishing her cocktail dress weren't quite so short. Not only because it was cold, but also because she felt exposed. She knew it was irrational. No one, least of all Sebastian, could see up her dress. But every time she sat, stood, or took a larger than usual step, a wisp of air floated between her legs; it set her tingling, reminding her of being with Kevin. Had that really happened? She couldn't believe it.

Such a short time ago this life with Sebastian had felt like a dream, and now it felt like a grim reality. Even thinking about Kevin made her heart ache. But he was reality, too. His warm skin. His strong hands.

Focus. Morgan looked at the buffet. She had heard about the molasses desserts at the party. They didn't use it as a drizzle anymore, Sebastian had said. But they still cooked with it. As Morgan tasted the sweet desserts, the tiny pecan tarts and the eclairs, she could feel the molasses on her tongue. That's what color Kevin's eyes were, molasses.

She chewed the sweets, the cream and pastry dissolving on her tongue, and she couldn't stop thinking about him.

But she didn't have time for that right now. To make that dreamy afternoon a reality, she needed to handle business tonight and get out of there.

Morgan stayed at Sebastian's slide. She drank slowly so she wouldn't need to go to the restroom. She watched everyone who interacted with him. Every waitress who handed him a drink, every colleague who patted him on the back. Every low-level employee shaking his hand for the first time and gushing. Were they handing him anything? Did Sebastian's hands go to his pocket after the interaction? Was anyone whispering in his ear?

Sebastian was the one who'd given the kitchen staff a night off to attend the party. People treated him like a folk hero. Not a billionaire who could easily spare the pocket change to hire caterers.

Morgan smiled and shook hands and stood and sat, trying to ignore the sensation between her legs that beckoned elsewhere.

Morgan had been keeping a sharp eye for anyone she recognized. She saw various oil executives, but they just seemed to come over for a frat boy, chatty laugh moment and then move on. Presumably, they had skirts to chase or deals to make.

But soon she saw someone she hadn't been expecting. Daphne Brightwell, wife of the man on the other side of the firewall. She was dressed in a sun-yellow gown, with emerald sequin leaves cascading down one shoulder to the floor. Leaves? Trying a bit too hard, wasn't it? For the wife of the man who was decimating the Amazon rainforest. But maybe not. Maybe they took leaves so for granted, she couldn't see the irony.

Mrs. Brightwell was alone. The trophy wife walked up to Sebastian with her hand out. Morgan smiled, as she had done a thousand times that night. But why would Mrs. Brightwell want to shake Sebastian's hand? They had hugged the night before. The wife had on white gloves with the dress. Her hand was extended, but the thumb was pressed against the palm. Did she have something for Sebastian?

Morgan stood.

"Mrs. Brightwell!" she said. "I never got a chance to meet you at the other party; we had to leave early." Morgan extended her hand. "I'm Morgan Faraday, Sebastian's girlfriend."

"Of course," Mrs. Brightwell said. Instead of shaking with the hand she had extended to Sebastian, Mrs. Brightwell used her left hand to squeeze Morgan's. "So lovely to meet you," the wife said. "Call me Daphne."

Morgan activated her small-talk engine. She loved Daphne's dress. Who was the designer?

Daphne butchered the name. He was an up-and-coming young man from South America. Brazil, she thought.

Morgan's smile almost faltered. Brazil? Really? She was wearing a dress that celebrated the very Amazon her husband was burning?

Sebastian slid over to Daphne's other side.

"Daphne," he said. "Thanks so much for coming."

A waitress walked by with a tray of champagne, and Morgan grabbed a glass, reaching between Sebastian and Daphne.

"Daphne, you don't have a drink, do you?" she asked. "Here you go."

Daphne's closer hand held the—whatever it was. She would have to take the glass with that hand or reach all the way across her chest with the other hand, which would look incredibly awkward.

"Thank you," Daphne Brightwell said, taking the glass with her closest hand.

A quick glance let Morgan know that her plan had worked. Daphne held the champagne flute awkwardly by the stem, her thumb still pressed to her palm.

Next to them, an older man engaged Sebastian.

Before Daphne could switch hands, Morgan took her free hand.

"Where are you sitting?" Morgan asked. "There's a spot at our table."

Could Morgan jostle her, get her to drop whatever it was?

Morgan went on: "Sebastian's assistant, Dawn, is out of town and wasn't able to make it. Won't you join us?"

"Sure," Daphne said. "I suppose I could. Sebastian, we can catch up at the table."

Morgan held Daphne's free hand in a tight grip as she

steered Daphne across the room. They moved around a few people with quick turns, but Daphne gripped tightly to whatever was in her hand. At the table, Morgan moved someone's purse to another chair so Daphne would be seated farther from Sebastian.

When she sat, Daphne set down the champagne glass on the table and clasped her hands for a moment, then slid her other hand briefly into her purse.

"I'm so glad to have gotten you alone," Morgan said. "I'm so sorry I'll never get a chance to meet Sebastian's parents. I think you and Mr. Brightwell are the closest I'll find to sort of surrogate father and . . ." what could say here? Certainly not "mother." Daphne looked only a few years older than Morgan. ". . . and his wife," Morgan finished awkwardly.

"Sebastian asked me to move in with him. I don't know if you know that," she said. "I was really clear that I didn't just want to be a live-in girlfriend. But I want to know that we have a future together. But he's so . . . so . . ." Morgan searched for the words. She couldn't find them until she thought of Kevin. How she'd felt when he withdrew? "Opaque," Morgan said. "You know, distant. He says he's just worried about business, but I wonder. I mean, I quit my job when I moved in with him, and now I just sort of spin all day, wondering if I'm doing the girlfriend thing right."

"Oh, honey," Daphne said, putting a gloved hand on her shoulder. "You have to step back and take a breath. Sebastian Reid is just a man. And like any relationship, it'll either work or it won't. Just . . . find your own interests. You should volunteer for the ReidCorp Foundation. That would be a future wife move."

Daphne tilted her head to the side and smiled. Condescending, but probably good advice, if Morgan really had wanted to be Sebastian's wife. Start acting like one.

"Thank you," Morgan said.

When Sebastian came back to the table, Morgan watched as Daphne made several moves to connect with him.

Every time, Morgan was there to interrupt, intervene, intrude. With every block Morgan made, Sebastian's smile got tighter and tighter.

Eventually he steered her to a dark corner by the sundae bar. Less popular these days, with so many people watching their carb intake.

"Morgan," he said, his smile so tight it was almost a grimace. "As my girlfriend, you need to understand that this is a work function. I need you to give me a little space to operate."

"A little space?" she asked.

"Yes," Sebastian said. "I need to be able to connect with colleagues and employees. I'm not going to be able to introduce you to everyone. Can you talk with other people while I'm operating?"

"Operating?" Morgan asked. "Is that what you're trying to do?"

"You do realize that this is my company's event, right?" he asked. He spoke slowly, like she was dense. "The Reid Corporation party."

"I do realize that," Morgan said. "I also realize that Daphne is not a colleague or an employee. Daphne is the only person I've impeded from talking to you. Because she keeps trying to get close to you, and you keep trying to get close right back."

"What are you talking about?" Sebastian asked.

"You all are having an affair, aren't you?"

"You've lost your mind," he said. "She's Mitchell's wife. My godfather's wife. It practically makes her my godmother. That's crazy."

"Don't tell me I'm crazy," she said. "I know what I saw. And 'godmother' is a stretch. She's younger than you are.

And looks like a bikini model. Of course she'd be interested in someone her own age after she married that old man."

"Morgan," he said. "I don't think this is working."

"Here we go again," she said. "You're dismissing me? You're gonna send me home?"

"Not this time," Sebastian said. "You need to pack your things and move out. Tonight."

"What?" Morgan said. "Are you having Daphne over tonight?"

"Just get out of my apartment," he said.

"So classy," Morgan said. "How am I gonna get a hotel room this time of year?"

"Call my assistant," Sebastian said. "She'll take care of it."

"She's on vacation," Morgan said.

"She's always on call for me," Sebastian said.

"Then I'll certainly call her," Morgan said. "I couldn't stay under the same roof with you for another minute." That part was certainly true. But even as she stormed toward the back door, she circled back and followed him.

Sebastian pulled an unfamiliar phone out of his pocket and dialed a number. "I'll be in the kitchen through the back hallway," he whispered. "Be careful."

And then, three minutes later, Daphne Brightwell came in. She had on a dark coat over her bright dress, but it was definitely her. Morgan slipped into the kitchen behind her with her phone out and snapped a burst of photos before Daphne could cross the room and get to Sebastian.

The room was dimly lit. They were turned to the camera. Faces bleached with the flash. Looking surprised and guilty with a rack of oversize pots in the darkened kitchen background.

"So who's crazy now?" Morgan demanded, loud, slurring a bit. "You're meeting her in a back room? Away from the surveillance cameras? Oh, but I've got a camera of my own. I got it all on camera. No wonder you were so eager to get rid of me." She turned to Daphne. "Are you fucking my boyfriend?"

"This has all been some kind of mistake," Daphne said.

"Mistake?" Morgan said. "You all are a fucking mistake. You fucking super-rich people act like you're so superior, but you're just fucking corrupt. No goddamn morals at all. You are disgusting."

"I—" Daphne said, backing away. "I should leave."

"Yeah, you should," Morgan said.

Daphne Brightwell left the kitchen in a swirl of black wool and emerald satin.

Morgan made to storm out as well.

"Morgan," Sebastian said. "Honey, let's talk this over."

"Nothing to talk over," Morgan said. "You threw me out, so I'm moving out. And going to whatever fucking hotel your assistant sends me to."

"Morgan, wait," Sebastian said. He seemed shifted somehow. His voice was nearly a whine. "Please," he said. "Just hear me out."

"I've heard enough," she said.

"One minute."

"I need to go pack," she said.

"Thirty seconds," he said, his tone desperate.

"Fine," she said.

Morgan turned around, crossed her arms over her chest, and regarded him coldly.

"It's—it's not what you think," he stammered. "It's not an affair."

"Why else would you meet a married woman in a dark kitchen?"

Sebastian hung his head. "It's something else."

She scowled at him. "What else could it be?"

"Her husband . . . Mitchell," Sebastian said. "I—I tried to bribe him. He was trying to give the money back. It was stupid. He couldn't get it to me directly, so he was getting his wife to do it. A favor for me. He knew my dad."

"A bribe?" Morgan asked. "Sebastian—"

"I know," he said. His voice cracked. Was he crying?

"I've just been under so much stress," he said. He sank down onto the floor, his head in his hands. "I've been making terrible decisions. But the worst of all was asking you to leave. This is the place when I always sabotage my relationships. I always push people away."

Whoa.

He was sitting on the floor in front of a shelf of large baking pans.

He looked up. Yes. He was definitely crying. In the dim light, she could just barely see the glint of tears on his cheeks. "Morgan, there's something about you. You're just so genuine. It scares me, but I know it's what I need. You're what I need." He reached for her hand. "I love you."

"Sebastian, this is too much," she said, pulling her hand away. "First you were kicking me out, now you're telling me that you love me?"

"More than just that I love you," Sebastian said. "I want you to marry me. Will you marry me?"

Morgan was flabbergasted. She was forgetting to act drunk. He was asking—what? An hour, two hours before, she would have turned him down flat, but something about his declaration moved her. The tears. He was totally broken down now. He was completely vulnerable.

This took it to another level. It would be one thing to get some dirt on Sebastian and Mitchell. But what if she could *turn* Sebastian? If she could get him to be a spy for the movement? Or a whistleblower? What kind of ammunition could they get on the entire fossil fuel industry?

"Sebastian," Morgan said. "I don't think I can say yes to you. Not here and now. Not like this. And it's never been just you and me. You're already married to your job. And your company, with all the drama of your family. That will always come first. And be this big secret thing in your life. Even if I become your wife, that job will always be your secret mistress."

"No," Sebastian said. "I need to change things at work. I need to—I don't know what I need to do."

"I know what you need to do," Morgan said. "Take some time off work. Get some perspective. Can we get away after Christmas? Just you and me. And we can tell each other our life stories? All our secrets. Really connect. Just the two of us?"

"Yes," he said. "Anything you say."

For the first time they both stood there and faced each other. He wasn't the billionaire. He was just a sort of messy guy.

"Do we go back to the party?" she asked.

"No," he said. "Let's get out of here. Let's just slip out the back."

"What will people say if you disappear from your own party?" she asked.

"I don't give a fuck," he said. "Oh God, that feels good. I don't give one single fuck. Let's go."

He grabbed her hand and pulled her down the hallway.

"What about our coats?" she asked.

"Fuck the coats," he yelled, and they went down in the elevator.

He called the limo, and they ran out into the cold, shivering and laughing.

The limo picked them up.

"I wasn't expecting you until much later, sir," the driver said. "Are you headed home?"

"I don't know," Sebastian said and turned to Morgan. "Are we headed home?"

"No," Morgan said. "We're headed to Brooklyn."

"What's in Brooklyn?" he asked. "I never go to any of the boroughs."

"The last vestiges of anything real in New York City," she said.

"Like what?"

"Like the best fucking Jamaican food you've ever tasted."

"Okay," Sebastian said. "Brooklyn it is."

She took him to Dashawna's favorite spot. A tiny place that did mostly takeout but had three plastic tables. They were the only people in the place that weren't dark-skinned. The two of them could not possibly have stuck out more.

"Are we gonna get mugged in here?" he asked.

"Calm down," Morgan said. "It's fine."

She turned to the woman behind the plastic partition. "Four beef patties, please," Morgan said, ordering for Sebastian.

She couldn't help but smile as she paid. Then they got the food and sat down.

As they pulled the patties out of the crinkling paper bags, it was awkward. Like a real date. She didn't know what to say. Her eyes strayed to the thin patches in the linoleum floor. The place was clean but well-worn.

"Oh my God," Sebastian said as he took his first bite. "There was this guy at Yale who used to throw Jamaican parties. He sold these. They were so fucking spicy." He breathed in to cool his mouth and stood up.

At the counter, Sebastian bought sodas for both of them. Green bottles. Ting. They tasted like grapefruit.

"This is what I mean, Morgan," he said. "This is where I need to be. Eating something unexpected and remembering my youth. When I cared about . . . things . . . more . . . things other than profitability. You take me to the places I need to go."

Morgan's mouth was on fire. Her eyes were starting to water, too.

"Let's get away," he said. "Let's go to Jamaica. A friend has a private beach. Just the two of us."

Morgan nodded. Thinking of Kevin. Her mouth full of spice and her eyes watering.

In the limo Sebastian reached for her. They were riding over the Brooklyn Bridge, the lights of the city sparkling ahead of them.

Morgan took a breath. "Sebastian, I just can't right now. It's been too much. Tonight. Thinking you were cheating. You throwing me out. Then proposing. I just—I need a moment."

"Fair enough," he said. "Take all the time you need."

She liked this kinder Sebastian. This vulnerable Sebastian. She leaned against him on the way home.

She couldn't sleep when they got home, although Sebastian knocked out shortly after they got home. She always slept well after a good cry, too.

This time it was a different tangle of emotions. The memory of Kevin, the unexpected turn of events with Sebastian. Morgan finally managed to fall asleep around four a.m. When she woke up, he was leaving for the day. Dressed in sweats.

"I'm going in to tell them that I'm taking a few weeks off," he said and kissed her.

"Wait," Morgan said. "What about the bribe money?"

"I don't know," Sebastian said. "I guess I'll figure that out in January. Maybe I'll let him keep it. Maybe I'll turn myself in for offering a bribe. I don't know. I don't fucking know. It feels so good not to know. Not to have to know."

This was going to work. She could turn him. She knew she could.

The moment he was out the door she texted Kevin for an urgent meeting.

*   *   *

At the bar she went straight to the storage room. She opened the door and saw Kevin waiting. She could feel her face leaping into the world's widest grin.

Kevin took one look at her and his own face split open in delight.

"You're done?" he asked, grabbing her around the waist.

"Better," she said, throwing her arms around him.

"Done and got smoking-gun evidence?" Kevin asked.

"Better," Morgan said, stepping back a bit to see his face.

"What could be better than a smoking gun and done?" Kevin asked.

"I think I can turn him," Morgan said.

"You what?" Kevin asked, his face falling.

Then it all poured out. Daphne. Her confronting Sebastian. Him breaking down. The marriage proposal. How he was different afterward.

"So, instead of being done, you're going to marry this asshole?" Kevin asked.

"Of course not," Morgan said. "This is so much bigger than that. Can you imagine what Sebastian knows? What would it do for the cause if he turned state's evidence? It's not just about stopping ReidCorp. Or catching him with his hand in the cookie jar. It's about taking down the whole consortium. If we could get one of them to turn? Can't you see it?"

"Of course I realize how valuable that would be," Kevin said. "But one little weepy moment with your billionaire boyfriend doesn't make a class traitor."

"No," Morgan said, feeling irritated. "I'd have to work on him."

"Think it through, Morgan," Kevin said. "Even if you get him to agree in a moment of weakness. The second his people get hold of him, they'll talk him out of it."

"I've thought about that," she said. "That's why I set up

for the two of us to go away and tell each other our life stories. I'll record the conversations. Even if he backpedals, I expect to get an incredible amount of evidence."

Kevin's mouth grew tight. "Are you maybe overestimating
your methods of persuasion?"

"What?" she asked. "My 'feminine wiles'?"

"I just mean—" Kevin said.

"Kevin," Morgan said. "I've known this guy for almost a
year. I've never seen him like this. Don't you think it's worth
a try?"

"And who's supposed to be bankrolling all this?"

"Sebastian, of course," Morgan said. "And I brought you
the cocktail dress to return. Thanks for the loan."

"He proposed and you said yes?" Kevin said. "You didn't
even say you'd think about it?"

"No way I said yes," Morgan said. "But my plan is that I
might say yes while we're on the getaway. As part of breaking him down. Getting him to turn."

"While you're fucking him?" Kevin said.

"Maybe," Morgan said. "My plan wasn't that specific.
Insert penis. Say 'Yes, I'll marry you.' You know I'm in a sexual relationship with Sebastian. We talked about this. You
were the one who said to spy on him and to just keep going
like everything was normal."

"But that was before," Kevin said. "Before . . . us."

"This has nothing to do with us," Morgan said.

"This has everything to do with us," Kevin said. "I can't
believe I'm fucking the same woman as Sebastian Reid. You
know what guys say? If I go down on you, it's like sucking
Sebastian Reid's dick."

Morgan could feel her rage rising. "No," she said coldly.
"No, it's not like that at all. What do you think I am? Some
bone that you two dogs are fighting over?"

"I just can't see—" Kevin began.

"That's right, Kevin," Morgan said. "You can't see. You

wanted me to be a spy, and you turned me into a spy. Now you want me to turn back into a regular girl? Maybe I could reclaim my virginity while I'm at it. You wanna take me to a goddamn purity ball? Well, I'm not turning back. This is an incredible chance for the movement, but you can't see it because yes, I'll have to do some fucking to get this evidence."

Kevin winced.

"Which is the fucked-up part," Morgan said. "When you were the spurned lover, you sent me in to fuck the guy I was learning to despise. And now that you want me again—and now that he's less despicable—you don't want me having the emotional intimacy with him that I'll need to get this information. But I'm done being your flunky, Kevin. I'm going. I'm getting that intel. And I'm going to take it as far as I can. This one's for the fucking planet."

She pressed the garment bag into his chest a little harder than necessary and crossed to the door of the storage room.

"You're making a mistake," Kevin said. "How long have you been an activist? Like for all of five minutes? You've still got a lot to learn."

"Fortunately, I won't be learning it from you," she said. "Let Yolanda know I'll be calling her when I turn Sebastian. Goodbye, Kevin."

She slammed the storage-room door behind her. It felt good to storm out—her whole body felt explosive. She took long, angry strides out of the bar. She kept going right past her subway stop. She wasn't ready to be contained yet. The weather was chilly today, but all she could feel in her face was heat.

People walked by her, huddled against the cold. She stood tall, her flushed neck exposed. But by the time she walked past the second subway stop and strode to the third, her rage had cooled.

There was so much finality to the goodbye as it left her lips. A lump of grief had taken its place. This was supposed to have been a moment of triumph. Just a delay on the way to something . . . wonderful. As she walked down the final block to the subway, she willed herself not to cry. As the wind whipped her face, she held her head high, acting like the tears were only a symptom of the cold weather.

She sat on the train in silence. Unable to read her book or listen to music or anything. Well, that solved one of her problems. How was she going to handle the situation with Sebastian and Kevin? It would be Sebastian. Who would have guessed?

Maybe if Sebastian wasn't busy being such a billionaire fossil-fuel asshole, he could really be her boyfriend. Men had turned from one side to the other in the past. She had read about Daniel Ellsberg, who had been a warmonger but had published *The Pentagon Papers* and really shaken up the military. In fact, there were a lot of veterans who had taken stands against war. Maybe Sebastian could become a big whistleblower. Who knew? She would keep an open mind. But there was a stinging in her chest and she couldn't shake it. Ever since she had walked into the bar grinning and watched the joy drain slowly from Kevin's face.

When Sebastian's jet landed in Montego Bay airport and Morgan turned her phone back on, she had gotten a notification from CFI. She'd been selected as one of three finalists of the quilt contest. At any other point before in her life she would have been joyous. But now she just felt disconnected from everything that represented.

Sebastian had held her hand as the plane went in for a landing. He had confessed that he was terrified of flying. That was part of why he had his own jet. Because he hated for anyone else to know.

He squeezed her hand as they touched down.

* * *

Jamaica was disorienting. She had never been out of the country before. Sebastian had to get her a rush passport. There were lots of Americans in the Montego Bay airport. But once they got into the limo, that was the last time she saw anyone who wasn't brown.

The moment they got to the guesthouse, she felt awkward with the people working there. The dark-skinned men and women who cooked and cleaned for them. Could they tell she was also of African heritage? That her mother worked as a cleaner? Did it even matter? Mostly, they probably saw her as American.

At first things were awkward with Sebastian, too. They hadn't had sex since his breakdown. Things were different between them. There was an emotional connection and intimacy. They had kissed once, on the lips, and it had been sweetly bumbling.

The beach where they were staying was a cliché. Pale sand. Turquoise water. Palm trees. Boiling sunsets. like walking into a postcard. Two miles of private coastline.

Every morning, before it got too hot, Morgan and Sebastian ran on the beach. She was always faster, but by the third day he didn't need to stop every so often to catch his breath, hands on his knees, while Morgan jogged in circles around him.

"Look at you," she teased. "Didn't you play sports at Yale? The billionaire lifestyle has made you soft. You have that treadmill at home, but you never use it."

"I have one at the office," he wheezed.

"Do you run on it?" Morgan asked. "Owning something isn't the same as actually using it. Telling your assistant to buy something doesn't improve your fitness."

She could tease him now. Things were different.

"Or are billionaire calories different?" she asked. "Let's see. 'I texted my assistant. That probably burned four hundred calories. Time for lunch . . .' "

"Keep talking trash," he said. "One of these days I'm gonna get my fitness back and catch up with you."

"Well, it won't be today," Morgan said, jogging backward with her hands on her hips.

They swam in the afternoons. On the third day Sebastian had just gotten out of the shower. Morgan was sitting on a couch when he walked into the sitting room. She patted the seat beside her and he sat down.

She leaned forward and kissed him on the lips, gently but without passion. They still hadn't had sex. Sebastian had made a few hesitant overtures, but Morgan had said she wasn't ready.

"Who are you really?" Morgan asked. "Who are we both?"

"What do you mean?" Sebastian asked.

"If there's any hope for this relationship," Morgan said, "we have to be honest with each other. About everything."

He looked wary. Almost as if he knew her phone, which lay facedown on the coffee table, was recording.

"I can start," Morgan said. "After I moved in, I wasn't really my authentic self. I was hoping to get a proposal. That was the original idea. But I didn't like living with you as a kept woman. I probably would have moved out even if we hadn't had that fight. In fact, I was just named as a finalist for an art prize and might have a windfall in my checking account soon. Either way, I'll have professional opportunities. I definitely was planning on moving out when that happened. But then you broke down and showed me this other side of yourself—showed me something real, not flashy and fake. I remembered what I liked about you in the first place. You have a genuine kindness, Sebastian. And a wit. If I could spend more time with this part of you, I might fall in love with you."

"I already am in love with you, Morgan," Sebastian said. "Maybe originally I was in love with the face you put on for me. You seemed so warm and easy to be with. My mother—my whole family—was really cold. And my parents died in that plane crash. I'm sure you know the story. I had all these nannies and guardians. I just—you weren't like a lot of women I dated from school and stuff. They had a future planned for us. They were all ambition but no heat. You're so *alive*. Like the colors you wear. You just brought this energy into my life, and I like it. It's no wonder I can't do what I've been doing up until now. I don't want that life. Why do I need to spend my time living out my father's dream, of running ReidCorp? I have plenty of money. I can just chill. This can be my life. This can be our life together. Let me—let me do this right."

Morgan could feel her heart start to beat hard. Was he—?

Sebastian slid off the wicker couch and got down on one knee.

He was. He definitely was.

Sebastian opened a small, red-velvet box. "Morgan, will you marry me?"

She looked at the ring. It was huge. Befitting a billionaire.

She laughed. "Yes, Sebastian." She wasn't sure what it meant. Was she saying yes for real? As a spy? Maybe if she turned him, it could become real.

He put the ring on her finger and kissed her. Not entitled. Sort of checking as he went if it was okay. She kissed back. It wasn't what she had with Kevin. But it was warm and different from what it had been with Sebastian before.

Later that night—long after she had turned off the recorder—as they had sex, she wondered if he would really go through with letting ReidCorp go. But soon he was going down on her, and she wasn't thinking of ReidCorp at all.

*   *   *

The next morning was overcast. Usually they had to come back after they ran because they had sweated off the sunscreen. But with the cloudy sky, they could go for a swim. The beach was beautiful, miles of pristine sand.

When they got back to the villa, she lay down in bed beside him.

"What are we going to do about that bribe to Mitchell Brightwell?" she asked.

"We can probably get out ahead of it," he said. "I can confess it and step down as CEO of ReidCorp."

"You would really do that?" Morgan asked. In that moment she felt a swell of hope in her chest. Maybe this could be something real.

"I don't want that life anymore," he said. "It killed my parents. My dad had them flying in unsafe conditions to survey some freshly discovered, potential new fuel. Because he had to get there first. He couldn't stand for anyone to beat him. That fuel didn't even pan out, but if the crash hadn't killed him, the heart attacks would have. He'd already had three. His chest was all plastic wires at that point anyway. I'm just pissed that he took my mom with him."

"Are you serious about stepping down and confessing?" she asked.

"Yeah," he said. "It's over for me. I already told the board I was taking a leave to sort things out. I let them know resignation was on the table. Now I'll just let them know it's for sure."

"What about . . ." Morgan began. But it was too early for that. She couldn't pressure him to turn. She should wait until there was an opportunity. Some crisis, or news about climate or something, where it would come up naturally. Although she wasn't sure when that would be. They didn't listen to the news. Had little contact with the outside world. They swam, ate, got massages, had sex, walked on the beach. In their wealthy bubble of relaxation, nothing about the climate crisis touched them.

Of course, with all the swimming she couldn't keep her hair straight. She would pull it up into a tight bun to disguise the texture. But one day they had sex after a shower, and she fell asleep right after.

She woke up to Sebastian playing with the ends of her hair.

"It's so curly," he said. "I had no idea."

"I usually keep it flat ironed."

"Why?" he asked. "It's beautiful."

"It's so unruly," Morgan said.

"Like you," Sebastian said. "I like it that way. I like you that way."

Morgan just smiled and shook her head. "Hair is complicated for Black women," Morgan said.

"I don't think of you as Black," Sebastian said.

"Well, I am," she said.

"Maybe half Black," he said.

"I'm not half anything," Morgan said. "I'm fully Black. I just have other heritages, too." Unapologetically Black was the thought, but she couldn't quite bring herself to say it. Could she?

But before she could decide, he grinned and stood up. "Morgan, there's something I'd like to do with you. Something I've wanted to do with all my girlfriends, but I never—"

Oh shit. This was the type of thing Dashawna talked about all the time. These guys had these whole scenarios built around being able to do things with Black women that white women were too good for. Was he gonna spring some fetish on her?

"Something in bed?" she asked.

Sebastian laughed. "No," he said. "Nothing like that. I— I like to watch . . ."

Morgan bit her lip and her brow furrowed.

"You should see your face," Sebastian said, laughing harder. "You look like: What kind of kinky stuff is this rich guy into?" Sebastian wiped his eyes. "Nothing like that. It's . . ." He trailed off and his voice got kind of shy. He couldn't meet her eyes. "I like soap operas," he said.

As he spoke, there was this whole new expression she'd never seen.

"It's just . . . there was this soap opera one of my nannies used to watch. I still watch it sometimes. Alone in my study. That's the real reason there's that flat screen in there. I put on headphones and watch this Argentinian show. And sometimes I cry a little. Just at the part where the boy's parents die in a car crash." He looked up at her then, his eyes wet. As many times as they'd been naked together, it was the most exposed he'd ever been.

Morgan threw her arms around him, and he began to cry. Really cry this time. Sobbing, crumpled face. The whole bit.

"God," he said. "Men are not supposed to cry. I feel like such a wimp."

"No," she said, wiping his eyes with the corner of a bedsheet. "It makes you human."

"Well," he said. "Now you know all my secrets. I'm a sap who watches telenovelas. I'm a failure at business. You still want to marry me?"

"Before I answer that," Morgan said, "I need to tell you my big secret."

She scooted up so that her back was against the bed's headboard and reached for his hand.

She turned to face him and his eyebrows were raised nearly to his hairline.

Now it was her turn to look down. "I'm poor," she said. "Barely scraped my way through college. I was basically homeless when we met. Sleeping on a friend's couch. My designer clothes are from another friend I met in fashion school. The friend I was staying with taught me how to reel you in. Your class doesn't like outsiders, but more than that, doesn't want gold diggers. I had to pretend to have money. I think I have about two hundred dollars in my bank account right now. No assets. A bunch of student loan debt. Which I'm defaulting on, by the way. I pretended to have money, and I was sort of using you to be a patron of my art. I was gonna get my career off the ground and leave."

His eyes were wider than usual, but he didn't let go of her hand.

"I have to say that underneath it all, I just didn't think I was good enough for a rich guy," she said, her eyes dropping to the cotton sheets, following the intricate wave patterns in the design. "People called my family trash sometimes. I figured, even if you liked me, you'd be ashamed of me with other people. You'd never take me seriously as a wife, or even a girlfriend. You know that song from the sixties, about how if a woman's father is rich you take her out for dinner, but if he's poor you just do whatever you feel like doing?" Morgan asked.

Sebastian shook his head.

"But I'm sure you're familiar with the sentiment," she said.

Sebastian nodded.

"I didn't want you to look at me that way," she said. "Like some trash you could use and throw away. I faked a lot of things with you. Money. Orgasms."

Sebastian's eyes flew open.

"Not recently," she said. "But . . . before. A lot of it was a big performance."

Sebastian nodded slowly. "It feels different, you know. When you fake, there's a lot of noise and movement, but down below, there's nothing happening."

"Welp," Morgan said. "Now you know all the secrets."

"Morgan Faraday," Sebastian said. "I plan to make up for your childhood. I'm gonna spoil you rotten."

Morgan shook her head. "I don't need all that," she said. "I just want to have a good life with you. And watch an Argentinian soap opera."

"Seriously?" Sebastian said. "You'd watch it with me?"

"Of course," Morgan said. "My grandmother used to be addicted to *All My Children*. I watched it with her every day when I was like three and four. I didn't understand any of it."

"Right?" Sebastian said. "That's why it's so satisfying to watch it now, as an adult. I finally understand what the hell's going on. As a kid, the only part I really understood was the car crash."

"Let's watch," Morgan said.

For the rest of the trip they cuddled up on the bed and watched the telenovela on his laptop, dubbed in English. It took Morgan a while to get accustomed to the words not matching the actors' mouths.

The show had run for several years, five days a week, so even though they binge-watched, they hadn't even gotten past the first two seasons when it was time to go home.

Morgan came back from the Caribbean with a tan, a new sense of optimism, and an IUD. A concierge doctor had come and implanted it right then and there at their beach villa.

Her contraceptive pills had run out and Sebastian suggested it. In her mind, she could picture Dashawna celebrating. "Girrrrl! That's some straight up *wife* birth control."

Chapter 14

The auditorium on the ground floor of ReidCorp was filled with cameras. Their cords snaked down the aisles and beneath the audience. Over a dozen microphones were attached to the single podium in the center of the stage. Every row in the thousand-seat auditorium was filled. Fossil-fuel industry leaders and ReidCorp executives. Every reporter in town, and even some who had flown in from out of town, wanted to be on hand for Sebastian Reid's big disclosure. Morgan had scanned the list. She was surprised to see so many environmental outlets included. But she was glad. He was really turning over a new leaf.

Morgan stood offstage with Sebastian. At first he had talked about going onstage with her at his side, introducing her as his fiancée. Morgan wasn't crazy about the idea, but she kept her mouth shut. Eventually he decided that the optics were better with just him, making his declaration and taking a few questions.

Sebastian was wearing one of his favorite navy-blue suits. He also had on a tie that was a nearly black shade of green and a shirt that was slightly off-white to green. That had been Morgan's touch. She thought he should go green all around.

"How do I look," he asked.

She straightened his tie. Although it didn't really need straightening. She just wanted an excuse to touch him, to seem needed. His assistant wasn't around today. He had given her a vacation when they had taken one, and apparently, she wasn't back yet. Good. Morgan could start to be the one who did things for him. Things she could keep up if she decided to become his wife.

She patted his tie into place. "You look perfect," she said.

"Here goes," he said, and walked out through the curtains into the blinding stage lights.

The buzz of conversation was strong in the room, until Sebastian walked out on the stage. Then everything quickly hushed.

He was small on the vast stage. Above him was a huge monitor that showed a close shot of his head and shoulders above the podium that bore the ReidCorp logo.

Sebastian cleared his throat. "Good afternoon," he began. "Thank you all for coming today." He looked down at the statement that he and his team had written.

"A decade ago, when my parents were killed in an airplane crash," he began, "I had no idea how I'd be able to continue to run my father's company. My father, as many of you know, was a force of nature. If he wanted something to happen, it happened. Which is why he was one of the early pioneers of fracking. 'What do you mean, there's no oil down there? What do you mean, we can't get to it? I'll make a way!' Of course, I was the one who shifted ReidCorp away from fracking." He made a fist and shook it at the sky. "You're not the boss of everything, Dad."

The audience laughed.

"But on a more serious note, I was really uncertain about how to run his company. My company. I was twenty-three and a mess. Irresponsible. Partying. Running up the credit card. Crashing my car. I'm sure some of you have dug up the

DUIs I have to prove it. But losing my parents was sobering. Not that I went to AA or anything, but it changed the trajectory of my life. I expected to get a nepotistic job in my dad's company and only pretend to work for a decade or even two before I had to settle down and really take any of my responsibilities seriously as the heir to ReidCorp. But when they died, everything changed. I only tell you this so you can understand."

He took a sip of water.

"I am proud of some of my accomplishments at Reid-Corp. Not only pushing back on the fracking, but also diversifying our portfolio overall. Investing in renewables. And, of course, a huge investment to continue my mother's work and the ReidCorp Family Foundation. I've had some real successes over these ten years."

He looked down at his shoes. "But I've also made some significant mistakes and missteps. The Calanez fire, for example. We took full responsibility for that. We paid huge settlements to those plaintiffs. Nothing can bring back lost loved ones or family homes. Still, we've paid restitution in every way we could. Or the Mercantile oil spills in North Dakota. Again, we paid huge settlements, and we invested half a billion dollars to make our pipelines stronger and safer."

He took a deep breath. "But I didn't come here today to tell you about the many, many mistakes we've made, because there are plenty more. I came to talk about how our company and I—as an individual—strive to take responsibility when we make a mistake. And I, as an individual, have made a huge mistake."

He cleared his throat and took another sip of water.

"When I was a kid," he said, "our family friend Mitchell Brightwell was like an uncle to me. When my dad died, he became a confidante, a surrogate father. I depended on him. When he became the chief of sustainable energy transition, I had to choose between keeping him as a surrogate father or continuing to run ReidCorp. I chose the company. I insisted that we have a firewall. I want to state for the record that Michell Brightwell always maintained that firewall. I was the one who attempted to break it down. He came to my apartment to confront me. He asked me to make a choice. I needed to step down from ReidCorp or stop calling him. But I wanted it both ways. I offered him a bribe to circumvent it, so we could continue to talk. He refused."

Sebastian looked down at his notes.

"But I wouldn't be deterred," he said. "I put a bag of uncut diamonds into his wife's hands at a fundraiser in mid-November. They were worth five hundred million dollars. Since then, Mitchell and his wife have been trying to give the bag back. It has been an awkward project since we are not supposed to have any contact. But as an uncle, he was hoping to give me a graceful exit. And his attempts to rectify my mistake have failed so completely. I don't want him to be at risk anymore in his attempts to save my ass. I did it. I take full responsibility. And I can see—in all this—that I am not a qualified CEO. I'm just a guy who misses his parents. Who has a lot of growing up to do before he could even consider running this energy corporation upon which so many people depend."

Sebastian took another sip of water.

"Today, I announce my resignation," he said. "I will be stepping down. I will be participating with the board and various advisers to determine how to move forward. When we have a new CEO, we will let you know. Meanwhile, I am willing to talk with any and all legal authorities and cooperate with any investigations into my misconduct. Thank you for your time."

It was like an explosion after he stepped back from the podium. A barrage of voices: "Mr. Reid! Mr. Reid! Mr. Reid" But he waved and walked off, as if they had merely been applauding.

* * *

Ever since Morgan returned from the Caribbean, New York seemed grimy. She walked past a pile of blackened snow that was slowly melting to reveal a pile of trash. Maybe she and Sebastian could leave. Move somewhere . . . beautiful. She could work with him over time to use his influence to work on climate. Scientists kept giving the human race a shorter and shorter timeline to turn things around in terms of fossil-fuel use, but she needed to take a little more time to get to know Sebastian to turn him around. He had moved so much already.

Marriage? They didn't have to rush. She wasn't quite in love with him yet, but she was getting there. She felt warm toward him. Really warm. The sex was so much better now. He was attentive and willing to put in the work. He didn't . . . quite do it for her the way Kevin did. But what could be more dramatic and romantic than a forbidden spy lover? That wasn't real life. Nobody could sustain that kind of intensity. She could have something real with Sebastian. And if they were both committed to putting in the work, they could have a really good life.

Three days after she got back she went out to brunch with Dashawna. It was time to tell her what had been going on, to show her the ring, and to let her know that she might get her big wedding planning payoff after all.

Morgan laughed to herself. She would also need to set up a time for Sebastian and Dashawna to meet. Her first thought was about how to coach Dashawna to make a good impression, but then she caught herself. Old habits die hard. Fuck that. She was going to be herself, and so should her best friend. She was on the subway to meet Dashawna in Brooklyn when her phone went off. It had been so long that she didn't recognize the sound. A clinking sound. What was that?

She picked it up and realized it was the audio-recording

device in the study. Someone was in there talking? How could that be? Sebastian had said he was going out to an all-day board meeting.

Morgan played the conversation back in her mind. Sebastian had asked what she was up to. She'd said she needed to catch up with her best friend in Brooklyn. He'd said he had a board meeting downtown. He'd be home by dinner. Did she want him to call her a car? No, she would take the subway. But it takes so much longer, he'd said. Only an hour each way; I'll be home by dinner time, too. Sebastian had kissed her goodbye and said he'd see her then.

But if there was noise in the study? Had he come back? That seemed odd. Then an even worse thought struck her. What if Kevin had somehow broken in? Was he getting the camera?

The train pulled into the next station, and Morgan ran across the platform to catch the train back uptown.

Morgan waved to the doorman on her way into the building and stepped onto the elevator. When she got up to the apartment, Sebastian was walking down the hall toward her.

"Darling," he said. "What a pleasant surprise." He kissed her.

Morgan pulled out of the kiss and laughed. "I forgot something," she said. "You, too?"

"A whole stack of papers," he said. "What'd you forget?"

"Some fabric swatches," she said. "It's great that you're home, I'd love to get a couple of things out of that storage space behind your study."

"Ugh," he said. "I'm redecorating right now. It's hard to get through. Can I get them for you tomorrow?"

"Of course," she said. "Let me just get the other stuff out of my studio."

"Sure," he said. "I'll wait and walk out with you."

Morgan offered what she hoped was a reassuring smile and walked to her studio. Something was off. What was he doing home? Why was he making excuses for why she couldn't go into his study? He never waited for her.

She walked to her room and snatched up some random pieces of fabric. She dug out the remote control for the camera, which she kept in a pile of old electronics in plain sight.

On her way back down the hall, she turned on the camera. She prayed it would work. She hadn't checked the batteries. But if—if something shady was going on, she would at least have the audio recording.

"Ready?" Sebastian asked.

She smiled at him. "Shows you how relaxed I am after our getaway," she said. "Forgetting the most important things."

He laughed, too. "Same here."

He locked the door behind them.

Sebastian handed a bill to the doorman. "Thanks, pal," he said. Morgan saw that it wasn't the usual twenty. It was a hundred.

He must have paid the doorman to alert him if she came home.

Sebastian had been outside the study, with the door locked, waiting for her? Who was in there?

Or was she being paranoid? No. The recording device had been activated. He was there when he wasn't supposed to be.

They stepped out front. His car was waiting.

"Drop you at the subway?" he asked. "I could even have him drop you in Brooklyn after he takes me to the meeting. You must be running so late by now."

"No, thanks," Morgan said. "I'm just going by her house to hang out. Besides, you know I'm an artist. It feeds me to people watch. It's like research."

"Of course," he said. "Whatever you want, darling."

First he wanted to walk her out. Now he wanted to keep her in the car? He obviously wanted to keep tabs on her. The doorman. The chauffeur. Was this what it meant to be the fiancée or wife of someone this rich? Maybe she was a posses-

sion to him. Maybe he was just upgrading her to a higher security clearance, with more scrutiny.

"I'll ride along with you until we get to Midtown," she
said. "You're going to ReidCorp HQ, right?"

"Of course," he said. "Whatever you want."

She picked a random subway stop and had them drop her
there.

She gave him a longer kiss than usual and grinned at him.
"Until tonight," she said.

He smiled back and she slipped into the subway, jumping
on the first downtown train that came.

Was it possible that she was being followed? It would be
hard but not impossible. She needed to assume she was. She
would need to go to Brooklyn. Meet with Dashawna. She
needed to contact Kevin on the way.

She texted Dashawna and asked to meet at one of their favorite restaurants.

Dashawna asked: **You treating?**

Morgan said: **Definitely.**

Dashawna texted back: **See you there.**

Morgan texted Kevin: **Something's up. Can you meet me?
I'll be in Brooklyn.**

Five minutes later, she gave him the address of the restaurant: **I need you to meet me there. Sit near us. No contact. I'm
not sure if I'm being followed.**

She waited to hear back from him but got nothing. Maybe
the signal was iffy. But when the train came aboveground,
there was still nothing.

Maybe he had stopped using the burner phone.

She took a deep breath and resent the first text to his usual
cell number: **Something's up. Can you meet me?**

I'm in the middle of a meeting.

She replied: **Something is going down right now. We need to
act fast.**

This better be good.

She forwarded the second message.

He wrote back: **I'm already in BK. See you there.**

Morgan arrived at Mi Viejo San Juan, a Puerto Rican restaurant decorated with paintings of the island—trees, landscapes, and small frogs with large eyes that seemed to be watching her. Dashawna had gotten them seats. There were two mimosas on the table.

"I waited for you," Dashawna said.

They hugged for a long time.

"I really missed you," Morgan said. She took off her gloves, hat, jacket, and scarf.

"Maybe you should get Sebastian to move to Brooklyn," Dashawna said. "Or better yet, have him buy something in Manhattan with a little apartment for me."

"Anything's possible," Morgan said and drained half her glass.

"So," Dashawna said. "Let me see!"

"See what?" Morgan asked.

"The ring!"

Morgan realized she had it turned around, with the stone in her palm, so it wouldn't snag on her glove.

She rotated it to the knuckle side, and Dashawna squealed. "Damn, girl," she said. "It's the Rock of Gibraltar."

Out of the corner of her eye, Morgan saw a tall figure walking toward them, Kevin, headed their way. The host seated him at the next table, his back to Morgan.

"So," Dashawna asked. "How did he propose? Did he get down on one knee?"

Morgan's face got hot.

"Are you blushing? Did he do it in some freaky way?"

"No," Morgan said. "Nothing like that."

"Uh-oh," Dashawna said. "Has the sex gotten any better?"

"Not really," Morgan lied.

Dashawna shook her head. "No amount of money is worth putting up with bad sex forever. Of course, you could always have a piece on the side. Do you think he's teachable?"

The waiter appeared. "Can I take your order?"

"The shrimp mofongo?" Dashawna asked.

"I'll have the same," Morgan said. "I need to go to the restroom."

As Morgan pulled her seat out to get up, she knocked hard into Kevin's chair.

There was a narrow hallway that led past the kitchen to the restroom. The only toilet was unisex, and it was occupied. As she waited, she heard footsteps behind her.

"Are you waiting?" Kevin asked.

"Yeah," Morgan said. She turned around to find they were alone.

She began to whisper. "The audio recorder went off this morning when I was on my way here, so I went back and—"

A young mother with a baby and a toddler walked into the hallway behind them.

"You can go ahead of us if you like," Morgan said.

"Oh, thank you so much."

They stood in silence until the door opened and a young man walked out.

The woman took her two kids in and locked the door.

Morgan continued: "When I got home, Sebastian was there, which was strange because he had left before I did, saying he had a board meeting. Those are usually four to five hours. I think the doorman tipped him off that I was coming up. I'm telling you, something's not right. Then, when he left again, he really wanted to have me driven out to Brooklyn in his car. He wanted to keep tabs on me."

"Did you activate the camera?"

"Yes," Morgan said. "I turned it on maybe twenty minutes after the audio started. I don't know who might be in there or if we'll have missed the most incriminating stuff. But here's what I do know: Nobody could have gotten out of that apartment through the front door in the time it would have taken me to get upstairs. I'd put money on the fact that whoever he had in the study was still in there when I left. He would have doubled back to finish his meeting. At the very least, the camera would have caught them letting themselves out."

"What's our play?"

"I need to get that camera out and bail."

Kevin's face was expressionless. "You'll do it after you leave here?"

"That's my plan," Morgan said. "Unless he's at home."

"Or maybe after he goes to sleep?" Kevin asked.

"It seems more dangerous that way," Morgan said.

"I'll be your backup," Kevin said.

"I'm not sure how to do this," Morgan said. "I think he might suspect something. Or just be suspicious in general. Why was he trying to control me by driving me around?"

"Could be either," Kevin said. "Those rich guys like to control the women in their lives."

The door opened and the woman came out with her two kids.

"After you," Kevin said.

"I don't really have to go," Morgan whispered.

"I do," he said. "Text me when you have an update. I'll be standing by." He stepped around her into the bathroom.

She heard the door click and walked back to her table.

"Damn," Dashawna said. "Did you take a shower?"

"I let the lady with the babies go ahead of me," Morgan said. "I think she had to change a diaper."

The shrimp mofongo arrived—a pile of fried, mashed

plantains with shrimp and tomato sauce. Morgan unrolled her fork from the cloth napkin. She was famished and realized she hadn't eaten all day.

"I'm proud of you," Dashawna said. "I didn't think you had the guts to reel in a billionaire. But you rolled up your sleeves and got a little muddy to make it happen."

"You have no idea," Morgan said and took a big bite of shrimp.

Morgan walked the two blocks from the subway to Sebastian's apartment. This part of the city was so much cleaner. The dirty snow had all been cleared away.

Maybe she was wrong about all of it. Maybe she was just being paranoid. She had been happy. Maybe not exactly happy but content. She had felt confident she could turn things around with Sebastian. She was a finalist in the CFI competition. But the events of the day had shaken her. She'd have to listen to the tapes to know one way or another. She took a breath and walked into the lobby.

Sebastian was home, alone, with tales of his "board meeting" going well. He had work to do and would be in his study until dinner. What did she want to eat? They decided on Ethiopian.

"Darling," she said, "I have some fabric I need to send to Pennsylvania. Can a courier help me with that?"

"Sure," he said. "Call Dawn. She'll give you the information."

So, as Sebastian worked in his study, Morgan arranged with Dawn to have all her most prized fabric mailed to her mother. She didn't like that Sebastian would have her mother's address, but it couldn't really be helped. Besides, he was a billionaire. He could probably get hold of that information without her assistance.

She sent four large boxes from her studio. Mostly the

clothes she had designed and her most precious fabric, but really all her worldly possessions.

She texted Kevin that she couldn't get the camera until later tonight or tomorrow morning. He texted back: **standing by**

She was hedging her bets. Covering herself for the worst-case scenario. She packed her backpack with the things she would need short term. She had no idea where she would stay or how far she would go.

Even after she had mailed several large boxes and packed it all, her studio looked the same. The furniture and knick-knacks she had thrown around weren't anything important to her. It had never really been her space.

On the dresser were the flat iron, the curling iron, the blow-dryer, and the pile of hair accessories. All her makeup. Most of her feminine toiletries: perfumes, body lotions, nail polish. The magnifying mirror that allowed her to look closely at her pores. Her eyelash curler. The fake eyelashes she wore occasionally, sparse and subtle, just a bit of additional length. Her tweezers for those stubborn eyebrow hairs that twirled unruly, like the locks on her head. She left it all. It looked like she still lived here. Really, it was everything that made up the artifice of her that still lived here. The real Morgan was already gone.

Dinner was uneventful. Like it had been before their trip to Jamaica, when she was spying and not a real girlfriend. He talked about his plans and she listened—only half tuned in—with an engaged expression on her face. After dinner they went back to their telenovela marathon. She just sat on the couch and let herself disappear into the drama on the screen. Tried not to feel his arm draped over her shoulder.

"I love that I can watch this with you," he said. "This is gonna be our life."

She kissed him on the cheek. "Lucky us."

* * *

They went to bed at midnight. She tried to get out of bed several times when his breathing became slow and even, but he always stirred. She dozed in between attempts to get up. When she woke again, it was after six. Too late to try. She'd have to wait until he left for the day. She fell back asleep. When she woke again, it was after eight. Sebastian was in the bathroom, and she heard the shower running.

She texted Kevin: **No chance last night. I think he's going out. Stand by.**

Kevin texted back: **Headed uptown.**

When Sebastian came out of the bathroom, she was pretending to wake up.

"Good morning," she said with a smile and kissed him. "Where are you going?"

"Early meeting," he said. "I'll be home in time for lunch. Wanna go out?"

"Sure," she said.

"I'll text you later," he said, and with another kiss he was gone.

Morgan got up and put on leggings. Sneakers. She wanted to be ready to head out at a moment's notice.

When she heard the door close behind him, she got her backpack and her winter jacket and set them on the couch. She took out her lockpicks and got to work on the study door. But before she could crack it, she heard someone at the front door.

"Hello!" the housekeeper called out. "Anybody home?"

Morgan jumped back, her heart in her throat. "Lena," she said. "I didn't know you were coming today."

Apparently, she had let Dawn know she needed to come in early.

"No problem," Morgan said. "I've got a bunch of things to do."

Morgan listened for the sounds of cleaning in the kitchen

as she worked on the study door. When she finally opened it, she slipped in and was careful to lock it behind her. Lena might move though the house and be unable to find her, but she wouldn't know where she had gone.

Morgan looked around in Sebastian's study. A few boxes were lying around. Was this what he meant when he said it was too messy for her to come through? She peeked into them. Looked like old books.

She had more privacy to pick the storage-room lock and worked without worrying about time or noise. When she was inside, she used a pocketknife to cut through the spackle on the Sheetrocked wall. She sliced out a square and pried it out. Behind it, the camera and digital recorder were now coated with a light film of dust from her work. She removed both the devices and brushed them off. She replaced the wall piece the best she could. It was noticeable. She put the screen over it. But when she slipped back into the study, she heard Lena vacuuming in the hallway right outside. *Shit.* She was trapped.

She texted Kevin: **Bailing out soon. You in place?**

Two seconds later, he texted back: **Out front in a white zone. Silver hatchback with a rideshare sticker.**

Okay. This was gonna be a piece of cake. She walked back out into the study.

Lena was still vacuuming. Damn.

She opened the camera and the digital recorder and removed both disks, making them much more portable. Should she keep the recorder and camera? Maybe they were an important part of the evidence? She had no idea. She put the pair of disks into the hip pocket of her sweatpants.

Outside Sebastian's study, the vacuum continued to run.

Morgan slipped back into the storage space and took her grandmother's quilt. She had grieved at the thought of leaving it behind. It was worn and nearly frayed, but it meant the world to her.

She shut and relocked the door to the storage room. Still, the sound of vacuuming was too close. She pulled her phone back out and texted Dashawna:

Hey D, I know this sounds crazy but I've been spying on Sebastian. For the climate movement. He's up to something illegal or shady, I'm not sure what. If anything happens to me, please let the authorities know that today was the day I planned to leave him with evidence of his misdeeds. But don't worry. Nothing's gonna happen. I've got a plan and support to get away clean.

She finished the text, and still the vacuuming sound was too close. As she waited, she rubbed the quilt between her fingers to soothe her nerves.

Finally, the vacuuming stopped. Morgan peeked out through the keyhole. She didn't see anyone. But it wasn't until the vacuuming started up in the living room that she dared to open the door.

Lena was standing outside the study.

Morgan jolted, putting a hand on her heart.

"Oh, there you are," Lena said. "You were in the study?"

"You startled me," Morgan said, forcing a smile. "He gave me a key, so I can get to my things that are stored in the back." She was glad she had the quilt covering the camera and digital recorder. "You know we're engaged now." She grinned and showed Lena the ring on her other hand.

"Congratulations," Lena said. "And such a beautiful quilt."

"It was my grandmother's," Morgan said.

Lena ran her hand along the cotton. Morgan was afraid she might feel the electronics underneath.

"Anyway," Morgan said, stepping back and out of range, "I'm heading out. See you next week."

Morgan stepped out of the building wearing a backpack that carried a change of clothes, her passport, a pocketknife, a dark wig, her grandmother's quilt, and her lockpicks, plus an empty camera and digital recorder. In the internal pocket of her sweatpants, she had two minidisks pressed against her hip bone, like a necklace of Spanish diamonds.

The December morning was bright. Morgan looked out onto Second Avenue for the compact silver hatchback, which was supposed to be on the street in the white loading zone. She couldn't see around a double-parked truck. She walked briskly toward a silver hatchback on the corner. A mother exited the hatchback and lifted twin toddlers out of their child safety seats. Wrong car.

Morgan stepped into the street to look around the truck. At the far end, on the other side of the block, a tall man beside a silver hatchback opened the door. She turned toward him, but a pair of security guards came out of The Excelsior and cut her off.

Damn! She had been so careful. Casual clothes. Small backpack. Leisurely pace through the lobby.

Morgan pivoted and fled toward the opposite corner, maneuvering past the double stroller that took up nearly the whole sidewalk.

This end of the street was more sparsely populated and she took it at a full sprint, dodging pedestrians and a man walking three dogs. When she hit the other corner, she glanced over her shoulder. The two guards were still chasing her, cutting out into the street to avoid the man and the dogs.

Around the next corner was the subway. She blended into the crowd walking below ground to the station.

Taking the stairs two at a time, she dug in her jacket pocket for a MetroCard. Four train lines stopped here. If she could make it through the fare gates, she could disappear. She swiped the card once, her hand shaking, and had to do it again. But then she was through.

She waited on the platform for the downtown N or R train in a sea of late commuters. A man in front of her was half dancing to music blasting in his headphones. Beyond him she saw frantic movement: the two guards. One of them was looking at an iPhone and the other was scanning in her direction. They pointed at her.

Her heart was in her throat. What the hell? What were the chances that they would know *exactly* how to find her when they couldn't have even seen her walk down into the subway? Had her cell phone been bugged with a GPS locator?

She threw the phone into the tracks, causing gasps among the bystanders, and backed away. She rushed toward the other end of the platform. Maybe she should run back out of the station. Maybe it was a coincidence. She could get lost on one of the other platforms. Or better yet, be just far enough ahead of them to jump onto a leaving train.

She ran down the stairs and ducked around a corner. She blended into the crowd heading to the 6 train. No way they could track her without the phone.

On the 6 platform, she looked into the tunnel to see if the train was coming on her side. Instead, she saw the two guards coming down the stairs. Panic twisted in her solar plexus. How the hell had they found her again?

She hustled past three men in suits, past a large advertisement for diamond jewelry. And then she realized. The engagement ring. The setting was big enough for a GPS microchip. The diamond must be worth a million dollars, but not worth her life. She twisted off the ring and flung it into the tracks.

The security guards gaped, and the one with the phone put it in his pocket.

Now she shoved past people to the edge of the platform. There were stairs to exit there. But a steady stream of people walked down, transferring from another train. If she tried to climb the stairs against the flow of traffic, the guards would certainly catch her. She was trapped. Except for the tunnel.

The next stop was six or eight blocks away. The guards were getting closer. She elbowed into the knot of people coming down the stairs and leaped off the end of the platform.

"Give me your hand and I'll pull you out," a man called after her. "Think about what you have to live for."

Fucking idiots.

She kept to the outer edge of the tunnel and soon found a narrow path for subway workers. As she sprinted along the edge, her running footfalls were the loudest sound.

Her heart pounded with the exertion. But then, the voice of one of the guards: "She's down there." She felt a spike of fear.

The train came down the tunnel on the other side, the blast of sound and wind nearly knocking her back. Still, she continued to run, her breath burning in and out of her lungs. The train passed. She heard the guards behind her.

A rat skittered ahead, momentarily throwing off her gait. She stumbled, but then righted herself and kept running. She saw the distant light of the next station. The tunnel was dim and dank with puddles of water. She ran on, splashing through them, hearing only one set of footfalls at her back. One of the guards had fallen behind. She said a silent prayer of thanks for her daily runs on the treadmill.

But the guard pursuing her was also in good shape. He was gaining.

A train came on her side. The noise was deafening as it passed her, but she kept running. She felt a stitch under her ribs. Her knees were getting weak. The train slowed up ahead for a moment. Could she jump onto it?

Morgan put on a burst of speed to catch up. Her chest was on fire. Her legs were fatiguing. She heard the running steps of the guard—closer now. The train ahead started to move. With her last ounce of strength, she accelerated, taking a final leap and reaching through space for the handle on the back of the train.

She caught it! The guard at her back reached for her, his hand stretching through air. His fingers slipped off the nylon of her jacket while the train lurched forward.

The train sped up. Morgan watched the guard stop and double over, elbows on his knees. Then the train slowed down again. He was walk-jogging toward her as the train ground to a halt. Should she jump off? Start running again? Could she still run? Her muscles were jangled from the adrenaline of the sprint, the leap, and the sudden cessation of movement in the cold air.

She was ready to jump when the train began to move again, picking up speed, as the guard fell farther and farther behind. She pressed herself against the blessed metal of the car, panting, her body so weak with relief, she nearly crumpled and lost her grip.

They pulled into the next station, and she slipped off the end of the car onto the platform. Her leg had cramped and she was limping, her hair plastered to her head. She hustled, looking back over her shoulder. This was how she bumped into the chest of a man in a suit.

"Excuse me," she said, and looked up into Sebastian's face.

Chapter 15

Sebastian stood on the subway platform with two more armed guards, his face cold as stone.

"Who the fuck are you?" he asked Morgan. "Who sent you to upholster my apartment and spy on me?"

Morgan looked at him and the two guards. Then around in the subway. It wouldn't do to play innocent. And they were in a busy subway station. He wasn't going to harm her in full view of all these people. Besides, it infuriated her that he couldn't imagine her thinking for herself.

"Nobody sent me," Morgan said. "I was just dating you when I found out what you do. Or, more accurately, what your company is doing to the environment."

"Are you kidding me?" Sebastian said. "The whiners got to you? Somebody talked you into this *after* you met me?"

"It wasn't really that hard," Morgan said. "Your company is destroying the planet. The earth might be uninhabitable for all of humanity because of your greed."

"That's ridiculous," Sebastian said.

"I can't believe that after all the scientists agree, you're still denying the reality of climate change," Morgan said.

Sebastian shook his head. "I'm not denying climate change.

I just don't agree that the planet will be uninhabitable for all of humanity. Just most of humanity. That Green New Deal shit? I don't want to live in a world where I have to raise my own fucking vegetables on a wind farm and ride around on a solar tricycle. I want my tech and my toys and my assistant and the best of the best in this life that my father built." His face was getting red. She had seen him cry. She had seen him sullen. But she had never seen him angry like this. And it seemed to be gaining momentum.

"There will always be winners and whiners. Winners come out on top," he said. "And you could have been part of it. You could have been saved from the apocalypse. You could have been the fucking queen of the salvaged good life. But you decided to spy on me instead?"

"Why do you care what I do if you have nothing to hide anymore?" she asked.

He didn't get a chance to answer because one of the guards who had been chasing her walked up to them. Morgan saw him hand Sebastian the ring.

"You were the one spying on me," she said.

"Not spying, tracking. I had assets to protect." Sebastian pocketed the ring. "I guess this means the engagement is off?" he asked.

Morgan didn't answer.

"I would have married you, you know," he said. Then his lip curled in the most bitter of smiles. "Wives can't be compelled to testify against their husbands in court."

The remark stung more than Morgan expected it to. Had he never really cared for her? Had it all just been transactional? Or maybe he did care, and he was hurt, so he needed to act like he didn't give a fuck? To save face for her? Himself? Maybe the guards?

Morgan shuddered. She might have married him. Now she just needed to get away.

"Hand over your backpack," one of the guards said.

Morgan swallowed and stood up taller. "I'll save you some time," she said and unzipped it. "I think this is what you're looking for." She pulled out the camera and the digital recorder.

"I still need to search—" the guard began.

She pushed the electronics into his chest, and when they fell, he dove for them.

As the guard reached for the devices, she pushed past him and ran down the platform, elbowing her way past commuters. Sebastian was right on her heels.

Morgan pushed aside an orange cone and ran up the nearest staircase. Only when she got to the top did she realize her mistake. Caution tape across the top of the stairs meant this pedestrian tunnel was closed for construction or some other hazard. But the only way back was down, and a glance over her shoulder yielded the sight of two security guards behind Sebastian, his face nearly purple with rage.

Morgan vaulted over the caution tape and took off down the empty tunnel at a sprint.

In the distance behind her, she could hear a train pull into the station, and the muffled sounds of the late-morning commute. She could detect no sounds ahead; the next station was a full avenue block away. A second later she could hear the footfalls of the three men behind her, the hard slaps of the two security guards in boots and the quieter padding of the custom Italian leather shoes of the billionaire.

Their footfalls seemed to be falling behind, but she was afraid to turn lest she lose her stride. She knew she could outrun Sebastian in his suit, but the guards were beefy. Maybe that meant they were in top shape, or maybe they were just big to intimidate people.

When the footfalls lagged farther behind, she took the chance at turning around. And then she did stumble, as she saw one of the guards was pulling out a gun.

Her heart began beating wildly. She could hardly catch her breath for the panic.

"Stop or he'll shoot," the man in the suit wheezed at her, his choking voice only audible because the tunnel was so empty.

Should she stop? Would he really shoot her? The tunnel curved a bit, and she could see the ribbon of caution tape at the other end, beckoning like a distant finish line.

He wouldn't dare. He wouldn't shoot an unarmed young woman in the back, in Midtown. How would he explain that?

Would they just shoot her and leave her there? The cops always suspect the boyfriend or husband when a woman is murdered. Could they cover it up? No. Three men couldn't drag a bleeding body out of the subway through the crush of late-morning commuters without being questioned. Maybe if they had planned, brought a stretcher, EMT disguises.

If she ran, they might take the chance at shooting her. But if she let them capture her? Let them march her out willingly through the crush of people, pile her into a dark limo? They could take her anywhere, do anything to her, and worst of all, they could get the two small disks in the inner pocket of her sweatpants, their hard plastic pressing against her hip bone with every stride she ran.

Her vision blurred a bit. Sweat had begun to drip from her forehead and into her eyes. She wiped it with the back of her wrist. As her vision cleared, she saw that a large chunk of cement lay in the center of the tunnel up ahead. It was perhaps the size of a couch cushion.

She glanced up to see the spot in the ceiling from which it had fallen, like the hole from a missing tooth. No wonder they'd closed the tunnel. Rusty water dripped down onto the chunk of cement from above.

She should keep running. They had ads on the subway

about harassment. She could say Sebastian had been harassing her. They believed women nowadays, didn't they? At least sometimes?

She had almost convinced herself when the first shot rang out. Nearly deafening in the silent tunnel. The cry that escaped her was involuntary. A sort of gasp shriek, as the bullet hit a wall tile off to her left.

As the sounds of the shot and her own cry echoed, some magical-thinking part of herself wanted to dive behind the fallen chunk of cement for cover. Why couldn't she be a little girl again, closing her own eyes, convinced that Mommy can't see her? She longed for the magic of invisibility, the gravity defiance of flight or any superpower that would bend the laws of physics:

Faster than a speeding bullet . . .

But she had only her two legs. A pair of lungs. A frantic heartbeat. Sweat soaked through her cotton top under the nylon jacket.

She ran past the chunk of tile where the bullet had hit—so far from where she had stood. Maybe they weren't shooting at her. Maybe just trying to scare her. Still, she began to weave. It slowed her down a bit, making her easier to catch but harder to shoot. From the sound of his footfalls, the guard wasn't even close. She realized that there was only one set of footfalls now. As she weaved right, she stole a glance over her shoulder. The man in the suit and one of the guards had stopped. Both were doubled over, catching their breath.

She could hear sound up ahead now: the murmur of commuters, echoes of trains, feet on cement stairwells. She was almost out of the tunnel. She could outrun them. She could.

The man in the suit cleared his throat. "That first—first shot was to get your attention," he rasped. "Stop or he—he won't miss the—second time."

Morgan did the opposite. Let the terror of the adrenaline

urge her to a burst of speed. She kept weaving, kept pumping. She was almost to the caution tape finish line when the guard pulled the trigger for the second shot, shooting to kill.

But she had just pivoted to weave in the other direction. The bullet tore through the spot where her back had been only a split second before, hitting her backpack, blowing right through it.

In an instant she was through the caution tape, running up the nearest stairwell. Her lungs heaving, the adrenaline starting to crash, but her will to live lifting her up, up.

"Did you hear a shot?" a man asked a woman in the tunnel above.

The woman pulled out her earbuds. "What?"

Morgan ran on. By the time she got aboveground, she was dizzy, sodden, crashing. She unzipped the jacket and slipped into the crowd on the sidewalk.

She staggered into a drugstore and got a burner phone. She tried Kevin but couldn't reach him. Tried his burner phone, but it was disconnected. Finally, she called Yolanda.

Morgan stood huddled in a bus shelter, the story coming out on a rambling whisper.

"His guards shot at you twice?" Yolanda asked. "But you lost them?"

"I think so," Morgan said. "I'm pretty sure."

"Where are you?" Yolanda asked. "I'll have our communications manager, Val, come get you. She's in the area."

"Where's Kevin?" Morgan asked.

"Sebastian's guys got him arrested," Yolanda said.

"For what?"

"Violating a restraining order," Yolanda said. "He's not allowed to be within one hundred feet of Sebastian's apartment."

"I forgot about that," Morgan said.

"He threw seaweed on Sebastian a while back," Yolanda

said. "But we'll get him out soon. Especially when we un-cover the evidence you have."

"How did they know he was there?" Morgan asked.

"They must've seen him," Yolanda said.

"I don't think they did," Morgan said. "They were chasing me, and I was heading in the opposite direction."

"Kevin said something about a mole in the organization," Yolanda said. "But I've been so careful. The only people who knew were me and Val. But that doesn't mean someone couldn't have overheard."

"Or worse, something might be bugged."

"Ugh," Yolanda said. "We might need to do a sweep. I'll get our tech guy on it. Meanwhile, sit tight, I gave your location to Val. She should be there any minute. She's driving a biodiesel VW Bug. Bright red."

"Hard to miss," Morgan said.

As she waited, Morgan kept her eyes open. If the line was bugged, would someone else have heard Yolanda giving her location to Val?

Traffic flowed down the wide avenue. Morgan kept scanning for anything unusual. But it just looked like regular people going about their uptown business. She kept her eyes open, looking from side to side, pressing her back against the wall of the building behind her.

Finally, the red VW Bug rolled up. An early '00s model with a flower power look to it.

Val turned out to be a thickset young Asian woman in a pair of olive-green overalls.

"Hop in!" she said brightly. She looked to be in her early twenties and intensely perky.

Morgan relaxed the moment she slid into the car and locked the door.

"Where to?" Val asked.

Morgan could only think of one place. "Do you mind driving to Brooklyn?"

"No problem," Val said. "Just let me get those disks from you. Yolanda wants them as soon as possible."

Morgan tried to reach into her sweatpants inner pocket, but it was pressed under the seat belt. She leaned back, but her waistband was soaked, sticking to her skin. And her damp fingers couldn't slide into the pocket.

"It's kinda stuck," Morgan said. "I'll have to stand up to get it out."

"Of course," Val said. "We'll get them out when we stop at Yolanda's building on the way to Brooklyn."

Now that she was safe, Morgan felt herself crashing. She closed her eyes for just a moment . . .

Morgan felt someone nudging her, heard someone calling her name. She felt groggy, disoriented. She opened her eyes to see an unfamiliar Asian girl with a ponytail and glasses. The girl was shaking her shoulder.

Morgan blinked, disoriented for a moment, then recalled where she was. She'd escaped from Sebastian. She had the disks. Val was waking her up.

"We're here," Val said. "At Yolanda's office." They were in the alley behind a large Midtown office building. Val had pulled the red VW Bug into a loading zone. Morgan was looking at a trio of dumpsters.

How long had she been asleep? They weren't that far from where she had started. Maybe a dozen or so blocks. But with the traffic, that could mean she had been out five minutes or half an hour.

"You wanna get those disks and I can run them in to her?" Val asked.

Morgan nodded groggily and stood up. She opened up the car door and nearly tripped on her way out. Her foot tangled in the strap of her backpack, which had been on the floor of the car. She set it on the seat.

Morgan pulled up her jacket and fished in the small inner pocket of the sweatpants for the disks.

"Finally," Val said. "We got the real dirt on Sebastian Reid."

Morgan had a photographic memory, but she didn't realize until that moment, that she had memory recall for audio as well.

Sebastian Reid. The voice that had answered her calls. As if it was her own name. It wasn't Val. This woman's name wasn't Val. It was Dawn. Sebastian's assistant's name was Dawn. Suddenly, Morgan's whole body felt cold and clammy with sweat, but she continued to dig in her pocket.

"Damn, it's stuck," Morgan said. "The—" she improvised. "The zipper is caught," she said. She feigned tugging on the zipperless pocket.

"Can I help?" the imposter asked.

"This happens sometimes," Morgan said. "I need to pull the sweatpants down. Is there a bathroom in here I can use?"

"Sure," Val said, stepping out of the car.

Morgan pulled her backpack off the front seat and Val locked the vehicle behind them. She used a keycard to open the rear door of the building.

They walked into a hallway lit with fluorescents, and Val led Morgan into the ladies' room.

It was an institutional restroom with stainless-steel fixtures. Morgan walked into the stall and took off her shoes. She pulled down her sweatpants and stepped out of them. Before she could lift them up to fidget with the pocket, Val had reached under the stall and grabbed them.

"What are you doing?" Morgan yelled as Val ran out of the bathroom with her pants.

Behind the stall door, Morgan held a pair of small, mismatched disks in her hand.

How long would it take for Val to realize the pocket was empty? Was this really Yolanda's building?

Morgan unzipped her backpack and pulled out a pair of jeans. The security guard's bullet had ripped through the left thigh. She pulled them on anyway, put on her shoes, and stepped out of the stall.

She texted Yolanda: **Val is the mole. is your office in Midtown?**

Yolanda texted back. **No. East 127th. Val? WTF?**

Shit. Morgan looked around the bathroom. It was a gleaming white box. No windows. Only the one exit. Morgan slipped out and into the sterile corporate hallway. She backtracked toward the door she had entered. She heard Val's voice.

"The pocket was empty," Val was saying. Morgan opened the nearest door, which turned out to be a custodian's closet.

The room was maybe six feet square. She only saw the contents for a moment, like a flashbulb illuminating a scene for a photo. Then the door closed and it was dark again.

She crouched behind a trash can and waited. No one followed. No sounds of people running past in the hallway.

Morgan needed to get out of this building. She turned on her burner phone for light and looked around. In the dim glow of the screen, she saw nothing but cleaning supplies and equipment. But there was also a bank of lockers. She pulled out her lockpicks and broke into one of them. It had a stash of beef jerky and a jumpsuit that said "Donovan" across the front pocket. It was way too big for her.

She picked the lock on a second locker and found a jumpsuit that said "Blanca." It was a little tight, the legs a bit too short. Five inches of her jeans stuck out at the bottom, a few shades lighter than the navy uniform, but it would work. She put on her dark wig, a straight brunette bob with bangs. She went back to Donovan's locker and took his baseball cap. Her best shot at getting out would be by pretending to take out the trash. She put her backpack and jacket into a black garbage bag and headed for the front door.

Her phone buzzed just before she left the custodian's room.

It was a text from Yolanda. **If you're coming to the office, I won't be here. Kevin is missing. He's not in the system, even though witnesses saw him being arrested. Something is very wrong.**

Morgan felt a twist in her chest. But she needed to worry about herself right now. And where was she supposed to go with these disks? As long as she had them, she had a target on her back. She tightened her grip on the garbage bag. It was time for "Blanca" to head home to Brooklyn.

When she closed the door behind her, she saw Sebastian heading her way from the other end of the hall, flanked by the same two security guards.

Morgan felt a clutch of panic at the sight of the man who had ordered someone to shoot her—to shoot to kill. Morgan ducked her head down and held the garbage bag in front of her chest like a shield. Her knees threatened to give out as she was nearly astride them. She could smell Sebastian's cologne. The scent nearly choked her. Yet as she walked past, garbage bag in hand, they didn't detect the hammering of her heart, her choking breath. Like magic, Blanca's uniform had granted her the power of invisibility.

Val walked into the hallway, trailing behind Sebastian. Morgan was certain she was done for. But Val looked past her, right though her, directly at Sebastian.

"Don't worry," Val said. "We'll find her. Everything is on lockdown. She hasn't left the building."

"And Templeton?" Sebastian asked. "Where is he being held?"

"Basement," Val said.

Kevin was in the basement. Morgan tried to take the service elevator, but she didn't have the custodian's badge. She tried the stairwell, but she needed a badge for that, too. She waited for one of the several regular elevators. When a trio of guys in suits entered, she stepped in after them. They paid her no mind and used a key to hit the button for five. While their key was in, she hit the button for the basement. They kept talking and ignored her, getting out on the fifth floor. Afterward, she could feel her anxiety spike as the elevator descended to the basement.

It opened again on the first floor. The elevator cars had wide doors in full view of the security guard at the front desk. She pushed herself over to the far edge of the car so she would be less noticeable. He didn't appear to be paying attention, but the door seemed to stay open forever. The doors began to slide shut. A woman was walking toward the elevator. Morgan crushed herself into the corner, kept her eyes down. Finally, the doors closed and the car began to descend.

On the basement level, Morgan landed in another windowless, institutional corridor lit with fluorescents. She found an evacuation plan on the wall with a floor layout. There was a large server room with the loud hum of technology that took up most of the basement level. In the corner was a cluster of small offices and a security section. Really, the security section was a series of rooms. Morgan suspected that one of those rooms would have guards looking at video feeds. She had seen several cameras on the first floor. There were a few inner rooms. Kevin must be in there somewhere.

Morgan looked around until she found the custodian's closet on the basement floor. It was much smaller. She grabbed a waste cart, one that had a bag for trash and separate receptacles for recyclable containers, and mixed paper, and brought it out of the closet. Morgan put the garbage bag containing her belongings in the clean and dry paper section and began to wheel the cart around the floor. The security section was locked. Morgan continued to circle around, unnoticed.

It took fifteen minutes of circling until she finally saw Val come in from the elevator with three cups of coffee. Despite the situation, it struck Morgan as so outrageous. One for Sebastian. One for each of the guards. Nothing for Kevin, of course. But nothing for herself?

Morgan began wheeling the cart after Val. When the door had nearly closed behind the assistant, Morgan put a foot in the way. She winced silently as the heavy door banged against her sneaker. Val walked down a narrow hall and through a second door without a backward glance.

Once Val disappeared, Morgan crept in. The hall was empty, with nowhere to hide. But Morgan had her lockpicks. She prayed that the room next to the one Val had entered would be unoccupied.

Morgan had gotten better at locks and quickly opened the door. She held her breath, worried someone would be there, would be looking up at her, startled. As she walked in, the light came on automatically, and she found no one. She slipped in, along with her custodian cart.

The room was a small, windowless box with a pair of worn folding chairs. She couldn't hear anything from next door. But when she looked around the room, she saw a small air vent. She pulled a pocketknife from her backpack and unscrewed and removed the grate. When she stuck her head inside, she could hear a little of what they said.

Muffled. Kevin's voice. But raised, so she could make out the words: "This is bullshit! This is kidnapping."

Another muffled voice. Maybe the security guard? She couldn't discern the words.

Then Sebastian, closer to the vent and easier to hear. "Is it kidnapping, or counseling? I'm trying to give you a chance, here. I'm trying to help you. We know she called you. We know you're in violation of your restraining order. We know how to get it charged as a felony. And we know that you're one strike away from being locked up for life. Just tell us where to find her and we can make this all go away."

"What?" Kevin's voice was loud after Sebastian's menacing whisper. "You think I care about being locked up for the rest of my life? If you get your way, our planet doesn't stand a chance. You're the architect of the end of the world."

"Yeah, but it'll be such a rough end," Sebastian said. "Remember how all those inmates drowned or overheated. How many might die in a pandemic? These jails aren't equipped for some of these supposed disasters. I'm trying to help get you in a position where you at least have a chance of saving yourself."

"I don't know where she is," Kevin said. "Your guys ran her off from your apartment, where we were supposed to meet. Then your fake cop collared me. That's all I know."

Morgan heard music, the instrumental ringtone of a bubble-gum pop song about unrequited love.

Val's voice interrupted: "Yolanda's calling me," she said. "Should I pick up?"

"No," Sebastian said. "Let her run around to police precincts looking for him. Eventually Morgan will call."

"No," Kevin said. "She won't."

Yes, Morgan thought. She would.

She pulled out her phone and looked at the time. She waited three and a half minutes. She couldn't run the risk of calling because if she could hear them, they might be able to hear her. She texted from the burner phone: **It's M. Where are you? Y's been calling you. Beware! V is the mole. She had me practically a prisoner at some midtown building. Waiting at our spot downtown. Get here ASAP. I don't know who else to give these disks to.**

Morgan heard the faint ding of the text arriving at Kevin's phone. Then Val's laugh. "You called it, Mr. Reid."

Mr. Reid. Mr. fucking Reid. She was responsible for laundering this guy's underwear and she had to call him by his last name?

"You know where the spot is downtown?" Reid asked.

"Yeah," one of the guards said. "Some bar. Never been there, but I have the address from the GPS."

"Let's head over, shall we?" Sebastian asked. "Dawn, keep an eye on Mr. Templeton."

Sebastian's assistant was named Dawn. Yolanda's communications manager was named Val. Which was her real name?

"You're gonna leave me here with him?" Dawn or Val asked. "By myself?" Dawn. Morgan had known her as Dawn first.

"He's zip-tied to the chair," one of the guards said. "He shouldn't be any trouble."

Morgan heard the door open, and the three men trooped into the hallway. By the time they had walked across the hall and the outer door had closed behind them, so had the inner door.

It would take maybe half an hour for the three of them to get to the bar and find she wasn't there.

It was so fucking quiet. Dawn would hear Morgan trying to pick the lock. Unless there was some way to distract her. It would have been easy if Morgan had her smartphone. But she only had the burner. Maybe she could use it. She recalled something from her childhood. Her mom didn't have a cell phone and would always set the house clocks fast to keep from being late. But sometimes they were faster than others. Morgan would call the time on their landline.

It took a few tries, but she figured out how to do it on the burner phone. Then she put it on speaker and set it in the vent.

"At the tone, the time will be ten fifty-eight and forty seconds," the voice said. And then there was a beep.

"What the hell's that noise?" Dawn asked. "Is that you?"

Kevin didn't answer.

Morgan slipped silently into the hallway. She rotated the wig so the longer part shielded her face. Wheeling the waste cart in front of her, she waited until she heard Dawn fumbling around the room. Then Morgan efficiently picked the lock.

She swung the door open, wide.

Dawn was kneeling in front of the air vent, with her back to the door. Kevin sat at the table. Morgan couldn't see any handcuffs but assumed he was restrained beneath the tabletop.

Morgan made eye contact with Kevin, then leaned down over the wastebasket so her hair covered her face. "How did you get in here?" Dawn asked, rising from the floor.

"Door was open," Morgan said. "Got any recyclables?"

"No," Dawn said. "This man is a suspect. Security caught him breaking into the server room. We're waiting for the police." She turned to Kevin. "I'd keep my mouth shut if I were you."

Morgan shrugged. "Not my business." She walked over to the three cups of coffee on the table, and the little paper coffee tray. "Can I toss these?"

"Sure," Dawn said. "Are you done here?"

"Yup," Morgan said, picking up the metal wastebasket. "Just let me toss these out." But instead of replacing the wastebasket, she walked toward Dawn and swung it, hitting her in the head. Dawn went down hard, crumpling onto the floor.

"Holy shit," Kevin said.

Morgan pulled out her pocketknife and sawed him out of the zip-ties.

"Were there any extra handcuffs?" she asked Kevin.

"In the drawer," he said, pointing to the desk.

Morgan pulled out a pair of them and cuffed Dawn as she lay on the floor. Around the woman's head, blood seeped into the seams of the linoleum.

"Did I fucking kill her?" Morgan asked.

"No," Kevin said. "She's breathing. Head wounds look

worse than they really are. We can call an ambulance when we get a safe distance away."

"No distance is safe enough," Morgan said, putting the wastebasket back.

On the floor, Dawn groaned.

"How are we gonna get out of here?" Kevin asked.

"Only one way," Morgan said, and pulled aside the plastic bags on the cart.

Morgan could have been hidden easily, but Kevin was a tight fit. Finally, by lying on his back in the fetal position, they managed it. The denim of his jeans showed a little. But it only looked suspicious if someone was squatting down beside the cart. Morgan hoped the security in the building had come down from code red when they thought she had already escaped.

Morgan took Dawn's keycard so they could operate the elevators.

She left the burner phone behind in the vent. Sebastian already had the number. When he and his guards found she wasn't at the bar, they would try to trace her. Let it send them back here.

As she wheeled the cart into the elevator, Morgan kept the cap low over her eyes. There was a camera across from the buttons. She pushed the lobby floor and held her breath.

On the street level she wanted to run, but she had to restrain herself to keep a casual pace. The cart wasn't used to holding the weight of a grown man, so the wheels jammed a little. Morgan had to really push. She backtracked through the corridor that led to the restroom and out the back door.

Dawn's keycard ought to work here. It had gotten them in the building. It certainly should get them out. But would it trip any alarms?

Morgan leaned into the cart. It was even slower going with the heavy load on carpet.

A pair of women in bright suits came down the hallway from the women's room. Morgan kept her eyes down. Women were always more observant.

But they swept past her as well.

At the alley door Morgan pulled out Dawn's keycard and swiped it. The light turned green. She pressed the door open and struggled to push the cart out over the doorframe. She whispered for Kevin to climb out.

He wriggled from beneath the plastic bags and Morgan retrieved her backpack and jacket.

She pushed the cart into the interior hallway and let the door close behind them. The red Bug was still in the back alley.

Morgan turned around and saw that there was a video camera just outside the door.

She grabbed Kevin's hand and the two of them began to run now, past the car, and down the alley.

"We need to call Yolanda," Morgan said. "Do you have your phone?"

"They took it," Kevin said.

It wasn't easy to find a pay phone in Manhattan anymore. But when they came out onto the street, she realized they were near Union Square. Kevin knew where they could find a phone.

Morgan pulled some coins from her backpack and Kevin used them. "Hey Yolanda, it's Kev," he said. "Morgan found me. She's got the disks. Who can we give them to?"

Through the receiver, Morgan could hear the attorney's voice, tinny and sharp.

"I'm uptown at the police precinct, accusing them of lying when they say you're not in the system. Who knew this time they were telling the truth? Meet me at the district attorney's office to deliver the evidence."

As Yolanda spoke, Morgan peeled out of the janitor's uniform, and left it crumpled beneath the pay phone. She took off the wig, too, and put it back in the backpack. Her body was starting to cool down from running. She put her nylon jacket back on and kept the baseball cap.

"Can we trust them?" Kevin asked Yolanda on the phone.

"In general? No," the lawyer said. "But I have a prosecutor friend who will make sure this evidence doesn't disappear." She gave them the address.

Morgan and Kevin walked downtown to the prosecutor's office. They didn't have phones to catch a rideshare. Morgan didn't want to waste cash on a taxi. And she was damned if she would allow herself to get cornered again underground in the subway.

"You okay?" Kevin asked.

"Yeah," Morgan said. "You?"

He nodded.

Suddenly, Morgan recalled the first shot in the tunnel. The moment the second bullet missed her. She faltered for a moment and Kevin took her hand.

She knew she should feel something at his touch. But she could only feel . . . disconnected. Numb.

"You sure you're okay?" he asked.

"Just shaken," she said. "Come on."

Half an hour later they arrived at a gray government building and entered through a bronze revolving door. Yolanda wasn't there yet. But they went to the prosecutor's office she had indicated.

When they opened the door, they faced a bank of cameras.

"What the—?" Kevin began.

Morgan elbowed him in the ribs before he could cuss in front of the press.

"Please come in," said a dark-haired woman wearing a trim navy suit and a red blouse. She introduced herself as Ivelisse Figueroa.

"This is a hearing to establish the chain of evidence for this exhibit," Figueroa said. "Sit down, sir," she told Kevin. "Miss, please remove your hat and raise your right hand."

Morgan took off her cap. She had a terrible case of hat head. Her curly hair was back in a braid, fuzzy and mis-shapen at the scalp from the cap, the wig, and all the sweating. But Morgan didn't care. The full numbness had set in after the morning. Dimly, she had the thought that Dashawna would be horrified. Morgan was truly looking her worst for all the world to see.

A man in a uniform came over and gave Morgan a Bible. "Do you solemnly swear to tell the truth under penalty of perjury?"

"I do," Morgan said.

"State your name," Figueroa said.

And then—question after question, in view of all the cameras—Ivelisse Figueroa established that Morgan had been Sebastian Reid's girlfriend, that she had met Kevin en route to Colorado, and that Kevin was part of a protest that identified Sebastian's company as one of the architects of the climate crisis. She had shortly thereafter become Sebastian's live-in girlfriend. And shortly after that she had agreed to get information about Sebastian. These disks had been in two devices in the wall of Sebastian's apartment. She swore to the address and that she and Kevin had placed the camera there.

"Have these disks been out of your possession since removing them from the camera and digital recorder?" Figueroa asked.

"No," Morgan said.

"Not at all, for any period of time?"

"No."

"Where are the recorder and camera?" the prosecutor asked.

"They were confiscated from me by two security guards

who were acting under orders from Sebastian Reid," Morgan said.

"But you had already taken the disks out?"

"I had."

"Let the record show that I am assuming possession of these disks," Figueroa said. "I have sent for two machines that will read them, and we will do so in full view of the press."

Morgan and Kevin exchanged looks.

A few minutes later a young man walked in with a media cart. Behind him, a petite African American woman came rushing in, breathless, wearing a charcoal-gray suit and a white blouse. Her hair was in braids pulled back into a bun.

She sat down next to Kevin and extended her hand to Morgan. "Yolanda Vance," she whispered.

Morgan shook on autopilot. Her left hand automatically attempted in vain to finger comb her hair into submission.

The young man with the media cart did some tinkering. Finally, he found the proper players and hookups. The prosecutor kept the disks in her hand and held them aloft the entire time in front of the cameras that were presumably still rolling. There could be no question of a sleight of hand.

"I invite the press to document that I am placing these disks into empty players."

The press recorded that fact, and she went on to insert the disks. First, she played the audiotape.

The recording was of a conversation between Sebastian and Mitchell Brightwell. Morgan had no idea how he'd been smuggled into the building. Maybe there was a back entrance for the servants that hadn't been totally sealed up. Or maybe he just boldly strode through the front door.

When Ivelisse Figueroa put in the videotape, it was clearly Brightwell.

The two men sat across from each other in Sebastian's office and the camera caught them in profile. The only light came from a lamp on Sebastian's desk. It was dim, but both men's faces were clearly visible.

At first the information they were discussing was too technical for Morgan to understand. But then Brightwell slid a small computer drive across the desk to Sebastian.

"It's all there," he said in the video. "The specs of what the DOE is looking for."

Morgan remembered that the DOE was the Department of Energy.

"So all the solar and wind shit has been for nothing?" Sebastian asked.

"Not nothing," Brightwell said. "You can sell it off at cost. But you'll never get in on the ground floor of any of it. The other guys are just too far ahead. The next big thing is wave power. All that offshore land you have for drilling will give you a big advantage . . . if you have the specs of what they're looking for. Plus, it'll give you an excuse to increase the oil production from some of those underwater rigs. The regulations have slowed it down to a trickle."

"But what if there's another big spill?"

"Those rigs were legally installed and legally allowed to operate for years," Brightwell said. "If you're operating there legally to develop wave power, they'll never be able to prove that you were pumping more than the legal limit. Not if you keep your guys in line and don't have any whistleblowers. Check it out. At the very least you'll be able to corner this wave market. There's still time to make your legacy, son. Your dad did it with fossil fuels. You can do it with wave power."

In the middle of playing the videotape the door of the prosecutor's office flew open. A middle-aged man ran into the room, red-faced and panting.

"I have an injunction," he wheezed. "Signed by a judge of

the Superior Court, to halt these proceedings. Further, I have a warrant to—to confiscate every video that has been taken of this evidence."

The prosecutor took the piece of paper and read it slowly, the video playing all the while. Then, after she had examined all the fine print, she turned off the playback machine.

She turned to the press. "You heard the man," she said. "You are required by law to turn over your footage to him to be destroyed."

No one moved.

"I said give me those recordings now," the attorney said, his face contorted with rage.

"What recordings?" one of the women camera operators in the front asked. "I was streaming live."

"Me, too," said another man with a camera. "Just like I am now."

"Does anyone here have recordings?" Figueroa asked.

All of the camera operators in the group shook their heads.

"Not a single disk or anything?"

None. Even the lone podcaster had gone live on Instagram via his phone.

"Every single one of you had a live feed?" she asked.

The group nodded.

"Well," she said into the bank of cameras. "This attorney, representing Sebastian Reid, has come into my office with an injunction to stop the playback of these tapes of evidence and to confiscate any and all recordings of this session, but unfortunately, there were no recordings of this session, only live feeds. I have complied with this court injunction to the best of my ability. I will now, in further compliance with this injunction, be disbanding these journalists, and will finish the documentation of this evidence in private. You are all dismissed."

Morgan looked at Yolanda, who mouthed, *Stay here.*

Morgan and Kevin didn't move as all the journalists filed out.

"What about him?" the red-faced lawyer demanded. He pointed to a lone camera operator who was coming closer.

"My assistant?" Figueroa asked. "He's documenting the chain of evidence for this office. Your injunction doesn't cover my staff."

"You fucking—" His mouth was pursed to form a word that began with the letter "b." Then he looked at the camera and thought better of it.

"Please clear the room," the prosecutor said. "My staff and I need to continue reviewing this footage. All attorneys and witnesses are required to exit, as per this injunction."

The red-faced guy turned and stormed out, only to be mobbed by the media.

"No comment!" he kept shouting. "No fucking comment!"

Morgan expected his voice to get further away, but instead it got louder.

"You cocksuckers need to let me the fuck out of here," he yelled.

"I'm sorry," Figueroa said to them. "The three of you need to exit."

Yolanda nodded. "Just keep your mouths shut," she murmured to Kevin and Morgan. "I'll do all the talking."

When they opened the door, Sebastian's attorney was shoving two reporters aside. He snatched one woman's microphone and threw it on the ground. He grabbed another man's camera and smashed it in his face.

"Did he just fucking attack that photographer?" Morgan asked.

"Keep walking, Morgan," Yolanda said.

Several of the cameras turned to focus on the attorney and the two journalists he'd assaulted. But the rest of the cameras turned toward Morgan, Kevin, and Yolanda.

Yolanda stood between them, an arm around each of their waists, anchoring them to the spot.

Several of the reporters yelled Kevin's name. He was a relatively well-known activist. Not like Greta Thunberg but known in New York City. Apparently, they knew Yolanda as well, although they called to her by her last name.

"Ms. Vance," they asked. "Are you also representing Ms. Faraday?"

"If you'll all be quiet," Yolanda said. "I'll be making a statement."

The reporters settled down as the other attorney stomped off down the corridor yelling loudly over his shoulder, "You cocksuckers think you're gonna sue?" he asked. "I'll fucking bury your asses."

"That show's over," Yolanda said. "Focus over here."

The camera operators who hadn't chased the attorney down the corridor pivoted over to Yolanda, Kevin, and Morgan.

"Let me say this," Yolanda began. "Any young woman who has read a few romance novels will be familiar with the idea of the billionaire as a leading man, a sort of magical Mr. Right," she said. "But in reality, as our country is finally coming to understand, that level of wealth has the danger of leading to corruption, leading individuals to believe they can do anything and are exempt from the laws of our nation. From not paying their fair share of taxes to sexual exploitation of minors to destruction of the environment to breaching every possible kind of business ethics. When profit and profit alone is worshipped as God, the whole world goes to hell. And you can quote me on that."

A ripple of laughter went through the press corps.

"In answer to your questions, yes, I am representing Morgan Faraday, in addition to my longtime client Kevin Templeton. After moving in with her boyfriend, Sebastian Reid, Ms. Faraday encountered certain evidence that suggested that he might be in violation of the law. She bravely investigated on her own and was able to document the conversation you saw in the prosecutor's office. Although Sebastian Reid acted quickly to quash that evidence, I'm pleased that the prosecutor, Ivelisse Figueroa, saw fit to share the video with the public, before Reid could use his undue influence to bury it."

"Ms. Vance," one reporter asked. "Is it true that your client is or was engaged to Sebastian Reid?"

"Both of my clients have had quite an ordeal today and deserve some rest. That's all for now."

The reporters began to shout more questions.

Morgan couldn't catch most of them in the barrage, although she did hear one clearly: "Ms. Vance, are your clients involved in a romantic relationship with each other?"

"Wait," Morgan said. "I want to say something."

Yolanda looked uneasy, but Morgan put up a single finger to ask Yolanda to wait.

"Something Ms. Vance said caught my attention," Morgan said to the cameras. "I do want to make a statement." From all the materials she'd been reading, she had thought about what she might say if she had the media's attention.

Morgan turned so she was full front to the cameras. She had put her baseball cap back on. Really Donovan's cap—so she didn't look quite as disheveled. "I was raised poor," she began. "My family didn't have enough of anything. Food. Shelter. Clothes. Health care. Education. Because I was lucky and worked hard, I was able to make it to college in New York City. And in the time since I got here, friends have pointed out that I was favored by teachers and counselors because I looked white, but I got here. Ever since I arrived in New York, I've been trying to be anything but poor. To fit in. To pretend. When I met Sebastian Reid, he was my ticket to the good life. He could guarantee that I never had to feel the sting of poverty again. Sebastian Reid thinks he can insulate himself and those he cares about from every single danger and pain in the world. Including the climate crisis.

"In my friendship with Kevin Templeton, Kevin has always referred to him as 'The Denier,' but today, after Sebastian Reid learned that I had been gathering evidence, he—he let me know that he is fully aware of the impact his company is having on the climate crisis. And that it's fine with him. Because he believes his money will insulate him and those he cares about from the impacts. Not only is that a brutal and callous response to human suffering, but it's not true. We only have one planet, and as the climate crisis worsens, everyone will be affected eventually. But also it's just— not something I would ever want to be a part of. Not something I would ever want to profit from. I guess through all this I learned that—that it's all of us in it together. If I want to honor that poor girl I was—lying in bed hungry, alone with my grandmother a lot because my mom was at work, with our roof leaking and holes in my shoes—it's not enough to get myself out of poverty, I want a world where we change things for every little girl and boy living that life today, living an even harder life in many other countries. We can do better now and for generations to come. We can end poverty. We can stop the climate crisis. And they have the same solution: Stop letting the ultra-wealthy profit from the destruction of the Earth and make them pay their fair share. Mobilize the full power of our nation to play a leadership role in getting the world to zero carbon emissions as fast as humanly possible. Thank you."

The barrage of questions began, but Yolanda steered them out the door.

"There's a car waiting for us," the attorney said to the two of them. The press kept shouting at them as they pushed their way down the hall, out the door, and down the steps.

At the curb they piled into a dark sedan.

"Wow," Yolanda said. "You did great." She turned to the driver. "Uptown." Then she gave him an address.

"What's uptown?" Morgan asked.

"I have to turn myself in," Kevin said.

"For what?" Morgan asked.

"Violating the restraining order Sebastian had against me," Kevin said.

"Are you kidding me?" Morgan said. "He kidnapped you."

"Oh, that will definitely come up," Yolanda said. "Believe me."

"We've finally gotten the dirt on him," Kevin said. "We can't let his legal team distract from his crimes because I'm a fugitive from justice."

Morgan reached for Kevin's hand. He had his sleeves pulled up now, and she noticed that his wrist was ringed with shades of plum and blue.

"You're bruised," she said.

"Damn zip-ties."

"Are you okay?"

"I'm fine."

"No, you're not," Yolanda said. "You're traumatized. You've been through a terrible ordeal. Wince when they examine you. We want to sue for pain and suffering."

Yolanda picked up her phone. "This is Yolanda Vance," she said. "Okay, I'm listening . . . Are you kidding me? My client was kidnapped by some rent-a-cop and held for hours while shackled to a chair. Your client oversaw the whole thing. You're lucky we're not pressing criminal charges against Reid."

"She's good?" Morgan asked.

"The best," Kevin said.

Morgan and Kevin didn't speak as they held hands.

Morgan leaned against him, inhaling his scent. Why couldn't they just stay like this? Never having to arrive at any precinct. Never having to face the ruins of her own life.

Morgan closed her eyes and let the fabric of Kevin's denim jacket press against her face all the way uptown.

They pulled up in front of a police precinct, and Yolanda stepped out of the car first.

"Let's go, Kev," she said.

He kissed Morgan on the forehead.

"I'll call you?" he asked.

"Yeah," she said. "I'll get a new phone."

Through the window, Morgan watched them. She felt rattled, disconnected, as they disappeared into the police station.

"Where to now?" the driver asked.

"Brooklyn, I guess," Morgan said. "Did Yolanda already pay?"

"Not Yolanda," the driver said. "I work for the prosecutor's office. I'll take you wherever you need to go."

"Anywhere in New York?"

He shrugged. "Could be the tristate area," he said. "Maybe beyond."

"Can you take me to Pennsylvania?" she asked.

He laughed. "Sure," he said. "I was afraid you were gonna say California."

Morgan gave him the address and he put it in his GPS. She leaned back against the leather upholstery and fell asleep.

Chapter 16

The GPS signal in Lundberg, Pennsylvania, wasn't great. But Morgan could direct the driver from the proper freeway exit down the narrow streets to the far end of town. The roads were even worse than when Morgan had left seven years ago. She hadn't been back since. Hadn't been home.

It was late afternoon, and an old local bus stopped in front of them, letting people out. Over a dozen women in domestic uniforms exited. Morgan hadn't ever really thought about it before. Where did people in the town work these days? Her mom had a factory job during her last two years of elementary school. In middle school she had gotten promoted to the front office. That's how she had scraped the money together to buy their house. That, and the fact that she was one of a few workers who was able to get a local job after the factory closed. Most people had to drive hours to the nearest jobs. Or worse, if they didn't have cars, they had to travel on slow, unreliable buses.

Eventually the car made its way through the rutted streets to a narrow lane that had a row of compact bungalows. The third from the corner, painted a dusty baby blue, was their destination.

Morgan used her key. No matter how long she lived in

NYC, she still kept the house key on her ring. Maybe because her mother had worked so hard to buy the little bungalow. Maybe because Morgan always suspected New York was just a dream she'd been chasing, and that she'd ultimately end up back in Pennsylvania.

The house was freezing and her mother wasn't home. As Morgan stood in the living room, she had the same feeling she'd had as a teen. When she was hanging out late with friends and having a good time, realizing her mom would be worried, realizing she should have called. Her mother would have seen her on the news. She could call from the landline. She went to pick up the wall phone but got no dial tone. Her mother had likely disconnected it to save money. She hadn't really used it for years.

Morgan peeled off all her clothes and took an Epsom salt bath. The old, clawfoot tub was comforting.

In the chilly house, she put on layers of clothes she had left behind. Fraying long underwear, sweats, and one of her mother's old cardigans. She washed all the clothes she had worn that day.

She crashed in her old twin-size bed under a triple layer of woolen and acrylic blankets, but she couldn't quite get warm.

It was after dark when she woke to the sound of a muffled cry.

"Morgan?" Her mother was standing in the doorway of her old room, having come home from her second shift as an industrial cleaner. "Oh my lord, it's so good to see you, baby," her mom said, advancing toward the bed. "I was worried sick about you. Cousin Jeanne called and said you were on the news. I been calling all day and couldn't get you."

Morgan sank into the hug, pressing against her mother's thick midsection. "I didn't have my phone," she said. "I'm so sorry you were worried."

"Baby, are you okay?" her mom asked. "Look at your hair. Wearing it wild like a real New Yorker. I love it. Have you eaten?"

Morgan looked back at her mother, her tighter, graying curls having been flattened under her winter hat. For nearly two decades, Morgan's mom, Elaine, had worn her own hair short and cut it herself.

"Mom," Morgan said. "You've been working a double shift. What are you doing worrying about me?"

"You're my baby," her mother said. "New York or not, I'm always gonna worry. Especially when your hotshot boyfriend sounds like a nightmare. You been some kind of spy up in New York or what?"

Morgan laughed. "Yeah, Mom," she said. "Some kind of spy."

"You wanna tell me about it?" her mother asked.

Morgan sighed. "Not now. Not yet," she said, tears filling her eyes. "But I do have something to tell you."

"What is it, baby?" Her mother asked.

Morgan went into her old bedroom and brought her backpack into the living room. Slowly, she unzipped it, as if what was inside might be too painful to see.

She pulled out the quilt and unfolded it on the floor for her mom, the bullet ripped through all four corners and again through the center of the quilt in three places.

"I'm so sorry, Mama," Morgan said.

"Are you kidding me?" her mother said. "This was Great-Grandma Lourdes keeping you safe. Plus," she added, wiping her eyes, "seven is a lucky number."

Morgan laughed so hard that she cried but then was laughing again.

"You gotta be hungry," her mom said. "I put some chicken stew on in the Crock-Pot before I left for work."

"It smells great," Morgan said.

They sat down to a midnight dinner.

*   *   *

Great-Grandma Lourdes was buried on a rainy day in September. Morgan was three. She stood in the rain under a large umbrella in her mother's arms, Grandma Betty leaning against her mother on the other side, all of them crying.

Lourdes had battled with cancer for the better part of a year, and Betty and Elaine had to take out a second mortgage on the house to pay some of her medical bills. They rented out the house and moved to a two-bedroom apartment to save money.

By then Morgan was in preschool, and Elaine had begun dating. She hoped to meet someone much more mature than her speed dealer ex-, but the dating pool wasn't great in Lundberg. Soon, though, Betty's health also began to fail. She had a heart condition.

When Elaine first met Brian, he seemed like the hero of the story. He wasn't a ridiculous white man-child, enamored of a Black girlfriend as part of some sort of rap fantasy. He was a legit businessman who respected Elaine as a hardworking single mother. In a whirlwind courtship, he moved all three of them in to live with him. Elaine knew it was too fast, but what did she have to lose? That crappy apartment? She could easily find another if it didn't work out. And if it did? It was everything she could have asked for. She was able to quit her lousy job managing the pizza place. Brian's house was huge, and they converted the den into a room for her mother. She and Betty still had the income from renting the house. And now Elaine could stay home to care for both Morgan and her mom. She was able to be a good partner to Brian. And he clearly enjoyed having a warm house full of love. He wasn't especially engaged with anyone other than Elaine. But when anyone asked how he was doing, he would say he was the luckiest man alive, having been suddenly blessed with a beautiful family.

Then Betty died of a brain aneurysm. Elaine had been right there. Had called 911 right away. They had come quickly, as they did in Brian's wealthy neighborhood. It was during the day, while Morgan was in school.

"There's nothing you could have done," the doctor later told her.

By that time Morgan was in second grade. Betty had just turned fifty-three. Elaine was still in her twenties.

This time, at the funeral, Elaine pressed up against Brian, and Morgan pressed up against Elaine. He was strong and stoic at first.

Elaine cried and cried. Morgan snuggled close to her in the bed after school.

After a couple of weeks, Elaine stopped crying. But she stayed in bed. Morgan would still come and join her. In second grade, she could already read a lot of words, and she would read her favorite picture books out loud to her mother. Some of the words she could actually read, but many of them she knew from memory.

"Just like when I'm sick, Mommy," Morgan said. "I'll read to you until you feel better."

But Brian didn't have any patience with Elaine's grief.

"I can't live like this," he said. "The house is a mess. Your daughter is making her own breakfasts and lunches. And the kitchen is sticky with peanut butter and jam and cereal and milk everywhere. And I'm sick of eating takeout. This isn't a free ride, Elaine. Everyone has to do their part."

At the thought of getting up, Elaine began to cry

again. "I don't know what's wrong with me," Elaine said. "Maybe I need grief counseling."

He rolled his eyes. "When my own mother died, I didn't miss more than a day of work for the funeral," he said. "After a week, you should have picked yourself up and gone back to keeping house and taking care of your family." By family, of course, he meant his needs.

Elaine tried. But she could barely get out of bed. She stumbled through days and did the barest minimum.

One night the dinner was slightly burned.

"Pathetic!" he said and slammed his fork down. He stormed off from the table, knocking over his glass.

It shattered on the floor and Elaine began to cry.

"Don't cry, Mommy," Morgan said. "I'll help clean it up. Besides, it's not your fault. He broke the glass, not you."

Morgan got her toy broom and dustpan and swept up the glass the best she could.

Over the next few months, "pathetic" turned to "lazy" and then "stupid" and then "disgusting." At first, he contained the verbal abuse to the times Morgan was at school. In the evenings he'd eat by himself in his study.

Words sail through the air to land in the ears of the intended party. They don't pay tolls. But the air is an indifferent medium. It accepts the passage of kind words as well as vicious ones. It accepts the passage of hands that reach to hold and to caress. But also with palms bent back that push, and with the curve of a wind up to slap. All the air steps back out of the way to let the hand sail by.

The first time he hit her, it was during the day. Morgan was in school. There was no one to hear the sound of the slap as it reverberated through the quiet house. No one to hear the gasp, Elaine's startled intake of air afterward. The air didn't protest. Neither did Elaine.

She simply went back to bed, the stinging side of her face pressed against the soft fabric of the expensive sheets.

Later, as she was cooking dinner, he came and made a nonapology. He was stressed, resentful. He had blown up because he felt he was being taken advantage of. Why was she living there without contributing financially to the household? She got all that rent from her house.

"But most of it goes to pay the mortgage," she said.

"Yes, but not all of it," he said. "Why aren't you contributing the rest of it to this household?"

Elaine was stunned. Even through the fog of her grief, her depression, and the shock of the spot on her face that was still warm. He wanted her money? He was supposed to be her salvation from being poor.

The depression became worse. She could barely get out of bed, and Morgan's teacher began sending concerned notes home. Morgan had arrived without her coat again. With only one mitten. It was almost winter. Did they need financial assistance?

Brian's abuse escalated, too. She moved slowly through the house. He shoved her routinely when he wanted to get past her, sometimes seemed to be waiting till she was in the doorway to push past and knock her into the doorframe.

He never hit her with a closed fist. But she never went to bed without having received a slap or a shove.

He didn't slap her in front of Morgan, but he did
shove her. Complain that she was always too slow.
And one day Morgan was too slow.
Elaine didn't see the shove, but she heard it. The
sound of seven-year-old bones hitting a doorframe
through girl-child skin. Somehow, the sound
penetrated through the layers of fog. The sound was
like an alarm clock. He had shoved Morgan, her baby.
No.

Morgan dreamed about Sebastian. Not quite a nightmare, but the feeling was ominous. She was sitting across from him at the table in his apartment. It was some type of elaborate, seven-course meal, and every time she looked down at her plate to take a bite and looked back up, there was someone else sitting next to Sebastian. First it was Mitchell Brightwell. Then his wife. Then one security guard. Then another. The table got bigger and bigger.

"Momo?" Morgan felt a hand on her shoulder. Her mother's touch, her voice, calling her by that childhood nickname.

Morgan opened her eyes. It was morning. She was in her old bedroom. The fabric she had put on the walls in high school. Everything the same except the sewing machine was gone. She had taken it to New York. Left it in Sebastian's apartment.

"Momo," her mom said gently. "I'm sorry to wake you, but I need to talk to you about something before I go to work."

"What?" Morgan asked, sitting up and wiping her eyes.

"I couldn't bring it up last night because . . . well . . . I hadn't seen you in so long and I just couldn't. It's about Brian."

At the thought of her stepfather, Morgan could feel her chest sort of collapse.

234 / Aya de León

"I watched that video of you during a break at work," her mother said. "About how you first liked that billionaire guy, and you thought he was a nice guy. And what that lawyer said about romance novels. And I couldn't help but feel sort of responsible."

"You?" Morgan asked. "How could you be responsible?"

"Well, that's just it," her mother said. "That was why I married Brian. Everyone talked about me as an 'unwed mother' or a 'teen mother.' And I was the only Black girl in town. They were certain this was the first step in me ending up in jail or on the street. And people acted like the proof of it was that I didn't have a husband. So, I thought that's what I should try to find. And then Brian showed interest. He had so much money. I mean, compared to your billionaire it was pocket change, but compared to me, with nothing, he seemed so rich. I'm sure I thought of him as rich at the time. I'm sure I filled your head with fantasies of how he was gonna rescue us and everything would be perfect. I mean, I was just sort of talking out loud to you because I was so young and scared. Anyway, it was pretty at first, but then it became so ugly—" She broke off and her eyes welled up. "Do you remember any of it?"

Morgan shook her head. "Only what you've told me. I know he hit you." Morgan remembered leaving late in the night. Running to a shelter. Sleeping in a room with what seemed like a hundred other women and children.

"I thought it was okay, you know?" her mother said. "I thought it was worth it. He could lose his temper sometimes. He didn't hit me all the time. It was like, the price I paid for everything. I made sure you never saw it. The hitting part. I didn't like how he talked to me. But I told myself that when you got older, I could explain. That I'd been a teen mom, but you could do it differently. You could go to college. Be financially independent and never have to depend on a man like I did. And later, when you did see him push me, I explained that he had been sorry. That being physical like that wasn't okay. That it wouldn't happen again. And then, when it happened again, I—I just thought it was better than being poor. Being poor was like being slapped over and over again in so many different ways. Always being humiliated. I felt like you would grow up and be able to understand my choices. And learn from them. And do it differently."

As her mother spoke, Morgan felt numb again. Like her entire torso was empty inside. No feeling. No organs. Barely any breath.

"But then he put his hands on you," her mother went on. "Just a push. And I was sure it was the first and only time. I hope it was."

Was it? Morgan didn't remember. She didn't remember any of the pushing. Only the yelling. The tone of his angry voice.

"You weren't ever alone with him," her mother continued. "He always made it clear that you were *my* daughter, not his. And then he pushed you. I knew it would only get worse. That one day he'd be hitting both of us. That was when I left. I couldn't do it for me, but I could do it for you. It was bad enough for you to watch me get pushed around, but what would you learn if I let him hit you? He was ten times your size."

Morgan shook her head. Her photographic memory failed her. Yet, from the hollowness in her chest, something about the sacrifice was familiar. That marrying the billionaire would be worth it. Not if he hit her, but other things she knew were wrong. Controlling. Withholding. Self-absorbed. She never would have accepted that from a man who didn't have money.

"Early on, he talked about adopting you, but once we got married, that talk stopped," her mother said.

And then, looking at her mother, suddenly she could feel something.

Rage.

"He promised you that we would be a family," Morgan said, her face suddenly hot. "Then he turned on you when your mother died. What an asshole."

"He was," her mother said, tears slipping from her eyes. "I just thank God every day that we got out. That I was able to get a good job, get this house. Get you to college. I guess I thought once you made it to college, you were safe. Home free. It just wasn't that easy."

Seeing her mother's tears, the rage shifted, and Morgan began to cry as well.

Her mother reached to comfort her, like a reflex. Like her own tears hadn't come first. That mothering instinct, to always reach out to your baby in pain.

For a while the two women just held each other and cried.

Finally Morgan sat up and wiped her face with the top sheet. "Mama, I never want to make that same mistake again," she said. "Pick a guy with money and make excuses for his behavior."

"It's easy to say that," her mother said, wiping her own face with her sleeve. "It's why I didn't date after Brian. I was just too worried that I'd do it again. Pick a guy who seemed different but turned out to be the same. You gotta be careful about that when the next guy comes along."

"I think he already has," Morgan said. "I don't know. Sometimes I think he's totally different from Sebastian, from all these bad-news men. Then, other times . . ."

"You've got a new guy?" her mother said. "Why aren't you with him in New York?"

Morgan sighed. "He's in jail."

Morgan talked her mother into taking the day off. The two of them talked late into the night. They told story after story. Morgan talked about her last seven years in New York. "I always wanted to get out of this town," her mother said. "But I had you so young, and then it was just about surviving."

"Move to New York with me," Morgan said suddenly. "Rent out the house and join me. We'll make it work somehow."

Elaine laughed. "First of all, nobody is renting houses in this town," she said. "And second of all, aren't you homeless? Sleeping on Dashawna's couch?"

"It's a big couch," Morgan said. "You could join me."

"No couches for me," Elaine said. "Plus, I have a job. But maybe if I retired early in a few years . . ."

"Yes!" Morgan said. "Mom, we could do this. And maybe in New York you would meet someone. Someone who wasn't white. Someone who was different."

"Oh come on," Elaine said. "I'll be over fifty by then."

"Foxy fifty," Morgan said. "You could grow your hair out because there would be people who could help you take care of it. You wouldn't need to marry anyone. You could just date. Have fun."

Elaine laughed and waved away the idea, like it was cigarette smoke. "New York has made you crazy."

"Forget the dating, then," Morgan said. "Just think about moving there. At least come for a visit."

Elaine shrugged. "I'll think about it."

They crashed late, and her mother got up midday to work another double shift. Two to ten and then graveyard: ten to six in the morning. She was out by early afternoon.

Elaine dropped Morgan in town on the way to work. Morgan walked into the town's biggest store for the first time in nearly a decade. The place was tiny, and it seemed like nothing had changed. But instead of the ancient German proprietor, his great-nephew sat at the counter now.

Morgan asked about where she could get a cell phone with a plan. The nephew shrugged and pointed over to a little display of electronics. There were a few overpriced burner phones with expensive monthly contracts. She passed on those.

There was, however, something that caught her eye. A small, random section of clothing dye. She bought a bottle in bright red and a white plastic bucket.

She walked home carrying the dye in the bucket and a few small groceries. It was unseasonably mild for January. Global warming.

When she got back to her mother's house, she took the jeans out of the dryer. Then she filled the bucket with water and bleach and bleached the jeans to a pale blue. After she had rinsed them and cleaned the bucket, she filled it again with hot water and dyed the jeans. By the time she pulled them out, they were a deep red that hinted toward magenta. She cut a large, circular patch around the bullet hole in the leg. Then, she cut the rest of the ruddy denim into arc-shaped strips. After she put those aside, she opened all the boxes of fabric she'd sent home.

Feverishly, she began to cut and lay out a new quilt. A black-velvet background. She cut generously from two bolts of rough cotton, one green, one blue. She had gold and copper silk, and a linen ombré that darkened from pale beige to ebony. For the big pieces, she used her mother's sewing machine. But much of it had to be done by hand. She had a rainbow of threads and needles in the old sewing basket that had been her grandmother's.

Morgan worked until the wee hours of the morning. She wanted to stay up to greet her mother when she came home but fell asleep on the couch, waiting.

After a week in Pennsylvania, she returned to New York on the bus, just like when she had come the first time.

She would have stayed longer with her mother, but she decided to withdraw her first quilt from the contest and substitute the new one she had made in Pennsylvania. A red target of circles on the planet with the actual bullet hole in the center.

The statement about women and money felt timeless, evergreen. But the statement of the new quilt felt utterly urgent. It was an intricate design of the planet in thirds, with air, wind, and earth as background. In the midground was an outline of her body, in a hands-up-don't-shoot stance. It was in the same color fabric as the background, but the fabric had a different texture, so you could only see her silhouette when you looked directly at the quilt. And on top of it all was the red target from the jeans material with the bullet holes. The one in the center of the quilt landing squarely on her heart.

There were no squares, it was all circles. The background was unpredictable, with different images in it when you looked from different angles. And in the background, the images changed. The line of a bird was also the line of a cat running across a savanna. And the line of the cracking earth in drought also morphed into the storm-ravaged trees in a flooding landscape. At the bottom were barrels and barrels of oil, coal mines, a line of fracking beneath the earth. At the top were the sun and the wind, delicately half outlined with metallic threads—not explicitly depicted as energy sources, just gleaming above it all. She titled the piece "Divest from Fossil Fuels/Defund the Police."

Morgan came in third place in the contest.

Dashawna was furious. "I can't believe they picked that white girl's quilt. It looked like a cheesy cottagecore photo on Instagram."

Morgan shook her head. "I said what I had to say," she said. "At least I got the third prize."

"Nah, girl," Dashawna said, shaking her head. "You shoulda got that big money."

The contest said the work was "too preachy" and they wanted art that "would speak for itself, creatively."

But after they announced the news, Morgan got a call from Yolanda that the *New York Times* Magazine was trying to get in touch with her.

"Yaaaasss!" Dashawna said. "That's what I'm talking about!"

Morgan mostly felt dazed as she talked to the reporter. Was it true that the quilt had actual bullet holes? Was it true that they were made by security guards employed by Sebastian Reid?

Morgan wanted to say, "Yes!" and tell the reporter all about it. But Yolanda had coached her not to comment as the trial was coming up soon. Sebastian's legal team would like nothing more than to slap her with a lawsuit for libel and have her legal team scrambling on defense.

Her chest burned with the anger at keeping quiet. But the reporter was savvy.

"Off the record, did he have his guys shoot at you?" she asked.

"On or off the record, I can't comment on what Sebastian Reid did or didn't do, or what he may have instructed anyone to do who was working for him," Morgan said. "But those are real bullet holes in my quilt. They were shot through a pair of jeans that were in my backpack. I don't know the identity of the shooter."

The reporter got some additional information and followed up on a police report of people hearing gunshots in the subway. They did find a couple of bullet holes in the subway walls. No bullets or casings.

The reporter wove it all into her cover story. How Morgan remained "tight-lipped" about the bullet holes in the quilt but connected the dots of evidence: the subway stop near Sebastian's apartment, the reports that the shooting was on the day Morgan had left, all folded into the feature on Morgan's journey to becoming a climate activist.

At the photographer's request, they had staged the photo-shoot on the Brooklyn Bridge, looking across the river toward Manhattan. Accompanying the feature were photos of Morgan wrapped in the quilt, displaying the quilt, wearing the quilt like a cape. The quilt was eight feet square, so Morgan requested a tarp under her feet. New York was filthy and the quilt was not machine washable.

When the article came out, Morgan was on the cover of the magazine, bundled in the quilt with the bullet hole over her chest. The interior photo had her holding it up in front of her. The photographer had caught the light, so that the gold silk threads gleamed. The photo editor had enhanced the image, so that the red of the target blazed, giving the blue and green and earth tones even more depth.

Dashawna went to the gym on Sunday mornings, so Morgan was alone in the apartment when the paper was delivered. Morgan cried when she saw herself on the magazine cover. The quilt was stunning, and the photo showed it off so beautifully.

The reporter also did a stellar job of capturing her journey. A struggling artist and the fantasy of a prince swooping in. Then a hidden price she wasn't prepared to pay and a change of allegiances. She had been anxious about what the reporter would say, so she was also crying with relief that the reporter didn't betray her in any way.

But there was a sadness, too. She had always sort of dreamed of being famous as an artist, but not like this. She also cried for her loss of anonymity. She knew that the big hook for the article wasn't her artwork, or even her climate activism, but rather the lurid breakup scandal and allegations of violence against a powerful man. They called her the "ex-fiancée and star witness in the upcoming trial against energy mogul Sebastian Reid."

* * *

Mitchell Brightwell had cut a deal. He had stepped down as chief of sustainable energy transition. Brightwell was in DC when everything blew up. He found a sympathetic federal judge to manage a quick proceeding in which he ended up with a misdemeanor conviction and probation.

Sebastian Reid wasn't going to get off as easily. He was being charged with seventeen counts of racketeering in New York State. Figueroa couldn't charge Brightwell with racketeering because he didn't stand to profit from the illegal dealings, and because he wasn't implicated in the kidnapping. Figueroa had hoped to also make attempted murder charges stick, but Sebastian had gotten to the two guards. The three men had an airtight story that the overly zealous guard had shot at Morgan and Sebastian had ordered him to stop.

Morgan was furious when Yolanda told her what Sebastian was saying. "He's lying!" Morgan fumed. "He told me if I didn't stop, he'd order that the guard shoot to kill."

"I know," Yolanda said. "But it's your word against three men saying the exact same thing. Figueroa has seventeen other charges."

The two of them were at a coffee shop in Brooklyn.

Yolanda continued: "If we fight this one, we'll just give the defense more opportunity to cast doubt on your other testimony. Without the kidnapping, the racketeering charges won't really stick. Sebastian is just another corrupt corporate CEO. Kevin's testimony will be seen as suspect because he has publicly vowed to destroy Sebastian. The jury is going to have to believe you."

Morgan was pissed. She looked out the window at pedestrian traffic walking by. She looked at the black-and-white photos on the café wall. She looked down at the table where Yolanda had a stack of newspapers.

On top was a tabloid, open to a page about the upcoming

trial: MEET THE PLAYERS. The article had a photo of Sebastian and labeled him "The oil man." They labeled Figueroa, the prosecutor "The lesbian lawyer," and had a photo of her and her wife at a GLAAD function. In his orange jumpsuit, Kevin was "The activist on lockdown." There was a coffee cup on top of whatever they were calling Morgan. She picked up the mug, but Yolanda swooped the paper out from under before she could read her new nickname. But she did catch a red-carpet photo of herself and Sebastian.

"Let's not get distracted from planning our strategy," Yolanda said.

"Okay," Morgan said. "What about Dawn or Val? Isn't there some leverage to get her to talk? Wasn't she spying?"

Yolanda shook her head. "There's no law against using more than one name," she said. "And just like it's not illegal for you to spy on Sebastian, it's not illegal for her to spy on our organization." Yolanda's mouth was tight. She and Dawn/Val had worked together for over a year. "Besides," Yolanda said. "She denies knowing anything about it."

At the end of their meeting, Yolanda handed Morgan an envelope. "It's from Kevin," the attorney said.

On the subway ride back to Brooklyn, the unopened letter buzzed in Morgan's purse. She couldn't bring herself to open it with Yolanda. Or in public. She was back to sleeping on Dashawna's couch. She waited until she got to the apartment and opened it with Dashawna.

Dear Morgan,
    If there's one thing jail does to a man, it removes his grandiosity. I was pompous in a lot of ways. I thought I knew best for everyone. I thought I was invincible. I'm not. I tried to control everything, even you. Especially you. I was so damn jealous. In part because . . . I just

244 / Aya de León

thought of you as a sort of pawn I could play in a chess game with Sebastian Reid. It was an asshole move. I'm so sorry.

I have a picture of you in my mind that I hang on to in this place. It's so weird being in a world with no women. I'm used to having women as my closest friends and comrades. But in a place like this, I can only think of you. Because with all the other women in my life, I can talk with them on the phone or write them letters and we have most of the connection that we had before. But with you, it's the fullness of your presence that I miss. The smell of your skin. The touch of your lips. The way your body fits into mine when we embrace. I know that sounds kind of cheesy, but hugs are what I give friends and colleagues. They fortify me and show me that I'm not alone in this fight. But when I embrace you, it's more than just knowing I'm not alone in this fight. It's knowing I'm not alone in some existential way.

I would understand if I've already blown it with you. So many asshole moves I made in my grandiosity. But even if you never want to be with me again—I hold on to the idea of our connection as the proof that I am capable of being more connected. That even if I can't have that with you, you've shown me that it's what I so deeply crave.

Love,

Kevin

PS: By the way, thanks for rescuing me.

"Damn, girl," Dashawna said. "That's a bona fide jail-house love letter right there."

Morgan read the letter through three times, her heart beating with equal intensity during each read through. She didn't know how to feel. Was he just saying this because he was locked up? Had he really changed or was he just missing her? Would it even matter if he got put away for a third strike?

"You gonna write him back?" Dashawna asked.

Morgan shook her head. "I don't know what to say," she said. "Besides, I'll see him in court day after tomorrow."

The night before Morgan was to testify in court, she could barely sleep. She dozed at around four and was up again at six. She pressed her hair with Dashawna's flat iron. She knew it was irrational. She had been wearing it curly since she had returned from Jamaica.

The case against Sebastian Reid involved overwhelming evidence. But she felt vulnerable when her hair was wild. Dashawna had showed her how to gel down the baby hair and tame it with oil and other products. But when she had tried those, Morgan always felt like she was pretending to be somebody she wasn't. For now, there were only two ways she was comfortable: natural, with her hair just curling and being wild, or tamed and hanging down like a shield. She had straightened it for every critical interaction with any type of authorities: college interview, job interview, her gig at Sebastian's house, and, of course, every single time she had seen him before their big trip. She was certainly not going to face the architects of the climate disaster in court without her armor.

During the week before the trial, Morgan did something she had never done before. She bought a new suit. A nice one. On credit: $400 on sale. She even took the tags off. It was like an offering to the gods, its crimson wool as a blood-colored sacrifice. Please, God, let us triumph. I'm not hedging my bets. I'm all in.

The day she was to appear in court, she wore pantyhose, a tall pair of black heels, and a cream-colored silk blouse.

Yolanda had coached her. Just answer the questions to the best of your recollection. Be honest. Don't let them rile you.

She and Dashawna went to the courthouse together. Dashawna was also a corroborating witness.

The courthouse was a massive gray building with large columns in front. Only among the skyscrapers of Manhattan would it seem unremarkable. In Morgan's hometown, it would have been visible for miles.

Even the interior of the courtroom was large, with high ceilings and a wide gallery for witnesses and observers. The judge had ordered all press banned from the room, so they prowled the hallways, waiting for news or photo ops.

Figueroa ushered her witnesses in through a side door.

When Morgan entered the courthouse, the first person she saw was Kevin, impossible to miss, tall in his orange jumpsuit and standing shackled and surrounded by guards. Figueroa had fought to have him testify in a suit, unshackled: "Your Honor, how is he a flight risk as a nonviolent offender in a courtroom in a secure building? The defense is just trying to prejudice the jury against the witness."

Sebastian's people wanted Kevin in full prisoner regalia and the judge sided with them.

But Morgan quickly stopped seeing the bright orange fabric. She just saw Kevin's face. The defiant angle of his jaw under the stubble. The broad shoulders in the jumpsuit. The narrow hips at the elastic waist. Kevin was still beautiful to her in that awful orange.

Morgan and Dashawna couldn't be in the courtroom except when they were testifying. Dashawna was on the witness list because she had received the text from Morgan about Sebastian. While Morgan looked totally professional, her bestie looked like something out of an old Perry Mason rerun, in a tight-fitting fuchsia suit with a pencil skirt, matching lipstick, and high black heels.

Morgan recognized the lead defense attorney as the middle-aged guy who had run into the prosecutor's office with the injunction—a dark-haired guy named Bret Halstead. He was clean-shaven, with a soft jaw and round glasses.

Morgan sat in the witness holding area, jangling with adrenaline and distracted by the knowledge that Kevin was so close by.

In the courtroom, the prosecutor started her case—Ivelisse Figueroa, the same woman who had taken their evidence. Yolanda had explained that she was Puerto Rican. "She lost her grandmother in Hurricane Maria," Yolanda said. "So for her, climate change is very personal."

The prosecution began by calling an expert witness and had him explain the complicated details of the law, and how the illegal contact between Sebastian Reid and Mitchell Brightwell fit the definition of racketeering under New York State law.

He was a smart guy who explained things clearly for everyone to understand. Figueroa thanked her expert witness and excused him.

"Next, the State of New York would like to call Morgan Faraday."

Morgan swallowed and stood up. She was grateful for her bulletproof hair and armor of a suit. She walked stiffly toward the witness stand, keeping her eyes forward. She didn't look at either Kevin or Sebastian. She swore on a Bible to tell the truth, although she hadn't been to a church since her grandmother's funeral.

She stated her name, residence, and occupation.

"So," Ivelisse Figueroa began. "How did you meet Sebastian Reid?"

"I was asked by a colleague to bid on a design job at his apartment in Manhattan," Morgan said. Her voice felt tight. Awkward.

"Thank you, Ms. Faraday," Figueroa said. Her voice was warm, approving. Morgan relaxed a bit.

Through a series of questions, the prosecutor then elicited the entire story of how she and Sebastian had met, began to date, and what their status was before she went on the trip when she met Kevin.

"Would you say that Sebastian Reid was your boyfriend at that time?"

"Objection," Halstead, the defense attorney, said. "Calls for a conclusion of the witness."

"Let me rephrase," Figueroa said. "Did you and Sebastian Reid use the language of 'boyfriend' and 'girlfriend' for your relationship at that time?"

"No," Morgan said.

"At that point," the prosecutor asked, "had you and Sebastian Reid made any commitments in your relationship?"

"Objection," the defense attorney said. "Relevance?"

"I'll allow it," the judge said.

"No," Morgan said. "He would call or text to invite me over or to go out or to go on a trip, and I would say yes."

"Did you always say yes?" Figueroa asked.

"I did," Morgan said.

"Why?"

"Objection!"

"Overruled."

"Sebastian Reid was a very attractive, charming, generous man," Morgan said. "I was hoping he would become my boyfriend, and that we might even get married."

"Make the romance novel stop," Halstead said.

"Is that an objection, Counselor?" the judge asked.

"Objection."

"Overruled."

"How did you see your relationship with Sebastian Reid?"

"I can't lie," Morgan said. "When we first met, I was dazzled by his apartment, his wealth, his generosity."

"Were you accustomed to such wealth?" the prosecutor asked.

"Not at all," Morgan said. "I grew up with a single mother. We were homeless for a time. At other times, we were on government assistance."

"And why were you homeless?" Figueroa asked. "Was your mother financially irresponsible?"

"No," Morgan said. "My mother was a victim of domestic violence. We left my stepfather's house and lived in a shelter for a while."

"And is your mother still homeless?"

"No, she works multiple jobs and owns her house."

"So—given your background—how was it to date someone like Sebastian Reid?"

"It didn't quite feel real," she said. "It was like a fairy tale. But I had a friend who coached me on how to date a guy like him."

"What do you mean?" the prosecutor asked. "A guy like what?"

"A guy who had a lot more money than I did. She said to hide the fact that I was broke because otherwise he would think I was just dating him for his money."

"And were you?"

"No," said Morgan. "Like I told you, he was witty and charming and attractive."

"And his money didn't figure at all into why you were dating him?"

"Of course it did," Morgan said. "But it was only part of what made him attractive to me. Not the whole reason."

"Would you call yourself a gold digger?" Figueroa asked.

"Absolutely not," Morgan said. "Sebastian Reid pursued me. He kept asking me out. He kept wining and dining me."

"But you deceived him about how much wealth you had?" the prosecutor said.

"He never asked me any point-blank questions about how

much money I had," Morgan said. "I never lied. But did I consciously create an inaccurate impression of my class status? Yes, I did."

"To get him to like you? To commit to you? To marry you?"

Morgan took a breath. "I did it so he wouldn't be prejudiced against me as a possible girlfriend," she said. "I wanted a chance for us to get to know each other, to see if we could be compatible. I didn't want his classism to rule me out as a possibility."

"Classism?" Figueroa asked. Like it wasn't a word Figueroa had coached her to use.

"Prejudice by middle- and upper-class people against working-class and poor people," Morgan said. "The presumption that people with more money are superior."

"Objection!" Halstead said. "Is our Marxism lesson over yet?"

"Sustained."

Figueroa went on to a methodical set of questions that clarified how Morgan was not in a committed relationship with Sebastian when she met Kevin in St. Louis.

"Did Kevin Templeton attempt to initiate anything romantic during that first meeting?" Figueroa asked.

"He invited me to dinner after we got to Colorado," Morgan said. "But I told him I wasn't available."

"Anything else?"

"He gave me his phone number," Morgan said. "And told me to call if I became available."

"And what did you do with that number?" the prosecutor asked.

"I threw it into the bathroom trash at the airport," Morgan said.

"So you had no way of getting hold of him?" Figueroa asked.

"I did," Morgan said.

"How?"

"By calling his number," Morgan said.

"But you just testified that you had thrown it away," the prosecutor said.

"I have a photographic memory," she said.

"Objection!"

"Sustained."

The prosecution spent the rest of the morning setting up their case for how and why Morgan had decided to spy on Sebastian Reid. Figueroa even asked Morgan to name some of the books and articles she had been reading.

"It really shook me up when I found out that scientists had said we only had a few years to stop our fossil-fuel dependency," Morgan said.

"Objection," Halstead said. "Counselor is attempting to have the witness testify about global warming in the courtroom."

"No, Your Honor," Figueroa said. "I'm simply attempting to help the jury understand the information the witness was encountering for the first time as she made the decisions she made."

"Objection sustained."

"At what point did you begin to develop romantic feelings for Kevin Templeton?"

Morgan shifted in the witness box. "I had romantic feelings for him from the beginning," Morgan said.

"Let me rephrase," the prosecutor said. "At what point did you begin to voice or act on those romantic feelings?"

"When I realized the impact Sebastian's company was having on the environment," Morgan said.

"You found it morally objectionable?"

"Objection!" the defense attorney said. "Leading the witness."

"I found it morally objectionable," Morgan said.

"And you moved out?"

"No," Morgan said. "When I went to talk to Kevin, I was planning to move out. But I stayed so that I could gather evidence about what I suspected might be criminal activities that Sebastian Reid was involved in."

"Objection."

Figueroa shifted tactics. Through careful questioning, the prosecutor drew out the story of Morgan and Kevin hiding the recording devices.

After a while, Figueroa leaned back and surveyed Morgan. "Ms. Faraday, how would you describe your relationship with Mr. Templeton?"

"Complicated."

"Sorry," the prosecutor said. "Can you describe the nature of the relationship? Was it personal? Professional? Romantic?"

"It was all of the above."

"Did you have a sexual relationship with Kevin Templeton?"

"I did."

"When did that begin?"

Morgan gave the date.

"Are you certain of the exact date?" Figueroa asked.

"I looked at the calendar that day," Morgan said. "I have a photographic memory."

"Objection!"

"Sustained."

The prosecutor questioned her for another half hour and then showed her a pair of mismatched minidisks.

"Do you recognize these?" She asked. "Exhibits A and B of evidence for the prosecution?"

"Yes," Morgan said.

"What are they?"

"They are disks I removed from a video camera and a digital recorder that was hidden in the wall between Sebastian Reid's study and a storage room in his apartment."

Figueroa had Morgan swear to the date and time she made the recordings, and they went over the events of the day she ran from Sebastian's apartment.

Then Figueroa turned Morgan over to Halstead, the defense attorney, for cross-examination.

Halstead stood up and took his time cleaning his glasses. As he walked toward the witness box, he gave her a look that was somehow simultaneously cold and eager. Like a predator, circling his prey.

"Ms. Faraday," Halstead began. "When you moved out of his apartment, what was your relationship with my client, Sebastian Reid?"

"We were living together," Morgan said.

"Is it true that you and my client made a commitment to your relationship?" Halstead asked.

"Yes," Morgan said.

"But by your own admission, you also had a sexual relationship going with Mr. Templeton, is that right?"

"It wasn't—"

"It's a simple yes or no question, Ms. Faraday," he said. "Did you or didn't you have a sexual relationship with Mr. Templeton while you were in a committed relationship with Mr. Reid?"

"I did not," Morgan said.

"So you were lying when you said you had sexual relations with Mr. Templeton?"

"No," Morgan said.

"Then how is that possible?" Halstead said. "It doesn't add up."

"I was lying about being in a committed relationship with Sebastian Reid."

"So you never said you would be faithful to Mr. Reid?"

"Faithful?" Morgan said.

"You never said you would be sexually exclusive with Mr. Reid?"

"I never used the word 'sexually exclusive,'" Morgan said. "I told him I would be his girlfriend and we would be in a committed relationship."

"And at the time did you understand that to include sexual exclusivity?"

"I did."

"Yet you had sexual relations with Mr. Templeton," Halstead said. He tilted his head to the side. "How does that work?"

"You want me to tell you how sexual relations work?" Morgan asked. "Don't you need an expert witness for that?"

A ripple of laughter went through the courtroom.

"Very funny, Ms. Faraday," the attorney said. "How were you able to have sexual relations with Kevin Templeton and still maintain your sexual exclusivity agreement with Sebastian Reid."

"I wasn't," Morgan said. "If you would have let me explain in the first place, I unilaterally rescinded my commitment to Sebastian Reid when I found out he was a liar and a criminal."

"Your Honor, I request that the previous testimony be stricken from the record." He turned to Morgan. "Ms. Faraday, did you inform Sebastian Reid that you were no longer committed to him?"

"No," Morgan said.

"So, as far as Mr. Reid was concerned, you were still sexually exclusive with him?"

Figueroa stood up. "Objection," the prosecutor said. "Calling for a conclusion from the witness."

"I'll rephrase," Halstead said. "Did you give Mr. Reid any reason to think that you had rescinded your commitment?"

"I did not."

"Didn't you—in fact—go to great lengths to convince Mr. Reid that you were still committed and sexually exclusive?"

"What do you mean by great lengths?"

"Didn't you, for example, spice things up sexually?" Halstead asked. "During the period when you were supposedly no longer committed?"

Was he really going there? Morgan wondered.

She looked at him levelly. "Can you be more specific?"

The attorney cleared his throat. "Didn't you engage in sexual acts that you hadn't engaged in previously?"

Yes, Morgan could see he was going there.

"Like what?" she asked.

"Oral sex," the attorney said, coloring a bit.

Morgan tilted her head to the side. "I do recall Sebastian going down on me after that point in the relationship," she said. "Would you like dates and times?"

Morgan heard a muffled "Ha!" from the gallery and had to work hard not to smile.

Halstead set his jaw. "Let me be more specific," he said. "I mean fellatio."

"Can you define that?" Morgan said. "It's not a term my generation uses."

"Oral sex on a man," Halstead said.

"Oh," Morgan said. "You mean that time after I found out what Sebastian's company was doing to the planet and I was so disgusted that I didn't want his entire body near me? Yes, I went down on him for the first time that night."

"So you admit that you escalated things sexually?" Halstead said.

"No," Morgan said. "I de-escalated things sexually. Oral sex is less intimate than penetration. I usually needed to be drunk to have sex. That night he came home early and I didn't have time to get drunk, so I went down on him."

"Were you or were you not trying to convince him that you were still his girlfriend?"

"I was."

"So how do you expect this jury to believe that you are being honest about the rest of your testimony, when you aren't even honest with your boyfriend, the man you were living with?" he sputtered. "You were intentionally using sex to confuse and mislead him, but you're supposedly being honest with us?"

"Objection!" Figueroa said. "Counselor is apparently trying to discredit the witness by slut-shaming her."

"Sustained."

"I can answer the question," Morgan said.

"Okay," the prosecutor said. "I'll withdraw the objection."

"I was spying on him for an urgent cause. I was intentionally misleading him for the greater good. I wasn't under oath to tell him the truth. Which is why testimony in court is weighted more highly than things people say to each other on the street."

Halstead rolled his eyes. "No further questions."

When Morgan got back to the witness room, Dashawna leaned over and murmured in her ear. "You were fucking fantastic, honey," she said.

Morgan squeezed her hand and tried to take deep breaths.

Back in the courtroom, they had to unlock Kevin for him to take the stand. That is to say, they unlocked the cuffs and the restraint that connected his handcuffs to the shackles on his ankles. But they kept his feet shackled in the witness box.

Clearly, he had done everything possible to prepare himself. Combed his hair neatly back. Trimmed his beard, although he was far from clean-shaven. Fair enough that they didn't allow razors in jail.

The prosecutor basically walked him through the same facts from Morgan's testimony.

After she finished, Halstead, the defense attorney stood up. "Just a few questions, Mr. Templeton."

Kevin looked up warily.

"Mr. Templeton, did you believe that any means would be justified to discredit Sebastian Reid?"

"I believed that we might have to escalate our activism," Kevin said.

"Including fabricating evidence?"

"There was no need to fabricate evidence," Kevin said. "Reid was caught red-handed."

"Red-handed?" Halstead said. "As in with blood on his hands? But weren't you the one throwing blood, Mr. Templeton?"

"It was seaweed," Kevin said.

"Objection!" Figueroa said. "Mr. Templeton is not on trial here."

"Sustained."

"Mr. Templeton, at any point did you lie to achieve your political goals?"

"Yes," Kevin said.

"And you encouraged others to lie?"

"I did."

"Including Morgan Faraday."

"Yes."

"Did you take any special pleasure in using Sebastian Reid's girlfriend to mislead him?"

"I hadn't thought about it," Kevin said. "Maybe I did."

"Did you take any special pleasure in having sexual relations with Sebastian Reid's girlfriend?"

"Objection!"

"I'll answer," Kevin said.

The prosecutor raised her eyebrows. "I'll withdraw the objection."

"Sebastian Reid destroyed everything he touched," Kevin said. "He never deserved Morgan. I couldn't wait until she got the evidence she needed just so that she could get away from him. Even if we couldn't be together. She deserved so much more than a man like him."

The defense attorney gritted his teeth. "Move to strike that from the record," he said.

The prosecution called Dashawna next. Figueroa didn't question her. Instead, it was a young black attorney. He had just a whisper of maybe a West Indian accent.

The prosecutor drew everyone's attention to the video monitors. There were three of them—each one huge—making the courtroom feel almost like a sports bar. No matter where you sat, you could always see the game, whether you wanted to or not.

He began asking routine questions of Dashawna, drawing out that she and Morgan had met at fashion school, were good friends, and sometimes lived together.

The young prosecutor stood in the center of the courtroom and stretched out a long arm to turn on the monitor with a remote.

On the screen was the text Morgan had sent the day she left Sebastian's apartment for the last time. Dashawna read it aloud.

"Can you identify this message?" he asked.

"Morgan Faraday sent it to me," Dashawna said, noting the date in December.

"Were you and Ms. Faraday in the habit of sending each other texts like this?" he asked.

"When women are young and single," Dashawna said. "We like to date. But when you're getting to know a guy, you never know if he'll turn out to be a creep. You gotta let your girls know where you are, who you're with, and what's going on. Unless things go well, and then it's just between you and your date."

Dashawna smiled at the prosecutor. Was she flirting with him?

"Objection," Bret Halstead said. "Relevance."

The judge agreed. "Sustained," he said. "Keep your focus. We don't need a dating advice guide here."

"Sorry, Your Honor," the assistant prosecutor said. He looked back at Dashawna and took a moment to gather his thoughts.

The prosecutor had Dashawna explain how their usual texting system worked.

Then the young prosecutor nodded. "Was the text in December different from previous texts?"

"Definitely," Dashawna said. All smiles gone. "She had never before said to call the authorities if anything happened to her."

"So you thought she feared for her life?" the prosecutor said.

"Objection!" Halstead said. "Calling for a conclusion from the witness."

"Sustained."

"How was that text different from previous texts of that nature?" the young prosecutor asked.

"The other texts were about dates," Dashawna said. "This one was about getting out of a relationship with a dangerous man who was up to something illegal."

"Objection!"

"Sustained."

"She suspected he was involved in something illegal," Dashawna said. "She was scared. She was running for her life with evidence."

"Objection."

"No more questions."

The defense cross-examined Dashawna but couldn't manage to shake her at all.

"Anything on redirect?" the judge asked the assistant prosecutor.

The assistant prosecutor was half a second late, eyes riveted on Dashawna.

"Uh, nothing more, Your Honor," he said. He tried to keep his focus as Dashawna strolled out of the courtroom, her ass swaying with each step in the tight fuchsia suit.

"I think you have a new fan," Morgan murmured when her friend sat down.

"I'd like to get prosecuted by him a few times," Dashawna said.

"Forget it," Morgan said. "He doesn't make enough money to be in your league."

"It's not about the money," Dashawna said. "He would be strictly for fun."

Next, the prosecution went through the process of stipulating and laying the foundation for the audio and video evidence. Then they played both.

Everyone in the courtroom watched the meeting between the two men. Sebastian and Mitchell Brightwell sitting across from each other in Sebastian's study. Their faces in profile, softly lit by the Tiffany lamp on Sebastian's desk. Both men clearly identifiable.

In the video, they saw the rerun of Brightwell sliding a USB drive across the desk to Sebastian.

"It's all there," he said. *"The specs of what the DOE is looking for."*

Ivelisse Figueroa stopped the video. "Ladies and gentlemen of the jury, let me remind you that the DOE is the Department of Energy. The US government entity at which, until recently, Mitchell Brightwell served as chief of sustainable energy transition."

The prosecutor restarted the recording with the remote control.

The two men on the screen went on to discuss wave power for five minutes, then Figueroa stopped the recording again. She paused for a moment to let it sink in, and the judge interrupted her.

"Ms. Figueroa," he said. "It's nearly five. This court is in recess until tomorrow."

"Yes, Your Honor."

As the court adjourned, Morgan took everything in through a fog. The guards taking Kevin out of court in shackles. Yolanda telling both Morgan and Dashawna that they had done great. Dashawna exchanging glances with the young prosecutor.

Morgan was crashing. The lack of sleep from the day before. Not enough to eat that day. Too much coffee. Too many surges of adrenaline.

She and Dashawna went home in a ride share. Morgan dozed on the way back to Brooklyn. She was asleep in earnest before 7 p.m.

The following morning Morgan had on a different, less-expensive suit.

She took a seat in the witness holding room next to Yolanda. Dashawna wasn't required to attend that day.

After the judge declared that court was back in session, Ivelisse Figueroa stood up.

"We'll continue playing the recording," the prosecutor said.

Bret Halstead looked at Sebastian, confused. Sebastian looked at the defense attorney and shrugged. Then the two of them began to whisper.

"Counselor?" the judge asked. "Is it something you can share with the entire class?"

"Sorry, Your Honor," the attorney said. "My client and I

were under the impression the prosecution would be resting its case."

"Not at all," Ivelisse Figueroa said. "We only played the first fifteen minutes of the recording. But it continues for over ninety minutes."

"We weren't aware of any other relevant information on the recording," the defense attorney said.

The judge frowned and looked at the defense team.

"Are you saying that you weren't given a complete copy of the tape in discovery?"

"No, Your Honor," the attorney said. "Just that we are not aware of any other relevant information on the recording."

"You can feel free to object if you find it irrelevant," the judge said. Then he turned to Figueroa. "Go ahead, Counselor."

"One thing I've learned," Ivelisse Figueroa said, "is that many of the important details of business deals and other critical conversations between powerful men happen during the more informal portions of a meeting. Which is why men make deals over golf or drinks or in strip clubs."

"The recording, Ms. Figueroa," the judge said.

"I would like to forward to the more informal portion of this recording," the prosecutor said. She clicked the remote, and the video began to play on all three screens:

Sebastian and Mitchell Brightwell still sat across from each other in Sebastian's home office.

"Now that we've got that settled, I need a cup of coffee," Mitchell Brightwell said. *"I hate meeting at your apartment, Sebastian. No staff."*

"Sorry, Uncle Mitchell."

Brightwell laughed. *"That assistant of yours looks eager to please,"* he said.

"Not everyone is trying to marry their secretary," Sebastian said, rolling his eyes.

Suddenly, Sebastian was whispering urgently to his attorney.

The defense attorney stood up. "Objection!"

Figueroa paused the video.

"On what grounds?" the judge asked.

"Irrelevant," the defense attorney said. "The rest of the conversation is strictly about their personal lives."

"Defense counsel introduced the entire area of their personal lives into the record," Figueroa said. "Including their sex lives."

"Objection overruled."

"Permission to approach the bench?" the defense attorney asked.

Next to him, Sebastian was gripping the table, his knuckles white.

The judge shook his head. "No, Counselor, I said I would allow it."

"But Your Honor," the defense attorney said. "There may be material that would be prejudicial to the jury."

"And we can instruct them not to consider it as part of their deliberations," the judge said. "You are aware of how a jury trial works, aren't you, Counselor? Continue, Ms. Figueroa."

"I'm going to wind it back a moment for continuity," the prosecutor said.

Brightwell laughed. *"That assistant of yours looks eager to please,"* he said.

"Not everyone is trying to marry their secretary," Sebastian said.

"Who said anything about marriage?" Brightwell said. *"I'm talking about the occasional blow job at the office."*

"No thanks, Uncle Mitchell," Sebastian said. *"That's not a face I wanna see after getting sucked off."*

The entire courtroom gasped. That hissing intake of breath through closed teeth. Maybe because the defense attorney had spent so much time priming them to be disgusted, to be horrified by something sexually untoward. But it was his own client who was eliciting the response. Not only because of the crude "locker room talk" between the men, but also because Sebastian Reid, usually so genteel, had participated.

The recording bungled on.

"Fair enough," Brightwell said. *"I guess that's an HR problem. Tell them the next Asian assistant needs to be a little more Hollywood and a little less Halloween."*

And then there it was, that telltale laugh. Sebastian threw his head back, and that unexpectedly high-pitched laugh tinkled from his throat like a bell.

In the video, he reached across the table and gave Brightwell a light and playful punch in the arm. *"You're funny, Uncle Mitchell."*

The prosecutor stopped the recording.

"Objection, Your Honor," the defense attorney said. "I move—I move that the testimony be stricken from the record as irrelevant."

"Sustained," said the judge. "Testimony to be stricken."

But it wasn't just the testimony that was stricken. Morgan looked over at Dawn—or Val, whatever her real name was—who sat frozen, her face blazing. The testimony would be removed from the words for the jury to consider. But the prosecutor's arrow had hit its target. In that moment Morgan could see that the insult and the injury wasn't just that Sebastian had said it. Or that Mitchell Brightwell had insulted her and Sebastian had laughed. It was that they had presumably previewed the entire tape and it hadn't even occurred to them that they were vulnerable if the prosecutor played that portion of their conversation. That she mattered so little. Or that they took her so completely for granted. One moment they could be insulting her, the next they could be asking her to bring their coffee. And perhaps she would also be expected to offer blow jobs in the office. The layers of humiliation were unbearable. Morgan felt for her. Every woman in the courtroom felt for her. Including the women on the jury.

"I would like to request a recess," the defense attorney said.

The judge banged his gavel, and before the sound had finished echoing in the room, Dawn or Val had walked out of the heavy wooden doors, with Yolanda on her heels.

Sebastian stood to follow her, but the defense attorney pulled him back, shaking his head.

"You'll only make it worse," the defense attorney said.

But it couldn't have been much worse.

Morgan stepped out into the hallway to find Yolanda with her arm around the young woman.

She was wiping her eyes. "I can't believe you're being so nice to me after I spied on you for all that time," she said.

"Men like Sebastian Reid are master manipulators," Yolanda said. "I don't blame you at all, Val."

"It's Dawn," she said through tears. "In all that time I was working for him, I was so sure he was different." Dawn wiped her eyes. "I could tell the other guys were total creeps, but I thought Sebastian was—was better. And he wasn't. All that time . . ."

And that was when Morgan saw it. Dawn was in love with Sebastian. Had been the whole time. Maybe imagined that with Morgan out of the picture, she would have a chance. And instead, she had been humiliated in front of the whole world. Not even worthy of a blow job under the desk?

A svelte redhead in a crisp and expensive suit rushed out of another courtroom and approached them.

"Excuse me," she said, looking at Dawn. "Can I speak with you for a moment?"

"No reporters right now," Yolanda said.

"I'm not a reporter," she said.

And then her photo popped into Morgan's mind.

"She works for Sebastian's law firm," Morgan blurted out.

"They sent you, didn't they?" Yolanda asked.

Dawn looked at her, defiant. "They're gonna send a shark in a skirt to try to reel me back in?" she said. "What? Do they think I'm stupid as well as unfuckable?"

The redhead winced. "I just want to advise you that your work for Sebastian Reid was confidential," she said. "And that you might be subject to liability if you disclose certain information."

"I would like to advise you that there are whistleblower laws," Yolanda said. "And these may apply to any information you might have as well and would shield you from any criminal or civil liability."

Dawn nodded.

Yolanda turned to the redhead: "Go tell the assholes at your firm that I plan to start by asking Sebastian Reid to drop all charges against Kevin, and then we'll take it from there."

The redhead turned and ducked into the courtroom, where Sebastian and the defense attorney were presumably waiting.

When court resumed after the recess, neither Dawn nor Yolanda was in the courtroom.

Ivelisse Figueroa said she would like to recall a witness. She turned to the courtroom. "Kevin Templeton."

Morgan looked for him in the front of the court near the bailiff, but he wasn't there. Then she saw movement in her peripheral vision. Kevin stood up in the back of the courtroom. He was clean-shaven and had on a blazer and jeans.

When they had first returned from recess, Sebastian and the defense looked drawn. But as Kevin made his way to the stand, they were downright pale.

As the prosecutor began to question him, Dawn and Yolanda walked back into the courtroom.

Figueroa's questions for Kevin went into greater detail about the kidnapping and he answered all of them succinctly and with confidence. The defense didn't even bother to cross-examine him.

"I would like to call Dawn Kim to the stand. She is known by some here as Val Kim," she said, her expression smug.

"Your Honor," the defense attorney said, standing up. "Permission to approach the bench."

He walked up and whispered something, then the judge looked at the prosecutor and motioned her over.

"He wants to make a deal," Yolanda whispered to Morgan.

The defense attorney was talking, but the prosecutor kept shaking her head.

"He's trying to get him off with a slap on the wrist, but she's not having it," Yolanda said.

"Excuse my language, but you've got to be fucking kidding me, Counselor." Figueroa said it loud enough for everyone to hear, and the courtroom exploded into whispers.

The judge banged the gavel. "Let's continue this in my chambers. Court is adjourned."

"Sebastian Reid is going to jail," Yolanda murmured as she stood up and gathered her briefcase. She hustled out of the courtroom.

Morgan looked around for Kevin but couldn't see him anywhere. She drifted into the hallway. Yolanda was deep in conversation with Dawn and Morgan waved a quick goodbye to them. Had Kevin left? Maybe he was desperate to go home and take a shower. Fair enough after weeks in jail.

She walked slowly down the hallway. She was eager to get out of there, but not completely sure where to go.

Brooklyn, she guessed. Back to Dashawna's. She pushed open the heavy wooden doors. She squinted into the February Manhattan sunlight. It was unseasonably mild. Higher temperatures everywhere.

On the courthouse steps, a bank of reporters had cornered Kevin. "That's all I've got," Kevin said. "My attorney, Yolanda Vance, will have a press conference later today."

Morgan made eye contact with him and retreated into the building, closing the door behind her. Kevin seemed to have all the press tied up. She slipped down the corridor, hoping to get out a different exit.

Morgan heard the door open behind her. As a rush of noise came in, she hustled down the corridor toward an exit sign. Kevin came running after her.

"It's Morgan Faraday!" one of the reporters yelled.

The next thing she knew, Kevin had grabbed her hand and the two of them were running out the side door. They cut around a corner and down the busy avenue block.

She hailed a cab and it pulled to the curb. The two of them tumbled in, laughing, as the press snapped photos and filmed them escaping.

"Brooklyn," Kevin said. Then he turned to Morgan. "Actually where are you headed?"

"I don't know," Morgan said.

"Do you—? I mean—" he stammered. "Would you like to maybe see my apartment?"

"I'd love to," she said. She suddenly felt shy. She wanted to kiss him, to embrace him. But the cameras and now the cab driver made her feel self-conscious.

Kevin gave the driver his address.

"Can we just not talk until we get to your place?" she asked.

"Sure," he said.

She let herself just collapse onto his shoulder and they drove across the city and over the bridge and through the most populous borough in silence.

Kevin's apartment turned out to be a studio in Williamsburg. It was a tiny box, cut out of what had probably been a warehouse or a small industrial building.

Kevin asked Morgan to have a seat while he took a shower. He felt grimy after the weeks in jail.

He ducked into the bathroom. He literally had to duck a bit to get through the door. That left Morgan alone in the main room, which was mostly taken up by the bed. There were two stools at a tiny table, which was apparently also the bed's nightstand. It had a stack of books and papers on it that spilled onto the bed.

Morgan heard the water begin to run. Why was she here? The man had just gotten out of jail. Maybe she should have waited. Given him a chance to settle in, collect himself. She herself hadn't even recovered from the shock of the trial. That it was over. That they were going to win.

Maybe when he came out of the shower, she should tell him she was heading back to Dashawna's. They could talk after things settled down.

She sat down on one of the kitchen stools and waited.

Kevin lived sparsely. Beside the tiny table was a cabinet and a half-size fridge. On the cabinet was a toaster oven. On the other side of that was a chest of drawers. That was the whole apartment.

But the walls were covered in art. There was a wall of maps above the bed of the Pacific Islands, the Phillippines, and several projection maps of what the continents might look like if sea-level rise continued unchecked.

In the center of the wall across from the bed was an illustrated poster of a brown-skinned woman holding a baby. Behind her was a globe with what could either be petals or flames circling it. The title text above said, "DEFEND OUR MOTHER" in bold capital letters. Morgan thought she recognized the artist's work, Favianna Rodriguez. At the bottom were silhouettes of people marching with their fists in the air. The text at the bottom said, "People's Climate Mobilization," and it was from 2014. Kevin had been at this for a while.

Part of her felt like an impostor, a sort of bandwagon activist. But no. Forget that. This movement was going to need everyone. Whether she had been involved for five decades or five minutes, she was committed now.

Abruptly, the hum of water from the bathroom stopped. Kevin's shower must be done. She wanted to wash her own hands, but when she looked around in the kitchenette, there was no sink. Maybe he washed his dishes in the bathroom. This suspicion was borne out when Kevin came out five minutes later in a T-shirt and sweatpants, carrying a coffee cup and a pair of small plates.

Kevin made a face as he put the dishes on the small table.

"That lovely perfume you smell is old almond milk," he said.

Morgan shook her head. Thank goodness it was winter. She didn't smell anything except that sort of spicy soap she associated with Kevin.

As she washed her hands in the tiny bathroom, she inhaled deeply and felt a crumbling of her resolve to leave. When she came back out, Kevin was sitting down on the bed, which was on a pallet just off the floor.

She pulled up one of the kitchenette stools. They were less

than two feet apart, but her face was higher than his. She could feel her pulse begin to race with the proximity. Morgan wasn't sure what to say.

He tried to make eye contact, but she looked out the window. The panes were really dusty. She thought she might die from the awkwardness.

"I got your letter," she finally said. "I didn't write you back because Yolanda said it might take a while for it to get to you. I didn't want to believe you would be in there that long."

Kevin reached for her hand. "Morgan," he said, looking up at her. "I'm so sorry. I didn't—"

She squeezed his hand and shushed him. "You don't need to apologize anymore," she said. "It was all in the letter."

"It wasn't enough, though," he said. "You risked everything. I shouldn't have been so . . . so . . ."

"Such a dick?" Morgan asked. She threw her head back and laughed, and it broke the tension. "Yes, you were a dick, Kevin. A complete and total dick."

He buried his face in his hands. "I'm so embarrassed."

"You should be," she said, the anger melting away with his apology. "But I think I can forgive you."

He looked up at her from the bed, eyes imploring. "Really?"

"Of course," she said. Then she leaned down and kissed him. And he pulled her down onto the bed, which was ten times firmer than she expected.

"What the hell is this?" she asked. "The futon you bought in college?"

"Yeah, actually," he said.

"What the fuck, Kevin? Why don't you just sleep on the bare floor?" she asked.

"I vowed not to replace it until I could afford a new mattress made entirely of recycled plastic bottles."

"Are you serious?" Morgan asked.

"It's supposed to be incredibly fluffy," Kevin said. "That's why they're really expensive to make. But in the meantime, I'd be glad to get some recycled foam to put on top. If you . . . wanted to . . . you know . . . sleep here."

"That's pretty presumptuous," she said. "You think I want to sleep at your apartment?"

"I'm really hoping you will," he said. "At some point."

"I'll think about it," she said, laughing, as she leaned in and kissed him, pushing him back on the hard bed.

Epilogue

Ivelisse Figueroa sat in the chair in front of the judge's huge mahogany desk. Beside her were Sebastian Reid and his attorney, Bret Halstead. They had recessed to the judge's chamber for the purposes of entering a plea with conditions.

Figueroa looked at a photo of the judge with a brown-skinned woman and several teenagers who looked like their kids. Was his wife Latina? South Asian?

The judge entered, sat down, and commenced the proceedings.

"Your Honor, we are willing to enter a plea of guilty in exchange for a fine and six months' probation," Bret Halstead said.

"Are you kidding me?" Figueroa asked.

"And community service," Halstead said.

"Stop wasting my time," Figueroa said, standing up. "I've got a smoking gun and a jury ready to convict. Your assistant is ready to turn."

Figueroa had walked halfway to the door when Sebastian Reid stood up and called after her. "I want immunity!" he said.

"Sebastian, please," Halstead said. He put a hand on Reid's shoulder and pressed him down in the seat. Halstead turned to the judge. "My client is falling apart under the strain. He doesn't know what he's saying."

Figueroa had stopped on her way to the door. "Whatever he's saying, I'm listening," she said.

"Sebastian," Halstead said to his client. "As your attorney, I'm cautioning you that we need to take a recess before you say anything else."

"I want three things," Reid said. He was looking over his shoulder at Figueroa, ignoring his attorney. "No felony conviction, no jail time. And immunity from future prosecution."

"Why on earth would I give you all that, just so that your corporation could continue on its path of destruction?" Figueroa asked. "Stop wasting my time." She turned again and put a hand on the doorknob.

"I could liquidate the corporation," Reid blurted out.

"Sebastian!" Halstead said. "You can't do that."

Sebastian turned to the lawyer. "You're fired," he said to Halstead.

"We can't have a sentencing conference without your attorney, Mr. Reid," the judge said.

"You have to be represented," Figueroa said, leaning back against the door. "Or whatever we come up with today will be too easy to reverse."

"Fine," Sebastian said. "You can stay, Bret, but keep your mouth shut."

"You're ready to liquidate ReidCorp?" Figueroa said, walking back to her seat.

"The writing is on the wall," Reid said. "Fossil fuels are basically finished. We didn't convert to green energy when we should have. I'm sick of steering a sinking ship with everyone hating me."

"The climate crisis isn't a popularity contest, Mr. Reid," Figueroa said, sitting down. "People are fucking dying."

"Counselor!" the judge said.

"Sorry, Your Honor," Figueroa said.

"Like I said," Sebastian went on. "I'll liquidate the company."

"It's worth over two hundred billion dollars," Halstead argued.

"Didn't he tell you to keep your mouth shut?" Figueroa said.

"And what are you proposing to do with the liquidated funds?" the judge asked.

"Maybe start a foundation," Reid said.

"Absolutely not," Figueroa said. "If you want to become a philanthropist, you can do that with your own private money. Any profits from the liquidation need to be disbursed in accordance with terms we set as part of the deal."

"There's no legal precedent for that," the judge said.

"First of all, a lot of that valuation is of fossil fuels that haven't been drilled yet," Figueroa said. "You would need to agree to keep them in the ground."

"There's no legal precedent for either of those things, Counselor," the judge said.

"What about New York's restitution laws?" Figueroa asked.

"That's quite a stretch," the judge said.

"I want to do it," Reid said. "Liquidate the company. Give the money away. Leave the reserves in the ground."

"What about all the barrels you've already drilled?" Figueroa asked.

"I don't know," Reid said.

"This is ridiculous," Halstead said.

"What part of 'shut up' don't you understand?" Figueroa asked.

"Counselor," the judge warned.

"I have dead family members!" Figueroa said. "The corpses keep piling up. Half the planet is on fire, the other half is freezing and flooding. I've been fighting with these assholes in court for so long, I can't always be fucking nice about it."

"She needs to be censured, Your Honor!" Halstead said.

"*This* is what I'm talking about," Sebastian said, standing up. "I'm sick of being the bad guy! My father started this shit. It wasn't me. He was Mr. Oil Man with his big money, and everybody loved him. But now I'm public enemy number one? I'm trying to go out to dinner and people are throwing blood on me? I can't live like this! I don't want to go to some country club jail and come back to this same fucking life. Take the goddamn company! I don't want this shit anymore!"

Sebastian looked almost like he might cry. Halstead seemed stunned.

"So, you want to rebrand as a good guy?" Figueroa asked. "A phoenix who rises from the ashes of ReidCorp with a private foundation and no felony record?"

"I don't know," Sebastian said. He sat back down, deflated. "Maybe. I just want out."

"You would need to endorse the fossil fuel non-proliferation treaty," Figueroa said. "End all new exploration."

"Sure," Reid said.

"End all your current production? Shut down the wells?" she asked. "Pay for the toxic cleanup?"

"All of it," Reid said.

"What about taking care of your workers?"

"Definitely," he said. "We would—? We'll just—" He blinked several times. "I don't know."

"You have some renewables, right?" Figueroa asked.

"Solar and wind," Reid said. "Developing some wave, too."

"You could transition those to worker-owned cooperatives," she said. "And pay to retrain and the fossil fuel workers and place them into green energy jobs. Maybe invest to expand those solar and wind cooperatives and place them there."

"Absolutely," Reid said.

"And you agree to give away the profits? Keep the fossil fuel reserves in the ground?"

"Whatever it takes," Reid said.

"Are we ready to get all this on the record?" Figueroa asked Sebastian.

"Yes," Reid said.

Halstead rolled his eyes and sat back in his chair. "Why not?"

The judge called in the court stenographer. It took her a moment to catch up.

"'Transition solar and wind to worker-owned cooperatives,'" she said. "'Pay to retrain the fossil fuel workers. Give away the profits. Keep the fossil fuel reserves in the ground'" the young woman quoted back to her.

"What do we do with all the oil we have?" Reid asked.

"I'm freestyling here," Figueroa said. "Maybe donate it to struggling nations in the Global South? They can use the savings to help fund their climate mitigation efforts and transition to clean energy? We'd have to research that."

"Okay," Reid said. "Sure."

"Counselor," the judge said to Figueroa. "I don't know if these international solutions are within the purview of this court."

"Why not?" Halstead asked. "And why not throw in a pony?"

"The relevant racketeering laws in this case are pretty broad," Figueroa said. "We're basically just talking about restitution. I agree we'd be breaking some new ground, but there is plenty of precedent."

"Yes, but what you're talking about is really more like reparations," the judge said. "At an international level."

"But the defendant isn't objecting," Figueroa said.

"Despite advice of counsel," Halstead said with a glance at the stenographer. "For the record."

"How could we enforce the restitution via liquidation?" the judge asked.

"We'd have to do maybe five years felony probation,"

Figueroa said. "Make completing the restitution a condition of probation."

Sebastian opened his mouth to speak, but Figueroa cut him off. "And signing the fossil fuels non-proliferation treaty wouldn't really be enough. You'd have to become a global champion of decarbonizing. Get all your corporate cronies on board."

"No probation," Sebastian said.

"No probation, no deal," Figueroa said. "If you do what you say you'll do, you can get your record expunged."

Sebastian turned to his lawyer.

"Oh so *now* you want some legal advice?" Halstead asked.

"Bret," Reid said. "I'm fighting for my fucking life here. I don't want a record and I don't want probation."

"Cry me a fucking river," Figueroa muttered under her breath.

"If you didn't want any of that, then you shouldn't have opened your damn mouth, Sebastian," Halstead said. "But you did. And now you'll pay the price. They're not going to give you this deal without some teeth in it. At this point you're committed. Take the probation. Do the restitution and you'll come out with no record."

"Okay," Sebastian said. "Deal."

"I'm glad your father never lived to see this," Halstead said.

"That's the whole fucking point," Reid said. "My father should be the one cleaning up this fucking mess now, not me."

"This will be highly irregular to implement, Counselor," the judge said.

"Does that mean you're willing to try?" Figueroa asked.

"My wife is from the Marshall Islands," the judge said. "Her childhood home is already underwater."

"Of course she is," Halstead said. "How did I miss that?"

"Okay, Your Honor," Figueroa said. "I'll take that as a yes."

Lourdes welcomed her great-granddaughter Morgan the way she had welcomed all her grandchildren—with a quilt. Elaine had chosen the name Morgan for either a son or a daughter, but Lourdes had dreamed about a girl-child standing on the roof of their house. In the dream, she was luminous in the moonlight, a halo of wild curls on her head, large brown eyes staring out at the stars. Lourdes was certain that baby Morgan would be a girl.

She also could tell that this would likely be her last quilt. Elaine had moved home from the boyfriend. No more babies with him. And Lourdes was getting up there in years. She was unlikely to live long enough to see great-great-grandchildren.

She looked carefully through her fabrics to select for the quilt. Some of her choices were simply what she'd included in all her previous quilts: a faded yellow square of the curtain from her first apartment in New York—a tenement really. A rectangle of the sky-blue bedsheets from her first night in this house with Colin Tehan. The quilts had a lot of white: squares from various dress linings, her wedding dress. The first communion dress that had been worn by both Betty and Elaine.

And then, in the bottom of the fabric box, she pulled out a garment she hadn't ever used in a quilt before. The green cotton dress she'd worn to America—the one piece of clothing she'd had when she left her husband's house in Spain. It was so thin that she would have to stitch it to a stronger piece of cotton fabric. Otherwise the pulling and tugging of a baby would surely tear it apart.

It was hard to find a section of the dress that wasn't too faded and didn't have any moth holes.

There was one panel of the skirt that was in pretty good shape, but she didn't want to use that one. She picked a section with a seam down the middle. A seam that had been sewn by her own mother, back in Spain. With this quilt she would stitch a lineage for baby Morgan that reached all the way back to her bloodline in Málaga.

This particular panel held the stitches her mother had made, as well as her own stitches that had hidden her necklace all those years ago. She stitched in that particular panel as a talisman for the baby. Life can be treacherous for girl-children. As Morgan grew up, she might find herself in a desperate situation. But Lourdes included the fabric with the secret seam as a hidden message to her great-granddaughter that problems—no matter how big—always had solutions. If only women were bold enough to take action, to defy powerful men, and were willing to face the unknown.